Jackpot

Dear Martin

Odd One Out

Dear Justyce

Jackpot

NIC STONE

EMBER

Text copyright © 2019 by Logolepsy Media Inc.
Cover art used under license from Shutterstock.com
Hand-lettering copyright © 2020 by Jordy Moses

All rights reserved. Published in the United States by Ember, an imprint of
Random House Children's Books, a division of Penguin Random House LLC, New York.
Originally published in hardcover in the United States by
Crown Books for Young Readers, an imprint of Random House Children's Books,
a division of Penguin Random House LLC, New York, in 2019.

Ember and the E colophon are registered trademarks of Penguin Random House LLC.

Visit us on the Web! GetUnderlined.com

Educators and librarians, for a variety of teaching tools, visit us at
RHTeachersLibrarians.com

The Library of Congress has cataloged the hardcover edition of this work as follows:
Names: Stone, Nic, author.
Title: Jackpot / Nic Stone.
Description: First edition. | New York: Crown, [2019] | Summary: "When Rico sells a jackpot-winning lotto ticket, she thinks maybe her luck will finally change, but only if she and her popular and wildly rich classmate Zan can find the ticket holder who hasn't claimed the prize"—Provided by publisher.
Identifiers: LCCN 2019002077 (print) | LCCN 2019006339 (ebook) |
ISBN 978-1-9848-2964-1 (ebook) | ISBN 978-1-9848-2962-7 (hardback) |
ISBN 978-1-9848-2963-4 (glb)
Subjects: | CYAC: Lotteries—Fiction. | Social classes—Fiction. | Popularity—Fiction. |
Family life—Georgia—Norcross—Fiction. | Norcross (Ga.)—Fiction.
Classification: LCC PZ7.1.S7546 (ebook) | LCC PZ7.1.S7546 Jac 2019 (print) |
DDC [Fic]—dc23

ISBN 978-1-9848-2965-8 (pbk.)

Printed in the United States of America
10 9 8 7 6 5 4 3 2 1
First Ember Edition 2020

For Mama. Thank you for your hard work.

Friendship and money: oil and water.

—Mario Puzo

- 1 -

~~Mo~~ *NO Money, Mo Problems*

Oh, the irony of counting out change for a fifty-dollar bill while "Mo Money, Mo Problems" plays in the background. "Sir, I'm out of tens and twenties," I say. "I'll have to give you fives and singles . . . is that okay?"

It has to be, obviously.

The man smiles and nods enthusiastically. "Perfectly fine," he says, dusting off the lapels of his (expensive-looking) suit. "Matter of fact, keep a couple of those singles and give me a Mighty Millions ticket with the Mightyplier thing. I'll slide a few of the other dollars into the Salvation Army bucket out front."

Despite my desire to snort—I know one shouldn't judge a book by its cover, but based on the Mercedes-Benz key fob lying on the counter, I'd say this guy doesn't *need* two hundred and twelve million more dollars—I force the corners of my mouth to lift. "That's very generous of you, sir." Barf. "Nothing like a cheerful giver!"

The man takes his $43.74 in change, then grabs his mechanically separated meat stick and bottle of neon-green

Powerade. "Thanks so much"—he looks at my name tag—"Rico?"

"That's me!" I chirp.

"Hmm. Interesting name for a cute girl such as yourself. And what interesting eyes you have . . . two different browns!" Now he's winking.

Oh God.

"Thank you, sir. And thank you for shopping at the Gas 'n' Go."

He tosses a *Merry Christmas!* over the checkout counter before rotating on the heel of his fancy shoe and strutting out like he just won the lotto.

Merry Christmas. *Pffft.* Not much real "merry" about a ten-hour shift on Christmas Eve. It'll almost *be* Christmas when I walk out of this joint . . . and then I get to spend thirty minutes walking home since the one public bus in this town stopped running hours ago. Good thing the crime rate in (s)Nor(e)cross, GA, is relatively low and it's not that cold out.

I look at my Loki watch—a birthday gift from my baby brother, Jax, that I never leave home without despite how childish it makes me look. Ninety-seven minutes to freedom.

"It's the Most Wonderful Time of the Year" comes pouring out of the speakers (note to self: ask Mr. Zoughbi who the heck made this playlist), and I drop down onto my stool and put my chin in my hand. Truth be told, the influx of holiday cheer really *has* been a nice reprieve. Seems like every day there's a new political scandal or gun attack or government-sanctioned act of inhumanity or threat of nuclear war, but then Thanksgiving hit, and it felt like a collective exhale.

The bell over the door dings, snapping me back, and the cutest little old lady I've ever seen makes her way toward the counter. She's tiny—definitely under five feet and *maybe* ninety pounds soaking wet—with dark brown skin and a little pouf of white hair. The Christmas tree on her sweater has real lights, and when I smile this time, it's for real.

"Welcome to Gas 'n' Go," I say as she steps up to the counter.

"Why, thank you, dear. Aren't you just lovely?"

Cheeks are warm. "Well, you're looking pretty lovely yourself, madam," I reply.

She giggles.

"I mean it. That's a gorgeous sweater."

"Oh, you stop that," she says. "And anyhow, shouldn't you be at home with your family? Take it from an old bird: you don't wanna work your life away, now."

I smile again. "Yes, ma'am. I'll be blowing this Popsicle stand in a little over an hour."

"Good." She nods approvingly.

"So how can I help you on this cool Christmas Eve?"

She leans forward over the counter a bit, and I'm drawn toward her like a magnet. "Well, I was on my way to church, and between you and me"—she pauses to peek over her shoulder—"I happened to look up as we passed one of those billboards that show the Mighty Millions jackpot. You know what I'm talkin' about?"

I nod. Drop my voice to a near-whisper so it matches hers. "Two hundred and twelve million, right?"

3

"That's what the billboard said. I wasn't gonna play this time, but then I saw your station loom up on the left, and . . . well, it felt like a sign. So I decided to stop."

Now I'm really smiling. *This* is the kind of person I would love to see win.

"How old are you, sweet pea?" she asks.

"I'm seventeen, ma'am."

"That's about what I thought. You remind me of my granddaughter. She's in her third year at Florida A&M University."

I feel my smile sag, so I look away and pretend to do something behind the counter. Really hoping she doesn't ask about *my* (nonexistent) college plans. I'd rather not deal with another adult customer's judgy raised eyebrow when I explain that instead of college, I'll accept the management position I've been offered here at Gas 'n' Go, and continue to help support my family.

When I turn back to her, she's rifling around in her purse.

"Thought I had a photo somewhere, but I guess not." She shuts the bag and smiles at me. "What were we talkin' about?"

"Umm . . . your granddaughter?"

"No, no." With a wave. "Before that. I've got a nasty case of CRS lately. . . ."

"CRS?"

She leans forward and lowers her voice again. *"Cain't Remember Shit."*

And now I'm really smiling again. Laughing, actually.

"I'm serious, now!" she says. "Where were we?"

"You were about to purchase a Mighty Millions ticket."

4

"Oh yes, that's right! Let's do that."

I step over to the machine. "Do you have specific numbers you'd like to play?"

"I do! Been playing the same ones since 1989." She calls them out, and as the ticket prints, I stop breathing: three of her white-ball numbers—06, 29, 01—make up my birth date. And her Mighty Ball number is 07. Which is supposed to be lucky, right?

"You've got my birthday on here!" tumbles out before I can stop it. Frankly, I do my best not to pay attention to the lottery at all. Mama's been obsessed with the idea of winning for as long as I can remember, but after years of watching her *make sure* she had a dollar for a ticket and continuing to cling to this impossible hope while our finances literally crumbled around her (no doubt she bought at least one for this jackpot cycle) . . .

Hard pass.

Seeing the day I was born pop up on a ticket, though?

The lady's face is lit up brighter than her Christmas tree sweater. "Your birthday, huh?"

"Mm-hmm." I point it out.

"Well, I'll be! Perhaps you're my lucky charm!"

My eyes stay fixed on the ticket as she takes it from me. What if she's right? Two hundred and twelve *million* dollars could be on that little slip.

"Tell ya what, print me one of those Quick Picks, too," she says.

"Yes, ma'am. Would you like to add the Mightyplier option to this one? For an extra dollar, it'll double any nonjackpot winnings."

"Oh no, we're going for the big bank!"

I laugh. "Coming right up."

The machine spits out the second piece of paper, and I slide it across the counter to her. She grabs it and then holds both tickets up to take a good look at them.

Then she shuffles them around and puts them face-down on the counter. "So whattaya think?" she asks. "Right or left?"

"Oh, definitely left," I say.

She nods and pushes the left ticket across the counter to me. "Good. It's for you."

Whoa.

"Oh wow, that's really nice of you, ma'am, but I can't take that."

"You certainly can," she says. "It's my Christmas present to you."

I look at it and bite down on my lower lip. *God, how amazing would it be to win even* part *of two hundred and twelve million dollars?* The old Bad Boy rappers say, "Mo money, mo problems," but they all had plenty of it. Me? I work at a gas station for $7.75 an hour, and most of *that* goes toward whatever bill Mama hasn't made enough to cover each month (you know, minus the dollars she spends on weekly lotto tickets).

"Go on now. Pick it up," the lady is saying. "Obviously someone over eighteen will have to claim the prize if you win anything, but perhaps one of us will get lucky." She winks. Very different feeling than when Mr. Fifty-Dollar-Bill did it.

Makes my skin tingle a little.

I take the ticket and quickly stick it in my back pocket.

Which is good because Mr. Zoughbi chooses that moment to exit his office. Not sure he'd be real keen on a customer buying his underage cashier a lottery ticket. The lady and I exchange a look. She gets it.

"Well, you've certainly brightened up my Christmas Eve," she says loud enough for Mr. Z to hear. "You finish your shift and hurry home now, you hear?"

I smile and nod again. "You be sure to do the same, ma'am."

"Merry Christmas, baby girl." She turns to leave.

I swear that ticket has turned radioactive and my right butt cheek is expanding in size right now.

When she gets to the door, it swings wide, and I hear her say, "Why, thank you, young man. My, aren't *you* handsome!"

I look up, and there holding it open for her, with his million-dollar smile, is Alexander Macklin ("Zan" to his friends/ groupies/loyal horde)—varsity quarterback, all-around teen dream, and heir to the booty-paper throne.

No, for real. His great-great-grandfather or something supposedly patented toilet paper on a roll, and now his family runs Macklin Enterprises, which is legitimately famous for its focus on ass-wipery.

Speaking of ass-wipery, rumor has it he only goes to *our* school because he got kicked out of his fancy private one. Something about a hacking scandal.

And yes, he's handsome.

I'm pretty sure he doesn't have a clue who I am despite the fact that I sit two desks behind him in US History. But still. Would rather the richest boy in school *not* see me working the cash register at the local gas station. Pretty sure my hair's a frizzy mess and there's a cheese stain on my apron from a hot dog I snarfed earlier.

"Uhh, I need to go to the ladies' room," I say as Mr. Z approaches the counter to restock candy bars.

He looks up at me with an eyebrow raised.

I glance at the door again. The lady is gone, and Zan is stepping inside now. I think our eyes meet, but I turn away too fast to know for sure.

"Girl problems," I say to Mr. Z.

"Ah." He lifts his hands. "Say no more."

I slip from behind the counter. Zan has turned down the chip aisle, so I do my best to make no noise. Avoid drawing attention.

Just as I get to the back, Mr. Z hollers, "Oh, Ms. Danger!" He mispronounces my last name. Doesn't rhyme with "stranger" like everyone assumes. It's actually *DON-gur* and I usually correct people . . . having *Danger* as a last name would be cool if it weren't such a misnomer.

Anyway.

"Check the toilet paper supply while you're handling the lady business, yes?" he says.

So much for a clean getaway.

- 2 -

Merry Friggin' Christmas

The walk home is trash.

It's colder than I thought, and I can't stop thinking about that dumb boy invading my outside-school bubble. In a year and a half of working at the Gas 'n' Go, none of the rich kids from school have ever come in there. They all fill up their fancy cars at the BP near their gated communities a few miles away.

Now, with every numb-toed step I take, I wonder if Zan is still out and about. If he's going to drive by, see me walking the mean streets of Norcross in the dead of a chilly night with no hat or gloves, and assume I'm a hobo.

I relax the tiniest bit once I reach the street my apartment complex is on, but my head is still messed up from the almost-encounter. Mama's door is closed by the time I make it home, but Jax is stretched out on the couch in our small living room, trying his damnedest to keep his eyes open while *Elf* plays on the television screen.

I look around at the off-white walls and sparse second-hand furniture in our two-bedroom place. Jax was two when we moved in, and he and I have shared a room ever since.

I wonder what Zan Macklin's room—what his *house*—must be like. Especially tonight. To the right of our couch, there's a sorry excuse for a prelit Christmas tree with two measly newspaper-wrapped gift boxes underneath. An image pops into my head of a massive pine, taller than double my five-feet-six-inch height, and draped with twinkling lights and crystal ornaments and jammed with so many wrapped boxes underneath, it looks like it's shedding gifts instead of pine needles. . . .

And Zan Macklin standing over it all trying to decide what to open first.

Ugh.

After slipping off my boots, I go over to Jax. He sits up so I can sit down, and then he lays his head in my lap. "Merry Christmas, kiddo," I say as I run my hand through his mess of khaki-colored curls.

He sighs, and his sadness drops down onto my shoulder so heavily, tears immediately spring to my eyes. While it's true he has no idea I squirreled away money from my paychecks over the last six months so I could buy him the bike he wanted, knowing he's sad because of how little we have really rips me a new one.

I know we're filthy rich compared to people in *places with genuine poverty*, as Mama likes to put it, but Jax is only nine years old. All he knows is that the other kids at his school already have lots of toys and video games and money, yet they still get lots of presents. Mama works up-wards of seventy hours a week just so we can live in this bougie-ass area and "go to good schools," but being poor in comparison with everyone around you sucks. Especially when you're just a kid. We won't even talk about the fact that he's brown where most of the (rich) kids around him are white.

The ticket in my pocket appears in my mind's eye. The things I could do with that kind of cash . . .

"You should go to bed, baby boy," I say, trying to force *some* kind of cheer into my voice. "Santa should be here pretty soon. No telling what he's gonna leave you."

"There is no Santa," he huffs.

I die a little inside. "What do you mean there's no Santa?"

He turns his head to look up at me. "Isn't it obvious, Rico? If there *is* a Santa, he certainly doesn't give a rat's butt about kids like me."

Wow.

"First of all, where's your Christmas spirit, mister? And second, what the heck do you know about the word *obvious?*"

His chin starts to quiver, so now I *have* to hold it together. Dear God.

"I'm *always* good, Rico," he says. "But he never leaves me more than one thing. So either he's not real, or he doesn't really care about me."

I can't handle this right now.

"Well, I know for a fact that he's bringing a big surprise for you this year."

His eyes light up. Hope. Which is almost harder to take than the despair. "You do?"

"Mm-hmm. He told me."

Jax's eyebrows tug together. "Are you sure?"

"Would I lie to you, baby boy?"

He smiles.

"Come on," I say. "I'll tuck you in."

We head into the bedroom, and I pull back the Ninja Turtle comforter I found at a thrift store and gave him for his most recent birthday. He climbs in. "Will you sing 'Smooth Criminal'?" he asks.

I grin. Our obsession with the Michael Jackson song has its origin in our stint at a shelter during Jaxy's first couple years of life: there was a family with a toddler who often struggled to fall asleep, and the only thing that would help was the sound of her mom's voice whisper-singing *Baby, are you okay?* the way MJ does in the song. I started doing the same to Jax, who was a very fussy baby.

Good to know that even in his sadness, our bedtime traditions still reign supreme. Come to think of it, I'm glad he waited up for me.

He curls into a ball on his side, and I pull the comforter up over his shoulder as I begin to sing, but he's out before I get through the first chorus.

Which is good because now I'm crying.

It's like no matter how hard Mama and me work or how much we do, it always feels like we're drowning. And now I've got images of the richest kid in school superimposing memories of our shelter days and smashing up against the helplessness and desperation constantly simmering beneath the surface of my *chill*. It's bub-bub-bubbling up, pouring out, and stinging my windburned face from walking home in the cold.

I get up and go to the bathroom for a tissue. Feel the weight of the little slip of numbered paper in my pocket.

I've yet to look at it because . . . well, I hate to admit it considering how low I try to keep my expectations, but the encounter with the cute granny planted quite the "what if?" in the rocky soil of my heart. Which ain't good: when you live as tenuously as my family does, there's nothing worse than having even the slightest glimmer of hope dashed against the ugly boulders of life. But after checking my watch, I head to the living room, pulling the ticket out as I go.

Truth be told, I'm nervous about seeing which of the two I got—it'll be a little freaky if I chose the one with my birth date on it. I drop down onto the sofa as the movie credits finish rolling, and when cheesy saxophone music comes pouring out of the TV speakers, my breath catches.

"Mighty . . . Millions . . . Today could be your luc . . . ky . . . DAY!"

My heart is racing. Which is so dumb. I know from looking at the machine all the time that the odds are one in over 302.5 million, which is more than the jackpot itself.

But still.

The first ball drops—

29.

17 and 46 come next, but then the final two white balls are 01 and 06.

06. 29. 01.

No clue what golden Mighty Ball number is called out because all the sound gets sucked from the room as I look at the ticket in my hand.

It's not the one with my birth date.

None of the other numbers are on my ticket either.

Fresh tears spring to my eyes as I feel that void from

earlier open up beneath me and try to pull me under, but I clench my jaw and quickly swipe them away. Nothing has changed, and it's fine.

It has to be.

No clue whether or not the other numbers match the ones on the old lady's ticket—seems unlikely, but either way, she just won seven dollars.

Guess depending on how you look at it, I *am* a lucky charm.

Sure hope *she* has a merry Christmas.

-3-

The Wrong Ticket

There's a shriek like someone's being stabbed.

My eyelids pop wide, but I can't move.

The bedroom door is thrown open, slamming against that little rubber-tipped metal thingy that protrudes from the wall near the floor, and before I have a chance to react, there's a body flying through the air and landing on top of me. "*Ooof.*"

"He *came*, Rico, he CAAAAAAME!"

Jax sits up on my belly and grabs me by the shoulders. "You were *riiiiiiight*. Santa DOES give a flip about me!"

So he saw the bike then.

"*THIS IS THE BEST CHRISTMAS EVERRRRRR!*" he yells right in my face with his nine-year-old morning breath *(blegh)*.

I furrow my brow. "What on earth are you talking about, Jaxy?"

"Santa came! He brought me this awesome Minecraft Lego set and the twenty-inch Raptor Freestyle BMX Deluxe bike with a welded cross brace, alloy wheels, and super-gnarly pegs! It's *exactly* what I wanted, Rico!"

15

"That's awesome, little dude!"

He jumps off me. "Just wait till Mason Bridges gets a load of *this*! HA!"

Mason Bridges. Jax's most ardent antagonizer. A kid who sees his family's position at the top of the mountain as a license to drop rocks down on the people who live at the base. (The little jackass.)

Of course I don't have the heart to tell Jaxy there's very little chance of Mason *seeing* his cool new bike, since there's no way Mama would let him ride it two miles to school.

He runs out of the room still screaming his head off.

I sit up and stretch. Swing my legs over the edge of my twin bed. Still got my brown-skinned Barbie comforter and sheet set from when I was Jax's age.

Vintage, yo.

And then I smell cinnamon. Which would mean French toast.

Odd.

When I step out of the bedroom, Mama is standing over the stove decked out in her Hilton housekeeping uniform. Her dark hair spills down her back in a long braid, and her light-brown, freckled cheeks are flushed.

And there's French toast.

"Wow," I say. "You're cooking?"

She snorts. "Don't sound so surprised. It's Christmas!"

"And yet you're going to work on Christmas morning." As usual, I fail to keep my "little resentments," as she likes to call them, in check. And I instantly feel a pinch of guilt about it.

Typical morning in the Danger household.

16

"Somebody's gotta pay some bills around here, Rico!" she replies in her sarcastic singsong voice. "We can't all be *Santa*, you know."

This time, I bite my tongue.

Did I know she'd be pissed about Jax's bike? Of course. It's three hundred dollars of financial relief she won't be getting (and I have no doubt she knows exactly how much the thing cost).

Speaking of Jax, he chooses that moment to rip through the kitchen screaming, *"EVERYTHING IS AWWWWE-SOME!"*

"Nice to see the kid happy for once," I say, even though it's a low blow.

She glares at me, then peeks around to make sure he's out of earshot. "You think this is cute?"

I shrug. "That my little brother gets to act like it's Christmas *on* Christmas? Looks pretty cute to me."

"Mm-hmm. Well, when they cut our goddamn lights off, perhaps you can teach him how to use that bike to generate some electricity." She shoves the spatula underneath a piece of French toast so forcefully, it pops out of the pan and plummets to the floor. "Shit!"

I pour myself a cup of Folgers from the coffeepot—largely to piss Mama off since she hates when I drink it—and carry it over to the dining room table she pulled off a curb two years ago. "That can be one of my pieces."

No response. Just a gust of icy air as she sweeps out of the room, pretending I no longer exist.

Whatever.

After about a minute, she returns with her coat draped

over her arm and an envelope in hand. "I'm pulling a double, by the way." She slides the card across the table at me.

Merry Christmas to her too, I guess.

"You do know I also have to work, right?" I ask. "Two till ten—"

"I'm aware. Can't really miss it on that big-ass calendar you've got tacked to my wall."

This is one of *her* "little resentments." The calendar. As a matter of fact, Stacia Danger resents anything that reeks of structure she didn't create. Likely linked to her resentment of anything that makes her feel like a "bad parent."

Problem is, her attempt to be a "good parent" got us into this situation in the first place: living paycheck to paycheck—hers *and* mine—in an area that's way out of our price range.

"So what about Jax?" I say.

"He'll go upstairs. I've already talked to Señora Alvarez."

Thank God for Señora Alvarez, the delightful Salvadorian woman who lives in the apartment above ours and has been playing pinch-hit parent since we moved here. In fact, Jax spends so much time with her, he speaks a little Spanish.

Mama turns off the stove, wipes her hands on a dish towel, and dashes out of the kitchen. "I'm gonna be late," she says.

"Jax, Mommy's going to work! Come give her a kiss!" I holler.

Now she looks like she wants to murder me and bury the evidence.

"You can't just leave him on Christmas without saying

18

goodbye," I say before rising from the table and taking the four steps necessary to grab a couple of plates from the cabinet. "Where's the syrup?"

She doesn't respond, and when I look, her eyes have dropped, and her chin begins to tremble before she can stop it.

Because there is no syrup.

This was one of her gifts to us. French toast.

But there's no syrup.

I sigh.

Jax tries to barrel past me, but I stop him to give Mama a second to pull it together. "Jaxy, Mama made us some yummy French toast! Whattaya say we cook up some strawberries with sugar to go on top?" Because no matter what's lacking in this place, there are *always* strawberries. It's our one splurge.

"Heck yeah!" Jax says.

"Go tell Mommy thank you for her hard work so she can get going, okay?" I kiss his forehead.

As he runs to her, Mama looks up at me and smiles. Weakly, but it's enough.

A moment of accord.

"Thank you so, so much, Mommy!" Jax says.

Mama laughs and quickly wipes her own tears from her face. "You're welcome, Jaxy-Boy." She squeezes him tight. I walk over to join the hug.

"This is the *best* Christmas ever!"

"Okay, okay," Mama says. "I really do have to run." She breaks free and grabs her purse from the computer table, where our dinosaur of a PC monitor sits stoic and judgmental.

"Jax, you be good for Señora Alvarez, okay?" She kisses his cheek and he darts off. "Have a good afternoon at work, Rico."

"You too, Mama." And I swallow my pride. "Thanks for breakfast."

She nods. Smiles.

As the front door closes, I get the strawberries out and start cutting them up. Little sugar, little water . . . who needs crappy fake maple syrup anyway?

"Jax, breakfast!" I shout once I've scrambled some eggs and gotten everything on the plate.

He comes out of the bedroom with a red Lego robot in one hand and a green one in the other. "Christmas botsssssss!" he says, thrusting them into my face.

I chuckle.

"You know, since Mama's gone, we *could* eat in front of the television," I tell him. "Care to get a little Grinchy?"

"Yeaaaaah!" He shoots his little fist into the air. "Fuck the ruuuuuuules!"

Oh my God. "JAX!"

"Oops . . . You weren't supposed to hear that."

I just shake my head and smack him upside his. "Come on, you little toilet mouth."

As he gets settled into the couch, I turn on the television and tune it to Channel 3. Reach for the power button on the Mesozoic-era DVD player (remote's been lost for about three years now), but then:

> In breaking news, some folks are having a very merry Christmas as *two* winning Mighty Mil-

lions jackpot tickets were sold last night. One was purchased in Wyoming, but the other came from a machine right here in Metro Atlanta! The owner of the Gas 'n' Go convenience store on Spalding Drive in Norcross will receive a twenty-five-thousand-dollar bonus from the lottery commission for selling a winning jackpot ticket—

My mouth goes dry.

It's been five days, and no one in Georgia has come forward with the winning ticket. I know because all I've been doing while I'm not at work is gathering information on state lottery rules.

Rule number one: tickets expire after 180 days. That's June twenty-third, exactly six days before my eighteenth birthday.

Rule number two: winnings are subject to 25 percent in federal taxes and 6 percent in state taxes.

Rule number three: big winners in the state of Georgia cannot collect winnings anonymously.

In conclusion: someone eighteen or over who visited *my* workplace on Christmas Eve is holding on to a slip of paper worth one hundred and six million US buckaroos (before taxes).

I'm at the register when Mr. Zoughbi steps out of his office to come restock cigarettes, but I wait until the store is completely empty before I pop the question. "Mr. Z, do you remember how many Mighty Millions tickets you sold on Christmas Eve?"

"Oh gracious no, child," he says. "So many sold, I couldn't possibly know."

"I sold . . . three. One to a middle-aged white guy and two to an elderly black lady. Don't you think someone would've come forward by now? The trucker guy in Wyoming took home a forty-seven-point-two million lump sum after taxes."

"Ah, you never know! Perhaps our winner is consulting with financial experts and creating a plan. Many winners tumble into financial ruin due to lack of *Preparation*." He wags a finger at me.

All about the Preparation, that Mr. Z.

"Few weeks perhaps, there will be news," he continues.

I sigh. What he's saying makes perfect sense, of course. . . .

I just can't shake the feeling my fairy godgranny has that ticket.

I know for a *fact* she matched at least three of the numbers. If the winner *definitely* came from our store and was *definitely* purchased on Christmas Eve according to the reports . . .

What if she forgot she bought it? (CRS was her phrase, not mine.) What if—God forbid—she *lost* it?

"Truth be told, what is it to us?" Mr. Z continues. "The lottery commission already delivered our bonus." He tries to wink, but it just looks like he has a twitch. "There's a portion for you in your next paycheck."

Whoa. "You don't have to do that, Mr. Zoughbi. . . ." *Curse this knee-jerk pseudo-selflessness!*

"Oh, but I do!" he says. "Bonus for me means bonus for my number one employee!"

22

My face heats. "Oh."

"I am very thankful for you, child," he goes on. "You will see how much very soon."

He shoves the last carton of cigarettes into the overhead case and dusts his hands off. "Whoever our ticket holder is, we wish them the best, yes? I wouldn't complain about some of those dollars winding up in our register. . . ." He nudges me with his elbow. "But as a claim that large must be directly handled at the lottery office, I doubt we will ever see the winner again."

And back into the office he goes.

He's right. I know he's right. Whoever bought that ticket really has no reason to come back to this store (unless they need gas and/or artificially colored and flavored slushies).

But that won't stop me from wondering if I had the opportunity to pocket a big winner—thereby instantly changing *everything*—and I chose.

The wrong.

Ticket.

A Word from the Right Ticket

Forgive the interruption, dear reader, but I'll have you know this is going to be an adventure for me, too. It's not easy being an inanimate object worth enough American dollars to feed a family of six in Chad for over forty thousand years. (Or 4,077 families of six for a decade each. How my value is distributed is of no concern to me.)

(That is no exaggeration.)

Right now, that dastardly George Washington has his ugly green face smashed against mine, and there's a month-old Chick-fil-A receipt pressed against my behind without my consent. To top it off, the person who shoved me into this lackluster billfold truly *has* forgotten about me.

The indignity of it all is appalling considering my value, don't you think?

- 4 -

Bonus!

Five thousand dollars. That was the number on the check inside the *Happy New Year!* card Mr. Z handed me alongside my regular paycheck.

And instead of putting it in the account my mother has access to, I cashed it. Put it in an envelope. Stuffed it in a hole in my trusty box spring, same spot I hid the money I secreted away all those months for Jax's bike.

Every night after he falls asleep, I close whatever book I'm reading, pull the envelope out, and count the hundred-dollar bills. I've never held that much money before, and feeling the paper slide through my fingers keeps me distracted from other facets of my life that often plague my brain in the darkness: the fact that we're always a few hours of pay away from not making rent; that Mama treats me more like a partner and co-parent than a kid; that my seventeen-year-old life consists entirely of school, work, and sleep; that I have no friends.

That last one's really been getting to me lately. Got really acute a few mornings ago when I happened to leave my apartment to head to the (school) bus stop at the exact moment Jessica Barlow—class president, head cheerleader, and popular kid on infinity—was leaving the adjacent apartment.

Like a ding-dong, I froze, deer-in-headlights style. I vaguely remember her moving in who knows how many years ago, but between never seeing her around here since and the incongruous-to-her-glittering-image bumps and shouts that sometimes filter through our shared walls, I'd forgotten she lives there. Don't know her situation—she's one of the bright lights in Zan Macklin's inner circle and certainly *looks* the Rich Kid part—so the whole thing was jarring.

Especially when she smiled at me.

I've always done my best to keep my head down—which is easy to do when it seems like no one realizes you exist (though I've admittedly been staring at the back of Zan Macklin's head a lot more in history lately, wondering if we *did* in fact make eye contact that night at the store). But knowing she *saw* me? Maybe before, I would've written the whole thing off. But ever since seeing my birth date on that ticket, it's like this world of possibility has opened up, and now I constantly find myself . . . curious.

Which feels dangerous. There are few things worse for a poor kid than working up the courage to hope and then having that hope pulverized down to subatomic particles beneath the weight of (another) disappointment.

So I count my money.

But then on the afternoon of January twenty-fourth, Mr. Fifty-Dollar-Bill strolls into the Gas 'n' Go while I'm

26

shelving magazines. He overlooks me as he grabs the latest issue of *Playboy*, but there's certainly no shame in his game once he sees me.

"Hey there!" he says, clutching the magazine to his chest. On the cover is some lady wearing a pair of open jeans and strategically placed suspenders.

I force a smile to keep from wrinkling my nose. "Hello."

"Rico, right? You were here on Christmas Eve?"

"Mm-hmm." I stick the last *Car and Driver* in place. Stand and dust my hands off. "Anything I can help you find today?"

"Nope, I think I found it!" He holds his magazine up.

(Can I please throw up now?)

"Okay then!" I turn to head to the counter, and he follows me. Tries to hand me the magazine to scan.

"Just hold it out," I say. Cuz I ain't touchin' it.

It scans. $14.37 including tax.

Of course he hands me a fifty.

"So did you have a merry Christmas, Rico? A happy New Year?"

I shrug. "Not too bad. You?"

"Well, between you and me, it woulda been a lot merrier had I bought that Mighty Millions jackpot ticket," he says. "Anybody come forward yet?"

So it's not him then. Unless he's bluffing . . . but why would he be bluffing? "Not that I'm aware of, sir." I count his change out and slide it to him. "I'm sure we'll find out eventually."

———

27

I don't sleep that night. Can't. Every time I close my eyes, I see the smiling face of the little old lady who made being at work on Christmas Eve a little less awful. Counting the bonus doesn't help because all I can think about is the fact that someone—maybe her . . . (aka, almost *me*)—could be missing an opportunity to count 1,059,950 *more* hundred-dollar bills than I currently have in my possession.

When the sun rises, I'm wrapped in a blanket on the balcony staring at Mama's beat-up old Nissan pickup truck. The red paint has faded from the roof and one of the back tires is low. I go back inside to start a pot of Folgers, and turn on *Rise 'n' Shine Atlanta*.

First story I see?

> "Wyoming Mighty Millions jackpot winner Wally Winkle is about to become a television star! The ten-episode reality show *JACKPOT!* will follow the former truck driver as he adjusts to his lavish new lifestyle. The first episode is set to air Thursday, February seventh, at eight p.m. Eastern on the MoneyVision network."

I turn it off. Chew my lip. Look around at the dingy walls and mostly secondhand furniture in our closet-sized living room.

A hundred and six million dollars. Just out there some-where.

The things a person could *do* with that kind of money . . .

I sold three Mighty Millions tickets on Christmas Eve

exactly a month ago. Two of them were not the Big Winner. Could Mr. Zoughbi have sold it earlier in the day? Of course. But I also now know that the winning Mighty Ball number was in fact 07, and that the odds of matching three white balls plus the Mighty Ball are one in 14,547. Which, yes, makes it almost 21,000 times more likely than winning the jackpot . . . but the odds of *two* tickets with those numbers being sold at the same store on the same day?

Come on.

How can I know for *sure*, though? And what am I supposed to *do* about it? It's not like fairy godgranny left me her name and number and invited me over for tea. . . .

There were three other people, myself included, inside the Gas 'n' Go when fairy godgranny exited, Christmas sweater alight, holding a ticket that contained at least four of the six winning numbers. I know one of those other people—Mr. Bashir Zoughbi—wouldn't condone me hunting down one of his customers, so he's not likely to *give* me access to the security footage I'll need to try and find out what kind of car the lady was driving.

I *could* try to get into the hella-high-tech, flat-screened monstrosity on Mr. Z's desk—stuff from the cameras outside the store would have to be on there somewhere, right? Then again, the only computer I really interact with on a regular basis is our Tyrannosaurus rex that's still rockin' Windows 8.1. So maybe not a great idea.

Which leaves me with one other (very rich, handsome, and intimidating) potential option.

My eyes drop to the hole in the couch that has widened

over the years because Jax picks at it when he's anxious (which is all the effing time).

I'm picking at it now.

Sure hope there's something of substance beneath Zan Macklin's hundred-dollar haircut.

And maybe those hacker rumors are true.

-5-

A Terrible Idea

And now I'm hiding in the bathroom.

"A hundred-and-six friggin *MIL*, Rico," I whisper from my perch on the abused-looking toilet. "Get your shit together!"

"Uhh . . . you all right in there?" comes a voice from outside the stall.

Oops.

"Yes, fine," I say. "Just . . . ate a bad breakfast burrito."

"Gross . . ."

But it does the trick. I hear a compact snap shut and the click of shoes exiting shortly thereafter.

"Okay. Deep breath."

I almost missed the bus this morning because I spent so much time fussing over what to wear. Figured if I'm gonna initiate a conversation with *the* pee-pee-paper prince, I should look as close to a million bucks as possible . . . but then I discovered that the most expensive thing in my closet is a forty-dollar body-con dress Mama found deeply on sale at T. J. Maxx—and the last time I wore *that*, my turd-brain chem lab partner held up the round-bottom glass chemical container we were using for our experiment, looked me over lasciviously, and said, "Forget *back* . . . baby got *flask*."

So that was a no-go.

The bell rings, signaling the end of second lunch/beginning of third.

The time has come.

I exit the stall as a gaggle of cheerleaders come in.

Not even the vaguest peek in my direction.

I push toward the exit and, before I can think too much about it, run my hands over the front of the billowy skirt I threw on when Mama started yelling about "punctuality," lift my chin, and make my way out into the cafeteria.

Not a single head turns. (Typical.)

Zan is sitting at the far end of his regular table, which *should* make this easy. Guess it depends on if he resists or not.

I reach the table, and I'm moving fast.

This whole thing is a terrible idea. Maybe I should just keep going. They probably wouldn't even notice me speed-walking by like a freak-and-a-half.

But then I catch eyes with Jessica Barlow. Who is watching me. She smiles (so *weird*!), and I force a tight-lipped smile back, but as I pass her, still booking it, her head tilts—quizzically.

No turning back now.

One of the guys tells a joke, and everyone laughs. Zander says something to the black kid sitting across from him (think his name is Finesse?), then sets his water bottle down . . . which is when I pass behind him, grab his upper arm, and pull.

"Whoa," he says, and I'm sure he's looking at me, but I'm trying to maintain my forward momentum, so I don't look back. I do, however, breathe life's biggest sigh of relief as I feel his weight give. "Guess I'm being summoned," he says, and he rises to let me tug him along while everyone laughs.

The sweater he's wearing must be cashmere or something. It's by far the softest thing I've ever touched. Biceps don't feel too bad either.

It's not until we pass through the open doors to the west stairwell that it hits me: *I just pulled Zan Mega-Money Macklin from his lunch table in front of everyone. And he actually came. Holy shi—*

"So is our final destination inside the building at least?" he says.

I stop and let go of his arm, but now I can't make myself face him.

Sweet mother of pearl I did not think this through.

"Hellooooooo? Kidnapper?"

I take a few breaths and turn around.

God.

The guy looks (and smells) like he just stepped off the cover of the J.Crew Christmas catalog.

It's disgusting.

He smiles down at me. "Hi."

"Umm, hi." I look at my feet.

No, Rico! Chin UP, dammit!

And . . . Huh. I knew he was tan for a white boy, but his eyes are a lot greener than I expected. His eyebrows are super thick, and he's got acne along his chin and the ruins of an angry erupted zit in the little crevasse beside his left nostril.

I exhale. And almost smile. "I need to talk to you," I say.

He chuckles. "I gathered as much from the cafeteria abduction."

"Oh." *What do I say to that?* "Uh, I'm Rico, by the way."

"Zan."

I swallow a snort. "I know."

"So did I," he says.

Hmm.

"K, I'm gonna come right out with it—"

"That would be nice . . . Didn't get to finish my lunch."

Asshole. "I . . . need your help."

"Do you now?" He crosses his arms.

I totally huff. Like so hard my on-the-verge-of-frizzy bangs flutter. He's kind of frustrating. And he smells really good. It's confusing.

"Yeah. I do."

"Aren't you the same girl who avoided me like the plague when I stepped into your place of employment on Christmas Eve?"

Is he for real? "My 'place of employment'? Who even talks like that?"

"Admit it. You were totally dodging me."

"No I wasn't."

"Fine." He shrugs and turns to leave.

"Wait, no!"

"So you *were* avoiding me, then?"

"This is completely irrelevant to—"

"My food is waiting. . . ."

UGH!

"Okay, *fine*. Yes, I was avoiding you."

He nods. "That's what I thought. Now how may I be of service, dear Ri—"

The bell rings.

I smack my forehead, and his brows dip just the slightest bit. The weird green eyes burn a haphazard trail as they roam all over my face, and his head drifts toward his shoulder until he looks like he's examining a piece of abstract art from another angle or something.

It's unnerving. Especially since he oozes *wealth*.

I can't look at him anymore. "Can we talk after school maybe?" I say as my gaze falls. "I have to work four to eight, but maybe you could meet me at Tensonwood Park at three-thirty? It's down the road from the Gas 'n' G—"

"I know where Tensonwood Park is, Rico."

I clench my teeth. Not sure why I wasn't expecting him to be this arrogant.

A hundred and six MIL.LI.ON, Rico!

Gulp down my dignity and force myself to make eye contact again. "Please?"

He rubs his chin and stares up at the ceiling in pretend thought as the stairwell starts to fill. Then back at me. "No more avoidance?"

Egomaniac. "No more avoidance."

"Promise?"

"Oh my God."

He laughs. "Okay."

"Okay?"

"Okay," he says. "I'll meet you on the swings."

-6-

Swing for the Fences

Imagine my shock when I get to the playground at 3:20 p.m., and *Zan-the-Man* (that's another one I hear in the hallways) is already there. Literally on a swing.

His too-long legs *pump-pump-pump*, and he flies so high, the chains go slack at the top. When he sees me, he jumps out at the peak of his next arc. His arms lift, and his dark hair flutters in the breeze as he drops.

I can't look away.

He dusts off his pants, spreads his arms, and smiles. "Rico!" he says. "Fancy meeting you here."

Totally roll my eyes, but if I'm honest, it's a cover for how wildly uncomfortable I am. Talking to Zan Macklin in the dim-ish hallways of Norcross High School with other people milling around was one thing. . . . This? Out in the open, sun blazing, one-on-one? It's like I can feel how dingy and overworn my clothes are—jacket, shirt, skirt, the whole nine.

He heads over to a bench to sit and pats the space beside him, so I take a deep breath and comply, putting my hands beneath my thighs and staring down at our feet. The contrast between his pristine brown wing tips (*what high school senior even wears those?*) and my scuffed thrift-store boots would be enough to make me literally run away were I not so desperate.

One. Hun. Dred. Six. Millllll . . .

Which is probably about how much this guy has in his trust fu—

"Speakest thou to the Zan, O Avoidant One," he says, flicking a neon-yellow fidget spinner that seems to have appeared out of thin air.

"Oh my God, will you let that *go*?" My face is a raging inferno of mortification.

"I will not." He sticks his nose in the air. "What did I ever do to you, huh?"

"I didn't think you even knew who I was."

Didn't mean to say that aloud, but when he doesn't respond, I turn to him. Like on some strange instinct.

One of those thick eyebrows is practically making out with his hairline. "You're not serious."

"Why wouldn't I be serious?"

"Well, for one, you've been in *nine* of my classes over the years."

"Has it really been that many?" *And is he really keeping count?*

"It has."

Hmm. "Go on."

"For two, your name is *Rico Danger.*"

"It's actually *DON-gur—*"

He's . . . aghast, it seems. "Why would you *ever* tell anyone that?"

37

"Because it's true?"

He shakes his head, gives the spinner another flick. "Do you have any idea how awesome it is to have *Danger* for a last name? If your future husband doesn't take *your* name, he's a dumbass."

"Future husband?"

"Or wife," he amends. "Spouse. Future spouse." His cheeks are pinkening, and okay, maybe I chuckle a little. Partially because Zan Macklin just suggested I'll get married one day. *Pffft.*

"Is that a laugh I hear? Is the Avoidant One warming up to ol' Zanny Zan?"

"You might have an ego problem, *Zanny Zan.* That's a lot of self-nicknaming."

Now *he* laughs. "Touché, Ice Queen."

He slouches down and stretches his arms across the back of the bench. The cologne punches me in the olfactory receptors and my head goes a little fuzzy. Man, what is *in* that stuff?

I swallow. "So what's three?"

"Three?" he says.

"You gave me a *for one* and a *for two* . . . which implies a *for three*, doesn't it? Don't things like this usually come in trios?" Also, am I really sitting here talking to Zan Macklin like I *know* him, know him?

Wild.

"Who's got the ego problem now, huh, Danger?"

The corner of my mouth lifts despite my inner protestations. "Whatever."

"Mm-hmm."

"Cut it out."

Gotta say: Zan Macklin's way down-er-to-earth than I expected. I'm (cautiously) pleasantly surprised—and optimistic.

He's smiling now. And looking at me. I can see it in my peripheral.

"There actually is a *for three*," he says.

"Okay . . ."

A couple of seconds pass. Then a couple more.

Nothin'.

Another instinctive nonresponse-provoked head turn . . . He's full-on blushing now. "Well?" I say.

"Well what?"

"What's *for three*?"

"Well, for three, you're . . ." He looks at me. "Well. You're *you.*"

"What is that supposed to mean?"

"You're like . . . aesthetically unique."

"Unique." I hate that word.

"Yeah. Different. Singular. Whatever you want to call it."

"Okay . . ."

"It's a compliment. Let's get down to business, yeah?"

I gulp then. And notice his watch. Which pretty much blasts a big-ass hole in whatever tenuous web of connection I was feeling with good ol' *Zanny Zan*. Despite the fact that he's playing with a fidget spinner my nine-year-old brother would be really into.

God, what the hell was I thinking putting my grubby little hands on the Sultan of Sanitary Supplies? Are my nails even clean?

39

I totally peek down at them.

"What'd you wanna talk to me about?" he says.

I can't respond. It's like the letters all tumble apart when the words reach the tip of my tongue.

"Rico, if you wanted me to take you on a park date, all you had to do was ask—"

"Whoa, that is *not* what this is about."

He grins. "So?"

Why is this so hard?

"Okay," I say. Deep breath. He's just a dude. With hella money, yes, but also a crater of a former zit giving me stank-eye from the side of his nose. "Remember how when you were coming into the store on Christmas Eve, there was a cute little old lady going out?"

"You mean the night you avoided me?"

"Stop. She was dark-brown-skinned and had white hair, and you held the door open for her. She called you handsome."

"Wow, Rico. And here I thought you weren't paying me any attention."

I glare at him.

Of course he laughs. "I'm just messin' with you. Sure. I remember her."

That's a relief at least. "Well, I need to find her," I say.

"Why?"

I anticipated this question. I really did. Just failed to come up with a viable response. "I . . . wanna reconnect with her."

"Ah-ha." He clasps his hands in his lap. "So what does this have to do with me?"

"Well, for one, you're the only other person *I* know who

40

knows what she looks like." Besides my boss, but hopefully he won't ask about that.

"And *for two?*" He winks.

I turn away. "Well, I heard you're maybe, ahh . . . good with computers?"

"Oh?"

"Something about you getting kicked out of private school for hacking the main server and giving the entire eighth-grade football team straight As?"

He lifts his chin, but not before I see the wicked twinkle in his eye. "I know naught of which you speak, Agent Danger."

"*Agent Danger?* Seriously?"

He blushes again!

Which makes *my* face hot. Thankful for my skin's high melanin content in this moment.

(This is getting ridiculous.)

Clear my throat. "I need to get into the security camera footage from Christmas Eve to see if I can get a license plate for her."

"She got into a taxi."

My head whips left. "She did?!"

"Yep."

"Do you remember the name of the cab company?"

He shakes his head. "Can't say I do."

"Okay. So the security footage is my only hope, then—"

"So you want me to hack the security archives at your place of employment?"

I swallow. "Basically."

"Nope." And he crosses his arms.

I sigh.

"Not unless you tell me why you need to find her," he says.

I take a deep breath. Inhale a whiff of his (sorcerous) cologne.

Which probably costs more than our weekly grocery budget.

Now every time I breathe, I wonder how obvious it is to him: the fact that I have so much less than he does. Can he smell the five-dollar (for the big size) Johnson's baby lotion on my skin or the two-dollar Suave conditioner I left in my curly hair? What would he say if he knew my skirt was held together by a safety pin or that I use the laces in these shoes for a different pair as well?

What kind of assumptions will he make if I tell him about the ticket?

Yeah, I could say what I planned to: I think the lady is holding on to a big winner and doesn't know it. That she made an impression on me, and I think she deserves to cash that ticket in and enjoy the rest of her time here in this often-unkind world.

But will he believe me?

Also: What happens if he decides *he* wants the ticket? Even rich people seem likely to jump at the chance to get more money. Hell, if Ponzi schemes and corporate fraud are any indication, rich people seem *especially* likely. . . .

"Danger? You good over there?"

"Yeah," I say with a nod.

Because what other option do I have? If he can hack the security footage, I need him.

So I take a deep breath. And swallow. And let the cooler-than-expected breeze blowing up my skirt jolt me back to reality.

Then I look Zan Macklin right in his money-green eyes. And I tell him about fairy godgranny and the ticket.

A Word from the List Rico Made
a Couple Days Ago and
Then Threw Away

While currently smeared in discarded—and rotting—milk/egg mixture (did someone make French toast?) and covered with stringy stuff from the old banana peel I wound up smashed against, I felt it important that you see me.

Our beloved Rico isn't much of a dreamer—years of forced adulthood and hindered ambition will do that to a girl—but in a fit of sleepless fervor, she scribbled me onto the legal pad where she makes the "monthly budget and bills" lists . . . then promptly ripped me out, crushed me up tight like I'd insulted her mama, and slammed me into the trash can.

Bit rude, but whatever. Observe:

Things I would do if I had a $47.2-million lump sum

- Buy a nice house—4 bedroom/4.5 bath, two stories plus basement, pool preferably in a subdivision with

"On the River" in its name and walk-in pantry in the kitchen
- ~~Health insurance~~ GOOD health insurance
- Probably buy a second, smaller house just for me
- Decent car for me
- Volvo XC90 for Mama
- Buy Jaxy every Lego set there is
- Give a crap-ton to charities that help poor kids, especially around Christmas
- Jaxy college fund

-7-

Can't Hack It

At 7:33 Saturday morning, Zan-the-Man Macklin shuffles into the Gas 'n' Go with his shirt misbuttoned and his thick, dark hair sticking straight up on one side.

It's way more attractive than I was distinctly prepared for. Gotta shake it off.

"You're here!" I say, rushing over to grab his forearm and pull him to Mr. Z's office.

He groans. "This relationship isn't gonna last if you insist on dragging me along, IQ."

I pull the chair out from beneath the desk and shove him down into it. Then I kneel in front of the desk. "IQ?"

"Ice Queeeeeeen."

"Don't be ridiculous," I say as I input the password that unlocks the fancy flat-screen-monitor/actual-computer-part-in-one: *getgasandgetitfast1*. "I'm as warm as freshly baked bread."

He snorts and lets his head fall back.

"Okay, so you have exactly"—I look at my Loki watch . . . and then shove it behind my back when I catch sight of

46

his fancy-spensive one. God—"thirty-eight minutes." Toss in a friendly and hopefully encouraging pat on the shoulder even though I feel weird touching him.

"Why am I doing this, again?" he says.

"Because you're a good guy doing a good deed. That money could change an old lady's final years into something she's never even dreamed of."

"Maybe she doesn't want her life to be changed." He yawns, and I shake my head, instantly irritated. This guy has no idea what it's like to constantly be on the brink of not having what you need to survive.

Must be nice.

"Mr. Zoughbi will walk back into the store at precisely eight-fifteen." I stand, frankly wanting to get the hell away from him. He reeks too much of *money* right now and it makes me wanna harf and punch him right in the sternum where his buttons are jacked up. Preferably at the same time. "All yours," I say.

No response.

Peek over the shoulder. He's knocked out. Mouth open and everything.

"Macklin!"

"Huh?" He shoots up. "What happened?"

"Did you hear a word I said?"

"Yeah, yeah." He rubs his eyes. "Forty-eight minutes—"

"*Thirty*-eight. Actually no . . . thirty-six now."

He cracks his knuckles and whips a pair of glasses out of his shirt pocket.

Of course he's even more attractive in nerd mode. Which

does nothing but increase my irritation in this moment. "I'll be out there restocking candy bars if you need anything. Leaving the office door open."

"Mm-hmm." He starts typing away.

I don't move. He's managed to pull up a black screen with a bunch of green letters and numbers and symbols scrolling on it. And still typing. I have no idea how long I stand there looking between the screen and his Concentration Face, but he suddenly stops typing.

He pushes his glasses up on his nose (*Stop it, Zanny-Zan-the-Man!*). "The doorbell just rang," he says.

"Huh?"

"Customer?"

"Oh my gosh!" I rush out of the office, and he totally snorts. It'll be a miracle to make it through the next half hour without steam shooting out of all my facial orifices.

Then I see the glistening bald spot of the man standing in front of one of the open cooler doors, and I immediately want to go back into the office and maybe hide under the desk.

It's Mr. Fifty.

When he starts to turn around, I pretend to busy myself with straightening cigarette cartons.

"Rico!" he says once he reaches the counter.

I look over my shoulder. Let my eyebrows rise. "Wow! You're up early for a Saturday."

"Ha! Look who's talkin'!"

"Employment calls." I shrug.

"Me too, kid, me too," he says. "You're having a decent morning, I hope?"

"Not too shabby. Yourself?"

He looks at his watch. (Which looks like Zan's. Figures.) "Late. But doesn't really matter when you're the boss, right?" A wink.

Blegh, go away!

He pays for his vittles and beverage ($44.17 in change), then smiles. "You have a good one, all right, Rico?"

"Will do, sir. Same to you."

As soon as the door closes behind Mr. Fifty, Zan speaks. Well, yells really. "Hey, IQ?"

"Stop calling me that!"

He laughs. "I take it you're alone out there?"

"Yeah . . ."

"Okay. Just thought you should know the security footage is encrypted."

Uhhhh . . . "And in noncomputer dork, that means what exactly?"

"Shut your hole."

A few seconds go by.

"No, for real," I say, kneeling to do the candy bars. "What does that mean?"

"Means more work."

Sugar biscuits. "How much more work?"

"Mmmm . . . For me? A good half an hour at least."

Watch check. "You got twenty-two minutes, Macklin!"

"Look, you *ingrate*, I'm working as fast as I can. Just letting you know I might not be able to crack it within your ridiculous time constraint!"

Inhale. Exhale. "Anything I can help you with?"

"One of those artificially colored and flavored mocha cappuccino things would be nice," he says.

I go to the machine and make the drink. Take it to him.

He's holding an active fidget spinner in his left hand—this one's gold.

"What's with those?" I nod toward it.

"Sometimes you just need something to do with your hands, you know?" He sets the spinner on the desk—still spinning—and reaches for the coffee. Looks into the cup, then up at me. "You're a god-awful barista, IQ."

"What?"

"Where the hell's the whipped cream?"

"UGH!" *Freakin' rich people!* I turn to go back to the machine, but he hooks a finger into my apron string and pulls me back.

"I'm messin' with you, Rico. Take a chill pill, will ya?"

"You're infuriating, you know that?" I set the coffee on the desk.

"And *you* are higher-strung than a superkite. We need to get you some good weed or something." He takes a sip of the coffee.

"Are you serious?!"

"About which part?" He goes back to typing. "I gotta say, though: I feel like I've known you for a long time. Is that weird?"

"Umm . . . yes."

"Hmm. Well, you have to admit we've got *rapport*, you and me."

I find myself silently agreeing in spite of the needling little voice telling me to compare his and my footwear (me: used and abused Keds I got for $2.50 at a flea market; him: what are surely the latest and greatest Nike Air Maxes).

Thankfully, though, before I have a chance to spiral and run away, some parking lot footage pops up on the screen.

"Oh! You're in!"

"Nope. Your boss has it set up where each month of footage has a different unlock passcode. This is January so I'm looking for some kind of loophole that will let me into the December stuff. Has he been hacked before?"

I shrug. "I guess it's possible. He got new software just after the store was broken into and trashed by anti-Muslim douchefaces last August."

Zan nods. "I'm guessing whoever did that got into the computer and messed some stuff up because homeboy's got this thing locked *down*."

The bell on the door chimes again, and I look at my watch. "Down to fifteen minutes."

"I'm on it. Go tend to your customer."

Except it's not a customer.

"Mr. Z!"

Oh God, oh God . . . crap crap CRAP!

"What are you doing back there, Rico? You leave the store open this way?" He walks toward the office.

My heart hops up between my ears. I'm so dead.

"You're back early," I say.

"Yes, yes. Dunkin' was fresh out of gingerbread cheesecake donuts." He shakes his head, thankfully distracted for the moment. "For shame."

"I'm so sorry to hear that, Mr. Zoughbi, Gas 'n' Go owner!" *Dear God, if you're real, please let Zan be hearing this and take the hint to frickin' HIDE!*

"You're acting very strangely, young lady. Is everything

51

fine?" He comes closer, and I try my hardest to block the way to the office.

"There was, umm . . . a minor problem." Man, I wish I were a better liar.

"Problem?" He looks down at the open boxes of candy bars on the floor. "What sort of problem?"

"Oh, no big deal . . . candy inventory mix-up."

"Ah. So you're ready to finish the restock?" He gestures to the boxes.

"Absolutely, Mr. Z." I smile and try to pull the office door closed, but then he says, "No, no, leave it. I'm going inside."

He gets closer. Closer.

I'm. So. Dead.

Though still smiling somehow. If only I could get my damn feet to move.

"Rico?" Mr. Z says when he's about five feet from me. "Are you—?"

"I'm just about done in here!" Zan says from the office.

My smile falls off.

"There is someone in my office?"

Mr. Z don't look happy. Matter of fact, the last time I saw a look like the one he's wearing right now, he was standing outside the store rubbing his beard as he stared at the broken windows and smashed-in front door.

I'm about to get fired. What if he calls the cops?

And there's Zany Zanny Macklin, who decides it's a good idea to come lean against the office doorjamb with his hands in his pockets like he owns the place.

Because he surely thinks he owns everything.

I hate him. I really, really hate him.

Mr. Zoughbi is understandably furious. "And who might this be, Rico?"

"Alexander Gustavo Macklin, sir," Zan says, extending a hand.

Gustavo?

"Rico here was having some trouble matching your physical inventory with what was in the system. Your computer apparently had a VV."

Mr. Z's eyes go wide. "A VV?"

"A Voldemort Virus, sir."

"Oh my . . ." Mr. Zoughbi is officially shook.

I gulp down a laugh. Even with my subnovice level of tech savvy, I highly doubt Voldemort Virus is an actual thing.

"It was causing a glitch in your spreadsheet software that doubled the number of bars in each box. Got it all cleaned up for ya."

Mr. Z puts a hand on his chest and exhales. He's buying this BS hook, line, and sinker. "Thank you so very much, young man! And good for you catching on and calling someone, Rico." With a pat on the back.

I clear my throat. "It was nothing, Mr. Z. Just didn't want you to worry." I'm lying to my boss. "I knew my pal Zan here could figure out the issue—"

"Wait just one moment," Mr. Z says, and his expression morphs into something indecipherable, at least for me.

That million-dollar Macklin smile falters.

Ah, fiddlesticks, he's onto us.

"Macklin, you say?"

Zan's Adam's apple bobs. "Yes, sir—"

"You!" Zoughbi's arms shoot into the air like torpedoes. "Here!"

Zan looks at me (like *I* have any clue what's happening?). "Umm—"

"What a day this is!" Mr. Z goes on. "There is something you and I must discuss."

"Uhh. Okay?"

"Wonderful you fixed my computer, but the customers, eh? They complain about the bathroom paper," he says. "Perhaps you might suggest something new? Two-ply or more with quilting, perhaps? If you give it to me at cost, I'll give your whole family a lifetime discount on cold beverages. . . ."

They disappear into the office, and my knees wobble with relief. No clue how long I stand there with my mouth open like an imbecile, but soon, customers are coming and going faster than I can count them. I end up sliding the box of candy bars behind the checkout counter.

Just as we hit another lull, the office door opens. "You're an upstanding young man, Mr. Macklin." Mr. Zoughbi throws an arm around Zan's shoulders and gives him a shake.

It bothers me to no end that my successful immigrant entrepreneur boss is referring to my high school classmate as "mister." What the hell has *Alexander* done to warrant that kind of respect?

Zan looks at me. "Great doing business with you, Mr. Zoughbi," he says, tossing a li'l winky-wink my way.

Vomit.

"You will bring me the samples?" Mr. Z says.

"I will, sir. The latest and greatest in rolled sanitary paper, and you'll be the first to see it."

"You hear that, Rico? First a winning Mighty Millions ticket, and now we will have the softest toilet tissue of any convenience store in the country—"

"The world, really, sir," Zan says.

"THE WORLD!" Mr. Z claps and lifts his clasped hands to the heavens.

There's no way any of this is real.

"I've gotta get going," Zan continues. "We'll talk soon, Mr. Zoughbi." They shake hands, and then he comes over to me.

"Rico, pleasure to see you as always." He stretches out a hand for me to shake. There's no mistaking the rascally twinkle in his eye. It's the same look Jax gets just before bragging about getting away with something mischievous.

When our hands touch, he presses a piece of paper against my palm . . . and yanks me forward. "C'mere, you." I collide with his chest—then he's wrapping his arms around my waist and lifting me off my feet.

What on earth?

He sets me back down, and I slip the note in my pocket, legitimately hot all over and *so* not okay with it.

"Wonderful citizens of Norcross, GA, I bid thee *adieu!*" He waves, and then the bell chimes as he exits.

What a weirdo.

When I turn around, Mr. Z is staring at me. "Rico Danger, you scoundrel! Why did you not tell me of your friendship with Mr. Macklin?"

"*Zan* is fine, Mr. Z."

"He is a very humorous young man, eh? Told me many stories of your shared childhood!"

Shared childhood?!

"I am grateful for you, young lady," he says. "You are one of many blessings to me."

Wow. I don't even know what to say to that. Especially since his thankfulness is built on a web of lies.

"You are fine out here? No need for a bathroom break?"

I just blink. "No, sir. I'm, umm . . . I'm good?"

"Excellent. I will look through the inventory spreadsheet once more to make sure all has been corrected."

I swallow. "Okay, sir."

He smiles and vanishes through the office door.

Once I'm alone, I pull out the note from Zan. His handwriting is surprisingly neat, but there are just two words.

And they make my heart do a little tap dance:

Got it.

-8-

Didn't Start the Fire

When I step into US History on Monday, Big Money Macklin is sitting in the desk beside mine. Not only do people kick palpable side-eye at me as I head to the back of the room, when I pass Zan's *regular* seat, the boy who normally sits next to me shoots glare-daggers at my face like I'm an accomplice to murder.

Which is . . . odd?

Zan nods at me as I sit. "Lady Danger," he says.

I shake my head, trying really hard not to smile. "Looks like Amit's pretty P.O.'d about you jacking his seat, Macklin," I say.

"Technically, it would be *P'd.O.* And anyway, I paid him twenty dollars. He's just mad because I wouldn't double it."

Wait.

"You *paid* him?" *To sit next to me?*

Am I flattered? Or annoyed at his nonchalance about flushing twenty bucks so frivolously?

This is confusing.

"Yep. You and I have much to discuss."

"Do we now?"

He throws his arms into the air. "Did ya *not* read my note Saturday, Danger?"

"Oh, this note, you mean?" I pull it from the breast pocket of the button-down I stole from Mama's closet this morning.

"Aww!" He puts a hand on my shoulder. "You keep it close to your heart!"

"Yeah, whatever." Pretty much didn't sleep all weekend because I couldn't figure out what the dang thing *meant*. "I've been so overwhelmed by the specificity, I can hardly stand it."

"I'm gonna need a coat of armor to survive your stabbing sarcasm, O Icy One."

"Why do you keep calling me that?"

He leans toward me. Cologne sorcery head-rush. "I think the more pressing question is why haven't you embraced it?"

I open my mouth to respond, but the bell rings, and Mr. Tripathi waddles in to start class.

Can't lie: knowing THE Zan Macklin is sitting beside me in class *on purpose* is a little distracting. Within five minutes, Mr. Tripathi is sounding like that teacher from *Peanuts* . . . *waaah wah waaah wah waaaaaah.*

I put an elbow on the desk and prop up my chin to keep my head from drooping as he babbles about some song called "We Didn't Start the Fire." Out of nowhere, something sharp pokes me in the forearm.

I yelp. Every head in the room turns.

"Is everything all right, Miss *Don-gur*?" Because of course, Mr. Tripathi says it correctly.

And I'm mortified.

"Yes. Sorry, sir," I say.

He nods and everyone faces forward.

"Geez, IQ. Think you could be any less discreet?" Zan whispers as soon as Tripathi rotates to tap on the SMART board.

I scowl at him, but he points to my desk. There's a note folded into a small triangle.

Of course he would make a paper football.

I unfold.

You know, we should probably exchange numbers . . .

Stab in the arm becomes stab in the gut with this acute reminder of my lowly "socioeconomic status," as Tripathi refers to it. Because while I technically *have* a cell phone—a prepaid imitation of the iPhones and Galaxies glued to everyone else's palms—it's solely for emergencies and I can't even text on it.

And this is why I keep to myself. My insides curdle at the very *idea* of the side-eye I would get were people to find out I don't have something that's considered such a staple to "this generation."

Ugh.

Umm . . . I don't really give mine out. You can give me yours though . . . If you want.

678.555.3525

I scribble it into the margin of my open notebook (that I haven't taken a single note in today).

Thanks.

So to update: I managed to retrieve a picture of your cute grandma from the security footage. Quality's garbage, but it's better than nothin . . .

I write back:

Awesome, but please don't ever say "your cute grandma" again.

K. She got into a cab that night.

Yeah. You told me that.

I got the license plate.

Score!

Gah, you're amazing!

I watch his cheeks go pink as he reads. Too much? Maybe too much.

I'm really not, but thanks I guess.

Modesty? Weird.

So what is it?

What's what?

The plate number?

Not important.

What do you mean "not important"?!

Trusteth in thine Zan, thou must.

What are you, Yoda Jesus now?

He snorts.

Of course everyone looks again.

"Mr. Macklin? Is there something funny?" from Tripathi. (I don't think Tripathi likes Zan very much. Not that I blame him. . . .)

"No, sir," Zan says. "Gnat flew up my nose. Please continue."

Everyone laughs, and Tripathi's jaw clenches, but he turns back around.

After about a minute, the note comes back to me. I kinda hate how excited I get when I feel the poke in the arm. It's just that . . . well, this is kind of my first time passing notes in class. Ever. A realization that serves to remind me of my dearth of, you know, *friends*. And free time. To make them.

You're funny, IQ, the note says this time.

Thanks.

You're most welcome. The reason the tag number isn't important is because I already made some calls and got the name of the cab company.

Okay, pause. Because why would he do all that? All I requested was assistance getting into the security footage. Now he's seeking out further information on his own?

Not sure I like this very much.

Oh . . .

We can go by the headquarters after school . . . try to get the name of the driver and contact him to see if he remembers where he took her.

So this is a "we" thing now? And I kind of *have* to go along with it: he's got the info. Except—

Can't today. Prior engagement.

Oh . . .

Yeah. Sorry.

Tomorrow then?

Gotta work.

So when are we gonna go, Danger?!

In addition to this skin-prickling suspicion about Zan Macklin's motives, I can now add annoyance at his flagrant lack of consideration that some people have to actually *work* for their money.

Perhaps asking him for help *was* a terrible idea.

Too late to turn back now, though.

Saturday?

Accepteth my lot, I musteth.

Okay, now you're just making shit up.

He guffaws. Like loud.

Tripathi whips around. "Mr. Macklin?"

"My apologies, sir," Zan says. "It's just funny seeing *Pope Paul, Malcolm X,* and *British politician sex* in the same line, am I right, guys? That Billy Joel was somethin' else!"

The whole class laughs.

-9-

Hard-Knock Life

Grocery shopping.

That's the prior engagement.

Twice a month on Mondays, Jax and I make our family's very tightly budgeted—by me—grocery run. I meet him at the apartment, and then we hop on the bus and hit what is probably our favorite place to go together: Kroger.

There's a list.

Coupons.

Strategy.

Teamwork.

When we step through the sliding doors, I release a shopping cart from the lineup, he grabs a hand basket, and I pass him his part of the list. "All right, kid, head in the game," I say. "You hit dairy, I'll hit produce, and we'll meet on the cereal aisle, got it?"

"Aye, aye, Coach!" With a salute.

Man, I love this kid.

We high-five and head off in opposite directions.

As I grab a big carton of strawberries, thoughts of a very specific, highly infuriating, ultra-rich turd of a boy fill my head. In addition to sitting beside me in class today, when I stepped into the cafeteria for lunch and took my regular seat—alone, in a back corner, slightly hidden by a large pillar—Zan totally popped up with the black guy he usually sits across from at *his* cliché-ass table full of popular jocks and cheerleaders.

"Danger, this is Finesse Montgomery," he said as they both stood over me like some kind of adolescent male sentinels.

"Sup?" Finesse said.

My mouth was full of turkey sandwich at that point, so I just smiled with my lips sealed.

"We've come from the far reaches of the Norcross High School common area to rescue you from this island of solitude," Zan announced.

I looked at Finesse. "What makes him think I want to be rescued?"

Finesse shrugged. "That's what I told him."

"Whatever," Zan said. "So you comin' to sit with us or what, Danger?"

Willingly place myself at a table with the richest, shiniest, most pleasantly fragranced kids in school? Me in my secondhand (maybe even third- or fourth-hand) jeans, "vintage" sweater, and a pair of Doc Martens I got from a church clothing drive?

Nope.

"While I appreciate the hospitality, Macklin, I'm gonna pass," I said with a wink. "Kinda dig my 'island of solitude,' as you so aptly put it."

Except now I can't stop thinking about it.

It's not only the fact that he invited me into his *circle*. It's really bothering me that I don't know why he's helping me. As much as I'd like to believe he's a nice guy, doing it out of the goodness of his heart . . . not buying it.

When I reach the cereal aisle, Jax is standing with That Look on his face. The one where he really wants something that's not on the list, but he knows we can't afford it.

Ugh.

"What is it?"

He points to a box of store-brand fruit snacks. "They're only a dollar if we use the Kroger Plus card!"

Pretty sure I no longer have a heart because it just shattered into a bajillion frickin' pieces.

But then an image of green rectangles of paper featuring the overly large face of Benjamin Franklin floats through my head. "You know what, Jax? You can get whatever fruit snacks you want," I say. Mama is definitely gonna flip, but whatever. I'll put a couple hundred dollars from my bonus into the account.

"I *can*?"

"Mm-hmm. Pick whatever cereal you want too. *AND* we're getting ice cream and microwave popcorn."

The kid looks like he's about to combust. He throws his arms around my waist. "You're the best big sister *ever*!"

Annnnnnd, about to cry.

"Okay, okay, enough mushy gushy," I say, prying him off me. "Pick your poisons, and we'll hit the frozen goods."

Once we get there, I send him to the ice cream while I grab the pot pies and TV dinners. The freezer door is just closing when I hear: "Well, whattaya know? An Ice Queen on the frozen aisle!"

Oh God. Not happening not happening not happe—

"You're totally powering all these freezers, aren't you?" Zan says, striding up the aisle with the confidence of a fella who likely owns a ton of stock in the Kroger Corporation.

I glance down into our cart full of cheap, store-brand food (minus the Gushers™, Fruity Pebbles®, and Orville Redenbacher's® Movie Theater Butter Popcorn).

Once he gets to me, pint of Häagen-Dazs® Butter Pecan in one hand, he reaches in and plucks out our box of Toaster Treats—aka Pop-Tarts® à la Kroger.

"*Unfrosted?!*" He looks up at me. "Jesus, Danger, you're a Neanderthal!"

"Get *out* of my basket." I pluck the box from his hand and drop it back in the cart.

He grins and shoves his free hand in his pocket. Blinks those long, heavy lashes. Exudes his . . . essence.

I hate him. I hate him I hate him I hate him.

"So. Prior engagement," he says.

I cross my arms. "Yes. Second and fourth Monday of each month is grocery day."

"I see."

Just then, Jax runs up. "Chocolate Chip Cookie Dough, or Fudge Brownie?" He holds up the two options.

"Both," I say.

"*Both?!*" His eyes go wide.

My heart beats a little faster. "Yes, both," I say. "Drop 'em in."

"Who's this little dude?" Zan asks.

"This is Jax."

"Jax, huh?" Zan squats so he and Jax are eye to eye. "Sup, man?" he says.

"Sup?" from Jax. With a gangsta-ish lift of the chin.

Absurd, this entire situation.

"I'm Zan." He extends a hand, and Jax shakes it. "Tell me something, man . . . is your mom always this grumpy?"

"Oh my God, I'm not his *mom*!"

Zan laughs and Jax looks up at me. "He was *joking*, Rico."

Ah, so they're best friends now. Fantastic.

Jax turns back to his new favorite (or so it feels. [Yes, I'm salty.]). "So you're my sister's boyfriend?"

"Eww, no!" My face and hands are *blazing*. Also, am I in kindergarten?

Zan laughs and ruffles Jax's dirty-blond curls. "Only in my dreams, kid." He stands up.

Mmmmmm . . .

"You guys done with your shopping?" Zan asks. "We can hit the checkout lanes together."

"That would be awesome!" Jax says.

And so we do. Could I have really said no?

Zan even bags our groceries. Which is so freakin' *weird*. Especially since he's good at it. As a matter of fact, I don't think I realized bagging groceries is something one can be *good* at until this very moment.

Actually, what's he even doing in Kroger? Don't people of his economic ilk shop at like Whole Foods or World Market or whatever? Do they even do their own shopping?

Who is this guy?

Once we're outside, he says, "So where'd you guys park? I'll help you load up."

And before I can make up something about a ride, Jax is saying, "We take the bus, dude."

Dude? Who is *this* kid?

Zan looks at me, but to my shock, the pity I'm bracing myself for isn't there in his face. "You want a ride?"

"No thanks. We do this twice a month. We'll be fine."

He smirks. Narrows his eyes. "Hey, Jax, you see that Jeep over there?" He points to a yellow four-door Wrangler with gargantoid tires, a light bar on the top, and the word TONKA printed in massive letters at the top of the windshield. A Jeep I—and probably most of our town—would recognize just about anywhere.

Jax nods. "Yep."

"You wanna ride shotgun in that guy?"

Jax turns to me, excitement twinkling in his hazel eyes. "Can I, Rico? Please, please, *PLEASE?*"

And, shit.

I glare at *Zan-the-Man.* My hatred intensifies.

"Well, big sis?" he says. More smirking.

Asshole.

"Rico, come onnnnnn!" Jax tugs on my arm.

I haven't seen the kid this amped since Christmas morning. But do I really want Mr. Money-Bags Macklin to know where my relatively shithole-ish abode is?

"Ashley Run Apartments, right?" Zan says.

No doubt the look on my face screams *How the f— do you know that, you stalker?!* 'cause then he goes, "Don't you live in the same building as Jess?"

69

"Jess?"

"Jessica Barlow? Blondie, cheer captain, National Merit Finalist, fierce leaderess of the NHS free world?"

Oh. Duh.

"Yeah. I guess I do." Not that I've seen her in the vicinity since the other morning.

Zan whips out a pair of sunglasses that I'm sure are worth more than my entire wardrobe. Slips them on all suave-like. "So let's ride."

"WOO-HOO!" from Jax.

Did I say yes? I don't recall saying yes.

But again, I can't really say no now, can I?

What I do know is I really didn't need another reminder of how few *real* choices I have in my own GD life. Fine, this is just a ride home, but it does feel like an encroachment on the little autonomy I prize probably more than any physical possession.

Man, how different would all this be going if I'd just *picked* the other ticket?

When we get to the Jeep, I climb into the backseat, and Jax sits up front with the toilet-tissue titan. I have qualms about this because Jax is such a shrimp and this monster-mobile has passenger-side airbags, but I can't crush the kid's dreams.

Have I mentioned I hate Alexander Gustavo Macklin? (And fine, *hate* is a strong word considering I don't actually know him, but like who even has a name like that?)

"Dude, this car is SO COOL!" Jax says. Bro can hardly see over the dang dashboard. "And are those *fidget spinners*?!"

I peek between the seats to follow Jaxy's eyes. There in one of the between-seat cup holders is a literal stack of the (variously colored) things.

"They are," Zan say. "You want one?"

"Uhh, YEAH!"

"Go ahead. Take your pick."

Jax grabs a royal blue one that has little spikes all over it.

"And thanks for the compliment on the Jeep." Zan starts the engine, and I swear the whole parking lot shakes from the rumble. "I bought it myself."

"You *did*?" Jax snatches the question straight from my lips.

"Yep. Hard work pays off, you know?"

"You have a job?" I blurt.

Zander looks at me in the rearview. Bah, stupid (serpentine!) green eyes. "Been working since fifteen, IQ."

"Doing what?"

"Started out bagging at Publix. When I turned sixteen, my dad put me to work at the family business."

"Ah, that doesn't count." I look out the window.

Zan laughs, but I'd be lying if I said it didn't sound forced. Did what I said bother him?

"I can almost guarantee you make more per hour than I do," he replies.

I snort. "Doubtful."

"I'm serious. Minimum wage-er up here."

So I have him beat by fifty cents. Big whoop. "Why don't they pay you more?"

"Not how my dad rolls."

Hmph.

Not like any of it matters, though. Job or not, he certainly didn't have to help pay any bills. I *wish* my income could go toward buying myself a monster truck.

Grumpy now.

"Jax, your sister's a really hard worker. You should definitely follow her example," Zan continues.

"I know, man. If it wasn't for Rico, we'd prolly be homeless. She makes the budget and really keeps us afloat. Our mom's *terrible* with money."

"Jax!" Is he for real right now?!

"You know it's true, Rico!"

Zan laughs, which kind of makes me want to set this precious toy truck of his on fire.

"It's a hard-knock life," Jax goes on, and I expect Zan to laugh again. . . .

But instead he says: "I get it, little dude. My mom's pretty awful with money too."

-10-

Checker Cab

For the rest of the week, Zanny Gusto, as I call him in my head, sits beside me in history *and* infiltrates my *Castaway*-esque cafeteria island.

But still: when he pulls up in front of my apartment building Saturday morning, I'm so nervous, I could collapse. I'm wearing the second-most-expensive thing from my closet: a maroon V-neck sweater dress that Mama splurged on for my Sweet Sixteen birthday dinner (that she also splurged on—definitely bad with money). Black tights, Goodwill coat, church-drive Doc Martens.

I still feel like a pauper.

Also not helping: pretty sure I caught Zomeboy semi-checking me out two days ago and now I feel like my ass has gotten bigger. When he pulls up, I'm waiting out front because the *last* thing I want is for Jax to invite him in to look at his Lego collection. It would involve him discovering that I, a high school senior on the cusp of full womanhood, share a room with my nine-year-old brother.

He whips his Tonka truck into a parking space—nearly sideswiping Mama's rust bucket in the process—and then

73

hops out and runs around the car to open the door for me. *He's* wearing a button-down beneath a nice cardigan, dark jeans, brown Clarks Wallabee boots, and a navy peacoat with gold buttons.

He looks me over. "Thou art lovely as a freshly bloomed rose this morn, m'lady," he says with a bow.

"You are *so* much weirder than I expected."

With a grin, he extends his hand to help me into the Jeep. The interior smells *extra* like his cologne today, aka warm sunlight and dizzy spins through an enchanted forest all while inhaling the holographic rainbow dust of hyper-masculine unicorn fairies.

I buckle my seat belt as he pushes my door shut, and then close my eyes and breathe in super deep, even though I should really be trying to stay focused. (*TICKET, Rico!*)

That's when I hear what I guess are chicken sounds—*bawk bawk!*—coming from the speakers.

He climbs in and pulls his door shut. Buckles up.

"What the holy hell are you listening to?"

"Project Pat, fool!" he says.

I just stare at him.

"Cardi B sampled the track for a semi-remix, but the original can never be topped."

"I haven't the slightest idea of what you're talking about, Macklin."

"Seriously?"

"Quite."

He gapes at me like I just confessed to not knowing the name of the first black president. "I know it's a little old-school, but . . . you really don't know Project Pat?"

74

Still staring. I blink.

"Three-Six-Mafia?"

"Oh, them." I look out my window as he finally backs out of the space. "Weren't they like devil worshippers or something?"

"Devil worshippers?"

"Yeah," I say. "'Triple-Six' Mafia, as in 666, the number of Satan?"

"I dunno about all *that*, IQ—"

BAWK, BAWK! Chicken head . . .

"What is this guy talking about?" I say.

"Father in heaven, what am I going to do with you, Danger?" Zan shakes his head. "The song is called 'Chicken Head,' which was a derisive term for girl who—" He stops and presses his lips together. "Mmmm . . . Well, we'll just say she's a rap groupie. I think the modern-day equivalent is *THOT*."

"How do you even understand what they're saying?"

He looks at me with his caterpillar brows drawn together (note to self: when I work up the courage, I must ask if he gets them threaded), then back at the road. "Okay, I've avoided asking you this because Ness told me it might be offensive—something about a microaggression. But your downright *baffling* response to this formerly very popular rap song has me really wondering." We stop at a light, and he looks at me. "What *are* you, Danger?"

A) Takes me a second to figure out he's talking about *Finesse.* B) I have no idea what to do with that question. "Huh?"

"Like ethnically. I've been struggling to figure it out."

Offensive indeed. But of course he asked anyway. "Does it matter?"

"Well, no . . ." He shifts in his seat and clears his throat. "Pure curiosity. Humor me?"

I sigh. This is a sore spot for me because honestly . . . I don't actually know all the pieces. I'm *black by societal standards*—something Mama's been drilling into me since I made the mistake of requesting a blond/blue-eyed American Girl doll for my sixth birthday (that's not to mention the fact that we couldn't afford a one-hundred-dollar doll). But I'd be lying if I said Zan's the first person to ever ask me the question. Apparently naturally curly hair and *high cheekbones* suggest other elements in my heritage?

Which is stupid and kinda confusing. And another thing that makes me feel out of place—not being *entirely* sure of where/what I come from.

Too many missing pieces.

Like a dad.

He's still waiting for a response.

And I can't seem to resist giving him one. "I'm . . . a mutt," I say, and I totally regret it the moment it's out of my mouth.

"Well, that's self-deprecating."

I shrug. "It's true. My mom's dad was a white guy. According to the story he told *me*, he had a one-night stand with an . . . *escort* he's pretty sure was black, then ten months later, my mom was left on his doorstep."

"Whoa."

"Uh-huh. Then the first semester of my Mama's junior year of college, she spent a month in Spain and came back pregnant with me. The Afro-Spanish guy she'd fallen in love with was named Rico."

"Ah, I see."

"Yeah . . . but she didn't know about his wife and kids until after she'd named me." And now she refuses to talk about him. Ever. Which is a point of contention between us.

He's silent.

"She never finished undergrad even though my granddad offered to take care of me so she could. Gramps died when I was six."

No clue why I'm telling him all this, but I can't seem to stop now. "When I was eight, she started dating this . . . white guy. Corporate lawyer named Tristan McIntyre. He let me call him Dad for a while, but when she told him she was pregnant with Jax, he broke up with her," I say. I *don't* say that good ol' Tris kicked us out of his penthouse and took out a restraining order on *pregnant* Mama to keep us from coming back. That for four months we lived out of the fifteen-passenger van my grandfather left to Mama in his will, and that a very compassionate black cop discovered us one night in a Walmart parking lot and threatened to call DFACS if Mama didn't move us into a shelter immediately.

That's where we were living when Jax was born. "Neither Jax nor I have ever even *seen* our dads. It's kind of shitty."

When Zander still doesn't respond, I quickly swipe at my damp eyes. "Really didn't mean to unload like that. I'm sorry." And humiliated. Despite the fact that I didn't tell the really ugly parts.

He looks over at me. "I'm sorry you and Jax have never known your dads, Rico."

Okay, walls back up now!

"So how long is it gonna take us to get where we're going?" I say.

(The words now coming out of the speakers: *Don't save her . . . she don't wanna be saved . . .* Highly appropriate in this moment.)

"It's in Decatur, so probably another twenty minutes or so."

Twenty minutes?

I clear my throat. God, what do kids my age even talk to each other about these days? "Soooo . . . where are you going to college next year?"

"I'm not."

I don't think my head has ever turned so fast. "But you're an honor grad, aren't you?"

"Geez, stalker. A little breathing room, maybe?" He makes those trimmed bushes above his eyes wiggle. (Definitely threaded.)

"What about the football thing?" I say. "You didn't get any scholarship offers?"

"I did."

"Well?"

"*Well*, not every high school quarterback is after a scholarship."

"Oh." I mean, clearly he wouldn't need one. . . . Leave it to the poor girl to assume all jocks are in pursuit of free college. "So where were the offers from?"

"Few places."

"Like?"

There's the blush again. "I don't wanna say."

78

"Oh come on. Can't be *that* bad." I gently shove his shoulder.

He sighs. "Duke, Stanford, and Notre Dame."

Holy shit! "Are you serious, Zan?"

His cheeks go redder, and he shrugs.

"And you're not going?"

"Nope." He shrugs. "College isn't for everyone, you know."

Hmm. There was some bite to that. And he doesn't sound convinced, but I decide not to push. Especially since I'm (uncontrollably) crunchy now. To have all *that* presented to you on a diamond-encrusted platinum platter for the taking and you just . . . decide not to? Seems so wasteful. "What are you doing instead?"

"Remember how I mentioned working for the family company?"

"Mm hmm."

"Well, it's always been in product development. You wouldn't know this, but a few of my ideas have become huge hits."

"Yeah? Like what?"

"Like the flushable moist wipe. Working on a prototype right now for a flushable damp wipe on a roll."

Dang. "Impressive."

"Yeah. Haven't quite deciphered how to keep the whole roll from drying out. Anyway, after graduation, I'll be stepping into a salaried, full-time position. I'll eventually climb the ranks and take over just like my dad did from my grandpa, but Dad feels it's important for me to start at the bottom so I'll '*appreciate the view from the top.*'" He narrows his eyes.

I mean . . . sounds valid to me. "And this is what you *want* to do?"

The pre-answer pause stretches so long, I begin to wonder if he heard the question.

Which makes me think . . . "Guessing the answer is *no*?"

"I mean . . . It's not really as simple as what I *want*."

"It isn't?"

"Of course not, Rico."

Touchy. "Why not?"

"Well, there are . . . familial factors to consider. Eldest bro is a lawyer, and middle bro died. Sister's a mechanical engineer, which leaves me as heir to the porcelain throne."

Now he's just oozing sarcasm. Which . . . I have no clue how to respond to. "Sorry about your loss."

He shrugs. "I wasn't even born yet."

And then I have nothing to say.

Air in the Jeep definitely feels different now, and I'm beginning to wonder what all is hiding beneath the overpriced clothes and helmet of perfect hair. It's a bit barbaric when I think about it now, but I assumed a dude—and a white one at that—with the kind of coin Zan has access to would think pretty exclusively about what he wants and the easiest way to get it.

So this is interesting.

"You okay over there?" he says once the silence grows legs.

"Yeah, I'm—" Surprised. "Sounds like your dad's a little tough on you."

He snorts. "You don't know the half of it, Danger. People

think I'm 'rolling in it,' 'ballin',' 'making it rain,' take your pick," he says. "But I'm not: my *parents* are."

An alarm bell rings in my head, but I let him keep going.

"Since I was small, my dad's drilled the fact that the only money that belongs to *me* is what I earn from working. Definitely don't come from rags, but he's determined to make me feel like I do."

Okay, so *definitely* possible he's after the ticket for his own gain.

Also: screw him for his entitled-ass complaint. Wonder if he'd feel like I was adulterating the pristine nature of his Tonka upholstery if he knew I'm basically wearing the *rags* he *doesn't come from*.

But I force a smile. We should be at the cab place pretty soon. Just gotta figure out a way to get the info without *him* having it.

He glances over and smiles back. "Thanks for asking me that."

"What?"

"If it's what I want. No one's ever bothered to ask before."

And just like that: a point of connection I would've never expected. Doesn't magically make our differences—or his potential motives—a nonissue, obviously, but I've certainly never had anyone ask what *I* want. Honestly don't even know that I'd have an answer.

"Hey, Zan?"

"Yeah?"

"Congrats on your offers," I say. "Even if you don't accept any, it's a huge accomplishment, and I'm proud of you."

He doesn't respond, but he doesn't have to. From the way his eyes shine and his knuckles go white on the wheel, I'd say it's exactly what he needed to hear.

The connection doesn't last: our investigative visit to Checker Cab Co. is almost doomed before it begins thanks to Zan McIdiot. Excuse me: *Macklin*.

When we walk into the dispatch center, which is located inside a run-down strip mall, this guy sees the brown-skinned, full-figured receptionist and decides to turn on the *charm*. "I got this," he whispers.

"How may I help you?" the lady says in the most nasally voice I've ever heard, eyes fixed on her computer screen.

"You doin' all right today, beautiful?" from Zan.

Oh heaven help us.

She looks up then. But does *not* look impressed.

"Hey, listen, we're trying to get some intel on one of your cabs," Zan goes on, leaning over her desk. "Think you could help us out, gorgeous?" He winks.

Takes everything I've got not to smack my forehead. If I weren't so determined to get this info, I'd leave his creeper ass in here and find some other way home.

The lady smiles. It doesn't go any higher than her cheeks. "Just one sec, okay, sugar?" She picks up a phone and presses a single button. Tosses us another (fake) smile. "Hey, hon, sorry to bother ya. Need some . . . *assistance* down here," she says into the receiver.

Zan cuts his eyes at me all smug.

This is when I know we're in serious trouble.

The door opens behind us and a brick wall of a black

man walks in decked out in his security officer uniform. KENNY is the name on his silver tag. "There a problem here?" There's something sickly satisfying about Dolla-Dolla Zan's smarmy smirk melting off his face like wilting ice cream on a summer day in Georgia.

At first I don't say a word. I want Macklin to *feel* the weight of this defeat. To sit in its cesspool-like nature and let the stink settle into his bones. (No moist-wipe proto-type to save him now.)

"You harassin' Ms. Delores, white boy?" Kenny says.

Now it's *my* turn.

"Oh my goodness, I'm so sorry," I say, stepping forward. "Officer Kenny, is it?"

He perks up at the sound of the word *officer. I feel you, Kenny: value validation is everything.*

"My friend didn't mean Miss Delores any harm," I con-tinue, quickly scanning Delores's desk space. There are two photos of her and a little girl.

Bingo.

"I lost a locket necklace inside one of your cabs on Christmas Eve, and I really need to get it back. I have the tag info . . . maybe you can give me the phone number of that particular driver?"

"Sorry to break it to ya, sweetheart, but no necklaces have been recovered," Delores says, glaring at Zan again. "Christmas Eve was over a month ago. That's an eon in taxi time."

I drop my head. "I know it's a long shot but I'd really like to speak to the driver and maybe look in the cab myself to see if it slipped into the crack of the seat."

"We clean our taxis *thoroughly* once a week."

Crap, I'm losing her. Time for the waterworks. "I understand. It's just . . ." I look at the pictures, and exactly as I hope, she follows my eyes. "That locket contains the only picture I have of my little sister. She, umm . . ." Now the fake tears. "She passed away."

"Oh no, that's terrible," Kenny says.

Zan's looking at me like I've sprouted a chicken head.

"Sorry for crying." I grab a tissue from the box on Delores's desk, wipe my eyes, and blow my nose elephant style. "That little girl in the pictures, she reminds me so much of Jada." *Sniff sniff.* "Is that your daughter?"

Delores's face softens and she puts her hand on her chest. Looks up at the pictures, then back at me. "Oh, sweetheart," she says.

I fake-sniffle again.

"You get over here, young lady," Kenny says. "You're in need of a hug."

Big ol' teddy bear, that Kenny.

Delores wipes *her* eyes, and then turns to her computer. "What's that plate number, honey?"

I look at Zan . . . who is still staring at me like I shot the moon out of the sky. "My friend here will give it to you, Miss Delores," I whimper from within Kenny's embrace. "I'd rather not talk anymore."

"I understand completely, sugarplum," she says. "Young man?"

Zan looks at her. "Huh?"

I swear to the taxi gods, if he blows my cover . . .

"You have the tag number?"

"Oh! Yes, sorry." He scrambles into his pocket and pulls out a crumpled sheet of paper. "It's TX 8429."

Delores punches it in. Then: "Uh-oh."

Oh no . . .

"That car was impounded two weeks ago. Driver's no longer with the company."

And now I really *do* cry.

Keep your head in the game, Rico!

"Do you have any contact information? I won't be able to rest until I know *for sure* that my locket wasn't found, Miss Delores."

"I get it, honey. I really do." She sighs. Eyes Zan. Scowls. Back at me. "All right, listen: I'm not supposed to give company information to anyone, so if either of you mentions where you got it, I'll tell the police you tied me up and stole it from my computer."

Geez, Delores.

She turns back to the screen and hits a few keys. "Driver's name is Beau Wilcox. Write this down for her, young man." She hands Zan a Post-it and pen. "The forwarding address we have here is in Birmingham." She calls it out and Zan scribbles. "No phone number."

I'm so relieved, I break free from Big Kenny and rush around the desk to hug Delores. "Thank you *so much*," I say.

"You're welcome, sweet pea. So sorry about your sister, and I truly hope you find what you're looking for."

I let go and stand up.

"And *you* need to learn some manners," she says to Zan.

"My apologies, ma'am," Zan says. "Won't happen again."

"It better not."

We say goodbye to Delores and Kenny and then head out. The shame of what I just did tries to settle on my shoulders, but then I think of Mystery Granny's twinkling eyes and light-up sweater.

She *needs* me to find her. (She *does*.)

Once safely inside the Jeep, I feel Zan eyeballing me.

"What?"

"It's terrifying how good of a liar you are, Danger."

I look at my chipped nail polish. Take a deep breath. "There's over a hundred million dollars on the line here, Macklin. Just did what I had to do."

"You enchantress," he says.

And we pull off.

-11-

Bye-Bye, Benjamins

Zan wanted to drive the two hours to Alabama right then—and fine, so did I—but we couldn't because I wouldn't have made it back to work on time.

So we make plans to go after school on Tuesday. (Because how else could I possibly get to Birmingham?) I tell Mama I picked up an additional shift and arrange for Jax to go to Señora Alvarez's.

Then I spend the next couple of days letting my mind wander without a leash—imagining myself, passenger-seat-reclined and feet up on the dash of Zan's Jeep during our out-of-state drive, daydreaming about making a pit stop at some random hole-in-the-wall restaurant, hoping the trip will get us that much closer to the ticket . . .

Which is stupid.

As far as I'm concerned, this is officially a *keep your enemies closer* situation. Zan Macklin and I are *not* gonna be friends and therefore will *not* participate in friends-on-a-road-trip activities.

Also, indulging in these Zan-centric vain imaginings is

maybe even a little bit masochistic considering my track record of crushed dreams.

In second grade, I saw a picture of Mae Jemison, laid and slayed in her orange NASA space suit with her giant helmet resting on her hip. From that point, I had one ambition and one ambition only: go to Space Camp.

I gathered the data—summer after fourth grade would be the earliest I could attend. And even through our van and shelter-living days, I kept hope alive.

That summer finally arrived, and Mama broke it to me that we didn't have the money yet.

Fine.

Same thing the following summer.

And the one after that.

Which meant I aged out. But no big. There was still Space Academy.

The next summer we moved to Norcross.

Cool.

The one after that is when I realized it was probably never going to happen.

I hit fifteen. Then sixteen. Last summer, I finally let it go. Cried every night the camp was happening 186 miles away in Huntsville, AL.

Then I sucked it up. Accepted my lot. Focused on Jax and trying to do all I can to make sure at least some of *his* dreams come true.

Trained myself to focus only on the day right in front of me—

And I should've stuck to that instead of letting my mind drift off into Zan-land. (Why is that even a thing?)

Because when I get home from work on Monday night, Mama is curled up on the couch in her pj's with Jax asleep beside her. As soon as I'm inside the door, she wipes the tears from her face and forces a smile.

Shit.

Probably literally.

Mama has occasional bouts of colitis, the main symptom of which is uncontrollable diarrhea . . . with blood in it.

I go and kneel beside her. "Another flare-up?"

She nods. "Had to leave the hotel early. Barely made it up the stairs." Which means she didn't make it at all.

She swears it's stress-induced. "I've been a little overwhelmed lately," she says. "Need to take a day or two off to get things under control."

Translation: *Rico, I can't work this week, so you're gonna have to pull doubles to ensure we have enough to pay rent next month.*

And there it is. The Hulk *SMASH* on tomorrow's ticket-hunt shenanigans. What *really* sucks is that the smash itself is a reminder of how useful that kind of money could be.

The worst thing about these flare-ups is we never know when they're going to end.

Did I mention my grandfather died of colon cancer? I try not to even think about that, but at times like these . . .

Why couldn't I have picked that other ticket? Certainly wouldn't be in this position if I had—surely millions of dollars would provide adequate stress relief to avoid any future bouts of Mama's gut-shredding plague.

"Mama, you really need to see a doctor about this," I say.

"Don't start, Rico. You know we can't afford that."

Right. Because no health insurance.

It'll never cease to amaze me that my mother's fear of unpayable medical bills is stronger than her fear of death. Yes, medical debt can and does sink families in situations like ours, but come on.

I think about those (now) forty-nine hundred-dollar bills hidden in my box spring. . . . But no. If I use that, there won't be any money if we have a *true* emergency. Mama's gotten over this every time before. . . .

Jesus, I'm doing the same thing she does.

She shifts, and Jax snuggles in deeper. God, what the hell will I do if she—

No. Can't think like that.

"We could move somewhere cheaper. I don't mind changing schools, and I'm sure Jax would be fine with it too."

She shakes her head. "The places I could comfortably afford with one job are all in areas I do *not* want you and Jaxy to live in. And we won't even talk about the schools."

I take a deep breath and look away from her then. Because this next thing I'm about to say . . . "Mama, I know you don't want to apply for public assistance, but thi—"

"I'm not having this conversation again, honey. We're fine. We don't need it."

And this is the problem with her. Clearly we *do* need health insurance, but the last time she tried to get it through the marketplace, we discovered that even combined, we don't make enough to afford the *cheapest* plan. All the site did was confirm what Mama doesn't wanna hear: for us, it's Medicaid or nothing.

I grit my teeth. Normally, I would just nod and go about my business. *Okay, Mama, that's fine*, I would typically say. Avoid an argument that would end with her being mad at me for days because I made her feel like a "bad parent."

But that was before I sold that ticket.

Before, I didn't have the courage to even *speak* to Zan Macklin, let alone plan a trip to Birmingham with him. A trip I can't make because now I really *do* have to work extra shifts while my mother waits for her inflamed bowels to return to normal. The stigma punches at her dignity to the point where she refuses to draw from a system she's helped feed for as long as tax money's been taken out of her paychecks.

Which means *I* get to bear the brunt of the slack.

Before the ticket, I would've held my peace because I do *get* it. Wearing scavenged clothes to *that* school is bad enough. Being the Medicaid kid on top of that would've been unbearable.

Now, though?

"You know what doesn't make sense?" I say. "You claim you moved us here for 'a decent education,' but I struggle to even get my homework done because I work so much to keep us from drowning."

"*Excuse* me?"

"I can't even *go* to college. So what exactly is the point, Mama? We live way beyond our means, and you can't say it's for Jax because *he* gets bullied so much for being the poor kid, his self-esteem is like . . . subterranean. You think a kid who feels as bad about himself as Jax does can muster up the motivation to get good grades? And God forbid me or him get sick—"

"*He or I*, Rico."

"Are you seriously correcting my grammar right now?"

She glares at me with so much vitriol in her face, if I weren't so pissed off, I'd probably cower and apologize.

But I don't. Because I *am* pissed off. For more reasons than I can even count in this moment. "This 'attempt at a better life for us' is failing, Mama. At what point are you going to accept that and make some changes?"

"You have no idea of the sacrifices I've made for you and your brothe—"

"I make sacrifices too!" Jax stirs, so I lower my voice. "Extracurriculars. Parties. *Friends*. A *normal* high school experience. I'm even sacrificing *college*—"

"You think I don't know that?" she snaps. "You think this is the life I *want* for my children? You think I *want* to always be at work? You think it doesn't scare the shit out of me every time I get sick? I can sell some of your granddad's stuff I've got in storage to give us some extra money, but I'm doing my *best*, goddammit!"

"Well, it obviously isn't good enough, is it?"

She looks like I just backhanded her, and I immediately feel like a garbage can overflowing with poop diapers and dirty Macklin wet wipes. Her hazel eyes shift back to the television. Full of tears (again) that will definitely overflow any second now.

Of course she's doing her best, Rico.

92

I clench my jaw to keep my own facial waterworks in check, then march into the bedroom. Before I can change my mind, I lift my mattress, shove my hand into the box spring hole, and remove the envelope.

Back into the living room I go, and into the air it flies. She catches it.

"My holiday bonus from work," I say. "Should give us a little breathing room, and maybe you can go see a doctor."

Before she can look at me again or form a response, I return to my bedroom and slam the door.

And then I cry.

A Word from the Benjamins

Rico will never know it, but after Stacia Danger put Jax in bed and confirmed that Rico was asleep as well, she took the forty-nine of us that remain—Rico placed Bill Fifty in a checking account to cover some grocery store splurges—into her closet. Then Stacia dropped to her knees, removed us from our envelope dwelling, and counted us one by one.

She counted again.

And again.

And again. (Don't these humans realize all that friction begins to chafe? Mercy.)

After the fifth time, she gathered us into a pile and stacked us against her knee a few times. Then she squeezed us so tightly, it became impossible to breathe . . . and promptly burst into tears.

"This isn't *fair*, Father!" she exclaimed. "Why is my life this way? How do *two* full-time jobs fail to cover the bills? Why is my seventeen-year-old giving me an envelope with forty-nine hundred dollars in it?"

"Gentlemen, we have another crier," Bill Nineteen managed to choke out.

"Who can understand these humans and the myriad emotions we engender within them?" from Bill Forty-One. "Sure wish she'd loosen her grip—"

"Where did I go *wrong*, Lord?" Stacia exclaimed, pounding our edges against her thigh within her closed fist.

"You know, fellows, the last time I heard a human say that, he was staring me right in the eye after losing a large stack of our brethren in a questionable card 'game' called Poking."

"I believe it's *Poker*, dear Twenty-Eight," Bill Seventeen said.

"Whatever the name, I've seen it turn quite ugly."

"Ay," from Seventeen again. "The things people do to get their hands on us. It's baffling!"

"I know I've made some mistakes, Lord," Stacia goes on, "but come on. *Rico* doesn't deserve this. Help me out for *her* sake, if nothing less. She and Jax deserve to have *lives*. To be *kids*, for crying out loud. To hang out with *friends* and have *fun* and go on *beach trips* —"

She droned on for a while, then sighed, shook her head, and gave us one last look before returning us to our envelope. We were lifted quickly enough to make our stomachs drop, then shuffly scuffling filled our ears before it got very dark and the smell of human feet filled our paper olfactory glands.

"I believe we've been placed in a shoe box!" Bill Twenty-Three exclaimed.

95

"Ah, well. Better than being tossed into the air and made to cascade to the floor like raindrops. I got trampled the last time that happened," from Bill Six.

"At least you're not torn," said Bill Forty-One. "One of my previous owners left me on a cold marble table next to his Rolex, and a downright beast of a miniature human got ahold of me. Almost ripped me right in two!"

"I've barely been touched," Thirty-Two said. "Came off the presses mere months ago."

"Count yourself lucky, son," said Bill One. "Eventually the humans will begin to treat you as though you hold the secrets to the universe. It's exhausting."

"That Rico sure was nice to us," Forty-Eight said with a yawn. "Very gentle."

"Too gentle, perhaps," replied Bill Seven, equally drowsy as the dark settled in. "From the way she cried when removing Bill Fifty from our stack, I suspect that if she had the choice, she would've never let any of us go."

-12-

Good for Him

When I tell Zan about my "family emergency" he's *way* more bummed than I expect him to be. His eyes drop, his shoulders slump, and he spends most of History sighing and tossing sad puppy eyes in my direction every few minutes. It freaks me out so bad, I camp out in the library during lunch to avoid seeing him again before the school day ends.

Right now, I'm thankful for the mindless task that is restocking Coke products in the soda fridge. I even take the time to make sure the label on every bottle is face-out. It actually feels pretty good, being in control of something.

Last night, I had a dream I found Mama . . . no longer alive. I woke up in a panic and reached under my mattress so I could ground myself by counting my bonus.

But of course it wasn't there.

I cried for a while before miraculously drifting back to sleep.

"Ricooooo?" my name rings out in Mr. Z's signature trill. When I come out of the cooler and pull off my hat and gloves (don't judge), he smiles at me from his perch behind the checkout counter. "Break?" he says.

I shake my head no. Gotta stay busy. Breaks equal wandering cyclical thoughts of lack ➔ ticket ➔ lack (that throws wrenches into plans to find the ➔ ticket).

"You work register then. Come. We'll refill coins while the store is empty."

I shuffle my way up front while he disappears into the office and closes the door to get coin rolls from the safe. As soon as I unlock the register drawer and pull it open, though, the bell on the door rings, and three voices flow into the store:

> **Guy #1:** *Grunt* Ness, can you hold the door for me? This box is kinda heavy.
>
> **Guy #2:** I look like a doorman to you, fool?
>
> **Guy #1:** Oh boy, here we go. You carry the box and I'll hold the door then.
>
> **Guy #2:** I'm not a butler either—
>
> **Girl:** Oh my God, I'll hold the damn door.
>
> **Guy #2:** No, babe, that's not your job. The white man gotta do for theyself someti—
>
> **Girl:** Can it, Ness!

And I watch with my mouth open as Zan practically tumbles into the store carrying a massive box with MACKLIN ENTERPRISES printed on the side. Finesse comes in after him, and bringing up the rear is Jessica Barlow.

Macklin makes it halfway to the office before he sees me, and when he does, he totally drops the box. Unfortunately,

Finesse isn't paying attention—too busy making goo-goo eyes over his shoulder at Jessica—so he crashes into Zan, and they both trip over the fallen box and go sprawling.

"Imbeciles." Jessica shakes her head at the guys and then turns her attention to me. "Hey, neighbor!" With a grin that could make a nun drop a habit.

"Uhh . . ." is all I can muster. Barring the two smiles she kicked my way—one on the shared strip of concrete between our apartment doors, and one on that fateful day in the cafeteria that started this whole Macklin Mess— those two-point-five words are the most we've ever exchanged. "Hi?"

"You know, I've never told you this because I didn't want you to be weirded out, but you're really pretty, Rico."

"No she's *not*," Zan says from the floor.

Wow.

Jessica turns to him as he gets up. "Asshole much?"

"What?" He's got the nerve to seem confused. Then he looks at my face.

Guess I look hurt?

He flushes bright red. "I didn't mean it like *that*—"

"So how'd the hell you mean it, Zan?" Jess punches the crap out of his arm.

"Ow!"

I think I like this girl.

Finesse comes and drapes an arm over Jessica's shoulders as Zan narrows his eyes and looks over my face. "*Pretty* is too flimsy a word to describe Rico," he says. "She's like . . . fuller than that."

Nobody speaks.

Then Finesse coughs, and Jessica glances back and forth between Zan and me with an unmistakable glint in her blue eyes. *I* peek at Zan to see if he's as uncomfortable as I am, but he's still visually dissecting my face.

Man, is it hot in here? Might need to hop back into the cooler area . . .

The office door opens, and Mr. Zoughbi comes out with the coin rolls, instantly spotting Zan-the-Man—who you'd think was Barack Obama (Mr. Z's favorite) based on the way his mustache quivers with excitement. "Mr. Macklin!"

Zan's focus shifts to him (thank God). "Hello, sir!"

"I didn't know you were coming today!"

Rich-boy shrug. "Was supposed to drive to Birmingham, but my travel companion had a 'family emergency.' "

He blinks enough times for the sarcasm to stab, then forces a smile.

"Oh no . . ." Mr. Z rubs his beard. "I do hope everything is all right?"

"As do I, sir. Haven't heard anything yet, but since my afternoon was suddenly open, I figured I'd bring some samples by."

So he's mad then.

Well, whatever. It's not like I could tell him *why* I was canceling and what I'd be doing instead. He'd never understand.

"Oh, wonderful!" Mr. Z claps the way he does when he gets excited. "Come, come! We shall discuss!"

Zan squats and picks up the box, but before he slips into the office behind Mr. Zoughbi, he looks at me again.

He's not mad. He's hurt.

Which makes *me* feel like I just got punched in the stomach.

The anger I could've dealt with. Chalked it up to Hyperprivileged Rich White Kid Syndrome—symptoms include abject fury over not getting one's way.

This, though, is making me feel as helpless and unmoored as when I handed over my bonus. No clue why, but I do *not* like it.

"Sweetie, will you grab me a Vitaminwater and a couple of PowerBars, please?" Jessica says to Finesse, snatching me back to, you know, my *job*.

"Sure thing, gorgeous." With a li'l smooch. Then he swags off in that way great athletes who know they're hot do. He and Jess are endlessly cute, and it's kind of annoying.

I start cracking open the coin rolls.

"So you and Macklin, huh?" Jessica says, stepping up to the counter.

"Mmmm, no. We're merely . . . acquaintances."

She grins. "That mopey face he gave you didn't look acquaintance-y to me. You're the travel companion who canceled?"

I shrug noncommittally.

"You really are gorgeous."

Who is this girl? And why are her compliments making me feel so warm inside? This is almost as confusing as dealing with Macklin. "Thanks."

"Between the two of us, I think you'd be really good for him."

I close the cash drawer. "Don't take this the wrong way, but considering you and I have never spoken before, that's a *strong* conclusion to jump to."

Finesse comes back and places her requested items on the counter.

"Oh drat," she says. "Honey, I forgot to ask for an ostrich jerky."

Ostrich jerky? "Umm, I don't think we—"

She cuts me a warning glance, and I'm so startled, my mouth snaps shut.

Finesse turns to me. "That would be near the beef jerky, right? Right." He walks off before I can answer.

Jess waits until he's halfway across the store before she faces me again. "Just because we don't talk doesn't mean I don't see you," she says. "We all do, babe. Zan most of all."

Babe, huh? I dump quarters into the register just to make noise. All this *attention* is starting to make me itch.

"I'm serious," she continues. "I haven't seen Zanny this *alive* in the eight years I've known him."

Zanny. Gross.

Finesse comes back to the counter. "No ostrich jerky, babe."

"That's okay, sweetie. Thanks for looking for me." Jess smiles at me.

The office door opens then, and Zan comes out with Mr. Z at his heels. "So the triple-ply recycled and the Ultra-Tough Quilted?"

"Correct, Mr. Macklin."

"And I'll send you a sample of the moist prototype we're working on through Rico."

"Fantastic!" Mr. Z says. "Thank you, Rico!"

Zan turns to me then. "You're off at ten?"

Mmmm . . . "Yes . . ."

"I'll see you then. Ness, Jess, let's roll."

And they're gone.

-13-

Ask Nicely

cash out, give the overnight dude a rundown, and at 10:04 p.m., I exit the store.

Zan is leaning against the front fender of his Jeep, with his feet crossed at the ankles, fidget spinner spinning between the thumb and middle finger of his right hand. When he sees me, he shoves the thing into his coat pocket and lifts his chin, half greeting, half beckoning.

There's a part of me that wants to walk right past his car to the bus stop—bus should arrive in approximately two and a half minutes. . . .

But then his gaze shifts off into the distance and he sighs. There's that *hurt* again. So I head toward him, feeling like I'm walking to my doom with each step.

"Rico," he says once I get to him.

"Zan."

And at first that's all. Once inside the Jeep and on the move, we take the shortest route to my apartment complex (aka the way the bus doesn't go): past the local tennis club, golf course, and the subdivisions of big houses most of my classmates live in. The only sound is some rap song about staying "fly till I die" playing softly in the background.

It's actually kinda nice—

But then we pass the Walgreens that denotes entry into the cheap pocket of town. Once we turn onto the poorly lit street that leads to my complex, he turns the music off.

Oh boy . . .

"So?" he says.

Of course I know what he's asking without asking, but screw him for refusing to just ask. "So what?"

"Family emergency?"

"I don't owe you an explanation, Zan." I cross my arms.

"That's fair," he replies. "But I'd appreciate it if you gave me one."

His eyes are muted in the light from the dim streetlamps outside, but they're still *so* intense, Jessica's words run laps in my head: *I haven't seen Zanny this* alive *in the eight years I've known him.*

It's like . . . confounding. Never in a hundred and six million years would I have expected to exchange a single word with Zan Macklin, let alone be sitting in the passenger seat of his Tonka truck with him *politely* requesting intel on my personal life.

But still. I hate how entitled he seems to feel to the information.

How entitled he seems to feel to everything.

To *me*.

He didn't ask if he could pick me up from work. He didn't ask me to get in his car. And he hasn't actually asked me to tell him why I really canceled. Not in a full sentence. With the word *please* tossed in there somewhere.

"You're really used to getting what you want, huh?" I say.

"What?"

"You don't really *ask* for things."

"What do you mean?"

"You like . . . demand them. The only reason I'm sitting next to you right now is because you basically *willed* it so by creating an expectation I didn't feel comfortable defying. Which I have a hunch is kind of a pattern for you."

"What are you talking about, Danger?"

I shake my head. "Even the fact that you insist on continuing to mispronounce my last name. You just do whatever the hell you want, and people go with it. Zan-the-Man Macklin, king of the world."

He just stares.

"And it's not that I don't appreciate the ride. . . . Actually, no. What am I even saying? I was totally fine without the ride. I've been fine without rides since I started this job. So why am I suddenly taking them? You say 'See you at ten' and post up outside my 'place of employment,' as you say, and I come out and just hop right in? What even *is* that?"

"I'm not understanding—"

"Of course you aren't, Zan. Why would you? I'm sure your whole life, you've never had to ask for anything. You say jump, people ask how high. Myself included."

He doesn't respond.

"My mom is sick."

Again, nothing.

"She can't work right now, so I have to work double my normal hours to make up the slack."

"The slack?"

"The income slack, Macklin." God. I figured he'd be a little out of touch, but *this* is . . . disheartening. "If I don't pick it up, there won't be enough money to cover bills this month."

He's back to not responding. Which I expected this time.

Soon we're turning into the neighborhood, and then he's pulling into the space next to Mama's truck. He sets the brake on the Jeep. "What can I do to help?"

"Nothing." It's knee-jerk, but the moment it's out of my mouth, I realize it's true.

"Come on, Rico. I know there's *something* I can do."

"There really isn't."

"Nothing at all?"

I can feel the rage rising from my gut, but I honestly don't know exactly who/what I'm mad at. At Mama for being sick? At myself for telling the richest boy in school my poor-kid sob story? At Zan for not being able to identify? At life for being so unfair?

"I don't need your charity," I say. "I take the bus to and from work every day. Even this *ride* was unnecessary."

And there's that *bewildered* look again. "I don't get it—"

"Tell me something I *don't* know, Zan."

He shakes his head. "Can you just explain how me wanting to help is a bad thing?"

"I didn't ask for your help!"

"But you did," he says. "If I remember correctly, you dragged me out of the cafeteria to ask for my help."

"This isn't the same!" Almost crying now.

"Why isn't it? Aren't friends supposed to help each other?"

"Oh, are we friends now?"

His face scrunches up so tight, it looks like a giant brown creepy-crawly is perched over the bridge of his nose. "Really? Are we *friends*? What the hell do *you* call it?"

"I don't need your money, Macklin."

"Who said anything about *money*?"

UGH! "What other kind of 'help' could you possibly mean?"

"How 'bout *rides*? *Food* while you're at work? Someone to hang with Jax so you can rest while your mom recovers?"

I don't say anything. Can't. Because at the end of the day, everything he mentioned falls under the category of *Stuff People Pay For.*

"So?" he says.

Again with that! "So *what*, Zan?"

He sighs again. Looks at me.

I wish he wouldn't. It makes me feel too many conflicting things. Especially with that crazy-ass cologne wafting over me.

"I'm sorry if I offended you, Rico," he says. "That wasn't my intention."

I hate him so much for apologizing. "*Good intentions* don't lessen negative impact, Alexander."

I reach for the door handle and shove the creaky thing open before he can see how wet my eyeballs are.

"By the way, we're going to Birmingham after school on Friday," he says once I've got my legs hanging out the door.

And here we go again! "Did you hear a single word I just said?!"

"Huh?"

I shake my head and take a deep breath. Guess I gotta pretend I'm talking to Jax. . . . "We're not going to Birmingham on Friday, Zan. For one: I have to work—"

"I made arrangeme—"

"Don't cut me off. It's rude."

He looks like I smacked him. Good.

"For two: even if I didn't have to work, I'd say no."

"Why?"

"Because you didn't ask me." I hop down.

"Wait!"

I turn to face him and cross my arms. More as a feeble attempt to protect myself from the *You can't talk to me that way, riffraff* statement I'm expecting to fly from his mouth than to look tough, but whatever.

"Rico, will you go to Birmingham with me on Friday?"

He cannot be serious.

"Please?"

Now he's just making me mad. "I have to *work*, Zan. I have a *job*. I mentioned that, but you clearly only heard the part that has to do with you, which is so utterly typical."

No overbearing rich-boy response this time.

"I'm going inside now." I start to push the (heavy) door closed, but then:

"Rico, can I please say something?"

"Oh, *now* you're asking?"

He sighs. "It just bums me out that one of the people

who *know* I don't always get what I want would say that I do."

"What?"

"The only other person who knows the real reason I'm not going to college is Ness."

Now *I'm* the one with nothing to say.

Can't seem to move either.

"Rico?"

GOD, he's infuriating. "WHAT, Zan?"

"What if you didn't have to work?"

"Didya miss *everything* I said about helping my mom?"

"What if you got a paid vacation day?"

"I don't *get* those, Macklin. *I'm going. Insi—*"

"What if you did this week? What if"—his gaze drops to his lap—"it were already arranged?" He braces like he's expecting me to throw something.

Which I might be considering. "What are you talking about?"

"I might've already asked Mr. Z if you could have the afternoon off. With pay."

"ARE YOU KIDDING ME RIGHT NOW?"

His head drops. "I'm sorry."

I huff. Hands on hips. (I can instantly hear Jax's voice in my head: *"Eww, you look like Mommy."*)

He looks at me. Sheepishly.

And I have to look away because to be honest, I feel like a gaping, festering wound.

Still don't trust him any further than I can throw him, but I do want—need—to get to Birmingham, and he is offering to drive.

Hate to admit it, especially after I just detonated on him, but he is nice to be around most of the time.

Not that I should let that part distract me . . .

One-oh-six, one-oh-six, one-oh-six.

(Plus six zeroes.)

I can cut him off once we get back. "We'll be leaving right after school?"

His head snaps in my direction. "You're serious?"

"Zan." *Why* is he looking at me like I offered him a trip to the moon?

"Okay, okay. Yeah," he says. "Straight after."

"Fine. Good night."

He smiles. Like *really* big. "I'll see you at school tomorrow, shrimp."

"You did *not* just call me shrimp."

"Oh, I did."

I clench my jaw and slam the door without another word.

-14-

Beau

Zan is waiting at my locker Friday afternoon, and as much as I want to maintain my force field of anger, excitement about this Birmingham trip manages to seep through.

"You're such a creep," I say once I get it open. "How do you even know where my locker is?"

"I find it hysterical that you think you're invisible, Danger."

"If you went to a school where nobody ever spoke to you, you'd feel invisible too."

"Goes both ways, though, doesn't it?"

"Huh?"

He waits until our eyes meet before he says: "Do you speak to people who don't look like they want to be spoken to?"

I don't say anything to that. Just finish swapping out my books and push the locker door shut.

"Ready to rock, Queen of Ice?" he says. "The day is ripe for a glorious adventure!"

"You're ridiculous."

112

He smiles and extends an elbow, and despite my inner protestations, I take it.

I was right to be reluctant: we pass a group of girls—Jessica's literal (cheerleader) #squad, though she's not with them—in the parking lot, and they give me stank-eye so intense, I have to fight the urge to do an armpit check.

Pretty sure Zan doesn't even notice. Which gets my gears spinning. Not that I've allowed myself to think of him in any way other than a means to an end (Is that awful? That's probably awful.), but I'm curious now. "So are you dating anyone?" I say the moment the Jeep doors are shut.

He starts the ignition, and some rap song about various types of checks comes pouring out of the speakers (fitting). He turns the music down and reaches for his seat belt. "Nope."

Huh. "Dated anyone recently?"

"I have not."

"When's the last time you dated someone?"

"What's with the line of questioning, Detective?" He taps around on the screen in the center of the Jeep's dashboard until the GPS pops up. Inputs an address and a route appears.

Should I tell him the truth? Guess it couldn't hurt. "The, uhhh . . . pep squad didn't seem too happy to see me with you."

Zan snorts. "I wouldn't date those girls. Got nothing in common with any of them."

I stifle a laugh at the irony. A disgustingly wealthy, good-looking boy having "nothing in common" with disgustingly wealthy, good-looking girls?

Okay.

"I see."

"They're about as deep as puddles, Rico. Wouldn't be too concerned if I were you."

"Who said I was concerned?"

He doesn't respond, but I see him grin. Jackass.

He takes the left that will put us on the highway, and reality comes into glaring relief: I'm about to be alone in a car with Zan-the-Man for two-plus hours on what could very well be a wild-goose chase.

Something I hadn't considered until just now: What if we can't find this Beau guy? Will Zan be super pissed because he wasted all this gas? Does he even *think* about gas? According to him, he bought this Jeep . . . does that mean he pays for the gas too?

And what are we even going to talk about? If anybody has "nothing in common," it's him and me.

"You catch the first episode of *JACKPOT!?*" he says, yanking me back from the ledge of the freak-out pit I was about to topple into.

"I didn't." Wanted to, but we don't have that channel.

"You didn't miss much." Zan shifts the Jeep over into the HOV lane and settles down into his seat. "Mark my words: Wally Winkle will be flat broke in five years."

Wow. "Well, that's epically pessimistic."

"I speak only the truth," he says. "The first show was basically an episode of MTV *Cribs*. We got a tour of the seven-million-dollar house he bought, complete with an indoor pool and racquetball court."

114

"So he wanted a nice home" is my tempered response. "He's still got forty million to live on."

Zan shakes his head. "The place was full of expensive furniture and electronics. He's already bought two luxury cars for himself, and a car and house for each of his three kids."

"What's your point?"

"Rico, giving forty-seven *million* dollars to a person with no financial acumen and little impulse control is a horrible i—"

"*Little impulse control?*" My voice totally cracks. "You don't even know this guy!"

"I don't have to. People who go from rags to riches overnight tend to be clueless about money management," he says. "There was this guy who worked at our factory ten years ago. He had a freak accident on one of the machines and wound up losing three fingers on his right hand. Got a five-million-dollar settlement."

"Okay . . ."

"Well managed, he should've been able to live a *pretty* good life for fifty-plus years—that's a little over eight thousand dollars a month. Honestly, invested properly, he could've stretched it even further."

"You sure know a lot about this . . ." (said semi-sarcastically).

"My dad's been drilling 'financial responsibility' since I was old enough to know the different coin values in my piggy bank. Read *Rich Dad Poor Dad* aloud to me for the first time when I was in pre-K."

"Ah." Damn know-it-all.

"Like I was saying, this guy who lost his fingers *should've* been set for a while, but within three years, he was begging to be hired back because he'd totally blown the money. Just like Wally Winkle, he bought a big-ass house and a brand-new car. Turns out he was also an alcoholic with a gambling problem."

I don't reply.

"People see the lotto as this Holy Grail that'll solve all their problems, but it's really nothing more than an ugly system preying on the hope of the poor and destroying lives. Wally Winkle has no idea what the hell he's doing, man. It's gonna get ugly."

I still don't say anything. This is the first time he's ever said this much unprompted, and . . . well, I'd be fine with him never speaking again.

If I open *my* mouth right now, fire might come out. What the hell does Alexander Gustavo *Macklin* know about "the hope of the poor"? I tuck my hands beneath my thighs and stare out my window at all the cars we're blowing past.

No clue how much time goes by, but suddenly he says, "You're mad at me."

"What?"

"I can feel it. You're mad at me because of what I said."

I sigh. "Can we talk about something else, please?"

"I wanna hear your thoughts," he says. "And don't tell me you don't have any because I know you do."

He's right. "It's just funny that the boy who's never wanted for anything has all this shit to say about people who spend most of their lives with next to nothing."

And there's that calculating look that gets under my skin.

"You have *no idea* what it's like to be poor, Zan."

"Fair enough. Please continue."

"People like Wally Winkle and the guy from *your* factory don't have the luxury of taking stuff like home and car ownership for granted," I say. "You probably never even think about it, but there are people who can't take it for granted that they'll have *food* on the table every week—"

"Like you and Jax?"

My mouth snaps shut.

He knows he said the wrong thing because he doesn't say anything else. After a few minutes of contemplating whether or not I should leap and barrel-roll out onto the shoulder of the highway when we change lanes, I muster the courage to peek at him. He's staring straight ahead with his lips sealed

"Why are you helping me, Zan?"

He peeks over. "Huh?"

"With this whole thing. If you think the lottery is evil—"

"I didn't say it was *evil*, geez."

"'Ugly.' 'Preying on poor people.' Whatever. If that's how you feel about it, why are you helping me look for the lady who has the ticket?"

Loooooong pause. "Because you asked me to?"

Mmmm . . . "Last I checked, all *I* asked for was help with the Gas 'n' Go security footage. You've initiated everything else, this road trip included." *So what are you after?*

He swallows. Like, more than once. Adam's apple looks like one of those bobbing ocean buoys.

Why do I feel like a bomb is about to drop?

He sighs. "Don't hate me, all right?"

"Ummm . . ."

"I was bored."

He—What? "Come again?"

He sighs. "Boredom," he says. "That's why I'm helping. I've been in that town doing the same things with the same people for as long as I can remember."

I pinch my lips together. Of course something that could change a person's whole existence would be nothing more than a boredom cure for Alexander Macklin. Clearly the *endless* crap he has access to All.

The.

Time.

isn't nearly enough to provide him with adequate entertainment.

He keeps going. "You dragging me out of that cafeteria was the most exciting thing to happen to me all year. Felt like being called upon to embark on some epic hero's quest."

I don't—

"So this is just a *game* to you?"

"I mean, not exactly. But also kind of?"

No idea what to feel. I guess on the one hand, I'm slightly relieved he's not after the ticket for himself. (At least I *think* he's not. . . . Who can really say at this point?)

But also: If this is a game to him, what does that make me? I gulp.

"I said the wrong thing again, didn't I?"

I sigh. Like, involuntarily.

Can I really be mad? I'm basically using him, aren't I? Though he has been volunteering.

"Can I say one more thing?" he says.

"We're in *your* car, Zan."

"Okay. Well, just know this is the happiest I've been in a long time."

"Huh?"

"This . . . journey we're on. It's fun, yeah. But it's also *nice.* Being at home—let's just say it's not always my favorite place."

"Really?" Now he's got my attention.

"It can be lonely and kind of stifling. With you I feel freer." He pulls his eyes from the road to stick them on me for a moment. Smiles in a way that turns my defensive mechanisms to vapor. "I'm living for it a little bit at this point."

And for a different reason than usual, I have to look away.

There's very loud, very upbeat music shaking the walls of the little clapboard house at the address Delores gave us.

So loud, in fact, we ring the doorbell and bang on the door, but nobody answers.

"Well, this is interesting." Zan looks at me. "What do we do now?"

I lean to the right and try to peek into one of the windows. Curtains are too thick to see through. "I have no frickin' ide—"

"Somethin' I can help y'all with?"

Zan and I both whip around. At the opposite end of the walkway leading up to the house is a tall white man so skinny, it's almost as if someone stood on his toes and pulled him up by the ears to stretch him out. His pants hover just at the top of his well-worn boots, his flannel shirt is misbuttoned, and there's enough hair on his forearms and sprouting out of his collar to replace all that's missing from the top of his head.

He looks petrified.

I'm standing there staring at him—his eyes are the palest blue I've ever seen—when Zan jabs me in the arm with his elbow.

"Oww!" I glower at him.

He moves his eyebrows up and down. (Dear lord, this boy is so obvious.)

"I'm sorry, sir," I say to the man. "We're looking for Beau Wilcox—"

"No Beau here!" He drops his head and makes a beeline to the door.

Zan and I part for him.

"Wrong house, wrong house," he says, fumbling with a set of keys. "Y'all get outta here now, will ya?"

The door flies open, and a heavyset woman as tall as Zander with a face as red as a tomato puts her hand on her hip. "Beau, where the hell have you been?"

"Woman!" The man straightens his spine and lifts his chin. "I'm the man of this house! Do not question me in front of guests!"

The woman frowns at Beau, then sweeps her sour gaze over Zan and me. "And who are you?"

"Don't question them either! That's MY job!"

She rolls her eyes and shuts the door. He doesn't turn around.

"Umm . . . Mr. Wilco—?" I start.

"Who are ya and whattaya want?"

"We're students from Metro Atlanta, sir," I say. "You drove a taxi there, right?"

He doesn't respond, so I go on: "I work at a gas station in Norcross, and you had a passenger on Christmas Eve. An older black lady. I have a picture here. . . . We're trying to find her, and we're wondering if—"

"I took her to the big church. We done here?"

Zan and I look at each other again, then back at Beau. "The big church?"

"Victorious Faith, or somethin' like that. She was my only passenger that night."

"Okay—"

"You're going now, right? That's everything I know."

Zan makes a circular motion around his ear with his index finger. Mouths "weirdo."

I shove him. "You're sure this was a small-framed, older black lady?"

"Well, yeah! I know who I drove."

"Short white hair?"

"Like a mini-Afro, that's right," he says.

"Victorious Faith Church?"

"That's what I said, ain't it? It was her first time there. She told me so."

"Oka—"

"Y'all get on now." And he walks into the house and closes the door.

A Word from Beau Wilcox's (Former) Taxi

mpound lots are pretty depressin', but I ain't never seen nothin' sadder than good ol' Beau the day he removed all his stuff from inside me. He was sobbing like a baby.

If you ask me, it's nothin' short of a travesty that they fired the fella. Lotto jackpot was $212 *million* buckeroos—course the guy couldn't resist stopping to buy a ticket! "Gambling on the clock." Tuh! That measly wage they paid was hardly enough for him and his family to scrape by! What the hell did they expect?

I sure do miss him and our adventures. That last lady we drove was sweet as pie too. There's still one of those little lightbulbs from her sweater sittin' on my backseat. She bought a lotto ticket too, and nobody gave *her* any flack for it.

People always talk about how badly blacks have it in this country, but Beau's skin's the same color as most CEOs and he sure ain't gettin' no legs up.

Poor guy.

I know I ain't been cranked in a while so I'm gettin' a little rusty, but I still think it's downright shameful the way working-class folk get treated round here.

-15-

Jessica Barlow

When I get home from work Saturday afternoon, Mama and Jax aren't there. Since my next adventure with Zan-the-Mack—a trip to the church Beau mentioned—isn't until tomorrow, I kick off my boots, stretch out on the couch, and try to relax.

It works . . . briefly. Just as I hit that spot between wakefulness and the edge of a dream, there's a loud *thump*.

I sit up and look around.

Then I hear the yelling.

The voices are muffled so I can't make out the words, but there are definitely two of them. Another thump; what sounds like glass breaking; a shout; another shout; then a door slams so hard, the walls of *my* apartment shake.

After a few seconds of silence so loud I wanna cover my ears, there's a knock on my door, and I stop breathing.

Do I answer? Surely Jessica's at cheer practice or student council or something . . . could that be her mom? Who does she even live with?

Another knock.

I take a deep breath and go to the door. Look through the peephole . . .

Pull back. Puzzled.

"Hey," Jessica says as I open. She's got her purse on her shoulder and keys in her hand, but her eyes are super red.

"Are you okay?" I ask.

She sniffles. "Not really. You, umm . . . you busy?"

"No." I peek over my shoulder at our overworn carpet and dingy furniture. "You wanna come in?"

She shakes her head. "I'm gonna go out."

"Okay . . ." *So why is she here?* Which must be written all over my face because the next thing she says is:

"I want you to come with me."

"You do?"

"Yes, please. Grab your stuff and meet me at my car?"

I look her over—Nike from head to toe beneath her North Face puffy coat. No idea how she affords that stuff when she lives *here*, but at any rate, *I'm* wearing a plaid shirt over a black tank and high-waisted ripped Levi's from like the eighties—all thrifted—with my secondhand Doc Martens, which are looking particularly grungy. "Should I change?"

"What?" She looks dumbfounded. "Are you kidding? You look perfect. Come on." And she turns to head down the stairs.

After standing in the doorway, staring out into space for a few seconds, I go back in and scribble a quick note so Mama won't worry: *Went out with a friend.* I toss on my trench coat, shove my wallet in my pocket, and step out to lock the door.

Then I jab myself in the palm with my key.

It hurts.

So not dreaming then. Okay. Down the stairs and around the bend to the parking lot I go. Jessica is sitting in the red two-seater Honda that's rarely here (or so it seems). When I get in, she's wearing a sweatshirt she didn't have on before, zipped all the way up to her chin.

Odd.

"Cute car." I fasten my seat belt.

She snorts. "Thing's a deathtrap." She pets the dashboard. "Pepper's my baby, and I'm thankful for him, but one crash in this thing, and I'm a goner."

"Ah. Comforting."

She laughs. Hard. "Are you always this funny?"

"Not sure I'm the right person to ask?"

Now she's smiling at me. Which makes me feel very warm. And also confused.

As I feel the corners of my own mouth lift, I look away.

"I totally see why Macklin's into you," she says.

And then we're off.

I expect the silence in the car to be heavy, but it's not. There's something disarming about Jessica Barlow. Which catches me off guard considering she's the prototypical hyperpopular high school homecoming queen (literally).

And now my wheels are spinning as fast as the ones on her car. Because why am I here? In the car of a girl I clearly know very little about. Going who the hell knows where. Just like Macklin, she didn't exactly *ask* me to come with her. She . . . beckoned. (Though she did say please, at least.)

125

And I went with it. Is it *because* she's pretty and popular and rich-looking? Is it because she's white?

I'll admit I'm increasingly curious about her the more we interact—and fine: flattered she "wanted" *me* to join her—but like what am I actually doing here?

I don't know how to navigate any of this.

She sticks a cord attached to the face of her radio into her phone, then holds the phone up to her face. "Migos, Rihanna, old-school 'NSYNC, or the *Hamilton* soundtrack?"

"Mmmm . . . you pick."

She taps the screen, and we hang a left out of the complex as Justin Timberlake says, *Dirty pop!* And then my head is bobbing.

"I love this song," I say.

"God, yes. Timberlake's old now, but I'd totally have his babies if I weren't so bent on having Ness's. Can you grab the wheel for a sec?"

I do, and she reaches into her purse and pulls out . . . a shower cap?

Once she's got all her luscious blond hair tucked into it, she rolls her window down and then reaches across me to pull a pack of Marlboro menthol cigarettes—I recognize the box from restocking them at the Gas 'n' Go—out of the glove compartment. "You smoke?" she asks.

I shake my head.

"Mind if I do?"

"No." It's her car, isn't it?

"I don't do it often because Ness won't touch me if he can smell it, but after these fights with my mom I like . . . *need* the buzz, you know?"

I don't, but I nod anyway.

This is almost an out-of-body experience.

"You mind rolling your window down? I'll crank up the heat so we don't freeze."

I do as she asks, and she lights up. Takes a deep puff and blows the smoke out her window.

"She just like . . . *God*. You ever have moments when you wonder how you could *possibly* be your mother's child?"

I shift in my seat. I've never talked to *anyone* about Mama and our issues, but the truth is, "Yeah. I have."

"I *know* raising me by herself has been hard, but I've done my part, you know?" she goes on. "I'm a National Merit Finalist and on track to be the goddamn salutatorian. And that's on *top* of being cheer captain, class prez, and holding down a part-time job since I turned sixteen."

"Dang . . ."

"Right? But it's like . . . not enough for her."

I don't know what to say to that.

"She's gotten into this thing where she's always asking me for money. Says I have to start paying rent when I turn eighteen next month," she says. "We got into it today because she found this bag of clothes I bought at work, and she went off about how I *waste too much money on unnecessary things*. First of all, it's *my* money that *I* work for, and second, she doesn't seem to get that I have to wear the brand."

Her take on money is fascinating to me: I've been working a year longer than she has, but I've never even *considered* doing what I want with what I earn. "Where do you work?" I ask.

"Nike."

Well, at least the apparel makes sense.

"It's just like . . . like it's not my fault she drinks away most of her paycheck, you know? I'm not the cause of her dissatisfaction with how her life has gone, and I hate when she makes me out to be the problem."

Alcoholism aside, that does sound familiar.

Though why she's spilling her guts like this, I'm not sure. "I know what you mean," I say.

We take the left at the YMCA that will lead us past the middle school to the richer part of town. Still no clue where we're going, but this doesn't seem like the time to ask.

She takes another deep puff of her cigarette, which is almost down to the orange part. "She's always yelling at me, and then she wonders why I won't *'spend any time'* with her. I can't even tell you how ready I am to graduate and get the hell outta here."

"Where are you going?"

Now her whole face lights up. "Ness and I are both headed to UGA. We have to live in the dorms freshman year, but we're getting our own apartment next summer. I can't even wait, Rico."

That . . . does something to me. And deep down, I know the *must be nice* thing doesn't work here—Jessica doesn't come from any more money than I do. There's no younger sibling for her to worry about, but that aside, our situations are virtually the same.

Space Camp was one thing, but being around Jess makes me wonder when I stopped dreaming.

Next thing I know, we're turning into Wellington on the

River, and I have an intense flashback of being in fifth grade and new to the area. This subdivision was under construction, and me, Mama, and Jax (who was a toddler at the time) would drive through and explore the houses as they were still being built. Mama would relay to me what furniture she would put where, and I would close my eyes and imagine it.

Back then, I actually believed there was a chance we'd eventually live in a massive house like the ones we're passing.

Now, though?

I wipe my eyes quick before Jessica can see me crying.

-16-

A Bit Much

We pull into the driveway of a gorgeous cream-colored brick house. Jessica, as she just insisted I call her, takes off the shower cap and sweatshirt before using the visor mirror to reapply her lip gloss. She pulls a little bottle of perfume out of her purse and spritzes a little on each wrist, and then rubs it behind her ears. "Do I smell like smoke?" she asks, sticking her swan neck in my face.

I sniff. She smells like magic. Mermaid sweat with a splash of *bibbidi-bobbidi-boo*. It's unfair, really. "You smell great."

"Good."

We get out, and when we reach the front door, she isolates a key on her ring and slips it into the dead bolt. When she pushes the door open, I almost pass out.

This house is like nothing I've ever seen.

The entryway has a soaring ceiling, adorned with what I'm guessing is a crystal chandelier, based on the prisms that appear when light hits the delicate pieces. The hardwood floors are spotless, the open room to the right features a huge fireplace and a stunning grand piano, and there's jazz music floating through the air like it's leaking from the walls.

Wherever we are, I instantly feel unworthy of being here.

Whose house is this, and why does Jess have a key?

A vaguely familiar brown-skinned girl appears at the top of the staircase. "Oh joy," she says, wrinkling her nose at Jess. "It's you."

"Hi, Sincere! You look pretty today!"

"Whatever." The girl rolls her eyes and disappears.

"Sincere's not a huge fan of my whiteness," Jess says. "Coat?" I pass it to her, and she deposits it into a closet. "Follow me."

We walk down a short hallway into a spotless kitchen. There's a beautiful black woman standing over the sink washing what look like collard greens.

"Hey, Mama," Jess says, going over and kissing the woman on the cheek.

The woman smiles. "Hey, baby girl!"

Then, "Jessie!" comes a thunderclap voice from behind us. I look over my shoulder as a tall, dark-skinned man steps into the room with his arms spread. "Get over here and gimme my hug, girl!"

As she complies, Jess says, "Parents, this is my good friend, Rico."

Good friend?

"Oh ho! Surname Danger, correct? We've heard about *you*, Miss Rico." The man spreads his arms in my direction, and I'm drawn into them by some strange gravity. "Pleasure to make your acquaintance! You're more stunning than

Alexander described! I'm Barry, and that's Cresida," he goes on. "You make yourself at home, all right?"

This is getting weird, but I force a smile. "Thank you."

"Are the guys downstairs?" Jess asks.

Cresida snorts. "Where else would they be?"

"I'll make sure he comes up to say good night," Jess says.

Barry gives Jess another squeeze. "Don't know what we'd do without ya, kid. You ladies have a nice evening, and tell those numbskulls we'll order some pizzas."

"Will do." Jess grabs my hand and pulls me toward a closed door.

"It was nice to meet you!" I call out over my shoulder.

As we descend the stairs, I'm more confused than ever. "Jess, sorry if this seems like a dumb question, but who are those people?"

She laughs. "If you really don't know, you'll figure it out in about three seconds."

And she's right. Because as we step into the open space of the basement, who's on the couch watching the largest, sharpest, highest-definition TV I've ever seen but *Alexander* Macklin and Finesse Montgomery.

Now I feel like a dumbass.

Doesn't last long: when Mack-Daddy Zan sees me, his mouth drops and he shoots to his feet. Looks at Finesse. "Did you know—?"

"Nope."

Focus shifts to Jessica, who blows him a kiss before she starts making goo-goo eyes at Finesse.

It's a few looooooong seconds before Zan finally turns his attention to me, but when he does? *"RICO!"* And he rushes over and scoops me up in what I can only describe as The Hug. Snatches the breath right out of me.

Once I'm back on the ground, he holds me by the shoulders and basically eats every inch of my face with his gaze.

Wildly uncomfortable, I turn to Jess hoping for help.

But Jess has entered the zone. She's locked in on Finesse like he'll disappear if she looks away.

Zan is still staring at me.

This is all a bit much.

Jess takes Ness's hand and pulls him up and toward a dark room at the opposite end of the basement. He wiggles his eyebrows at us in passing, and once they're in with the door closing, a light goes on, and then there's music playing.

Feeling a little awkward now. (Which is definitely a step up from *like a filthy blight on the pristine Montgomery home . . .* but still.)

Zan sits back down, so I follow suit. The leather couch is so deep that if I sit all the way back, my feet won't touch the floor. I look over my shoulder at the door, then at Zan (who's still staring at me with a goofy smile on his admittedly glorious-in-this-moment face). "Are they, uhh—"

"Yep."

"But Finesse's parents are—"

"Yep."

"Ah."

He laughs. "I'm glad you're here so I'm not alone this time."

Oh. "So this is a frequent—"

"Yep."

"Okay then."

He smiles, and we lapse into silence, but he doesn't stop glancing over at me.

It's strange: now that I'm *in* it, I think this is totally what I've secretly wanted—being a normal teenager with *friends* that I hang out with in basements on Saturday nights—but it's so much new, unexpected stuff at once, none of it feels real.

It makes me wonder what Wally Winkle felt when he realized he was holding over a hundred million bucks on a little slip of paper. Surely that was the fulfillment of one of his deepest longings . . . but it had to be surreal.

What about when he bought his house(s)? Car(s)? Not that I know his background, but at what point would a person who's only ever scraped by get used to having way more than they need?

"You should come closer," Zan says, knocking me out of my ponderings.

I lift an eyebrow and cross my arms.

He laughs again. "You have my word that I won't disrespect you."

I scoot closer, but just barely. There's still a good two feet of space between us.

In truth, it's not *him* I'm worried about. Just dropped back into the feeling that me and my *rags* don't belong on this side of town, let alone inside this house on this immaculate piece of furniture with the illustrious Zan Macklin.

"Aww, come on, Danger." He grabs my arm and leg and literally *pulls* me over to him. Once his arm is draped across the back of the couch, my right side is completely flush against his left.

Father in heaven.

"It's chilly down here, you know?" he says. "Gotta sit close so we stay warm."

I shake my head. "Macklin, you are so utterly full of shit."

"Fine, I'll admit it: I missed you, buddy!"

"You just saw me yesterday."

"But that was like . . . an eon ago."

"You're ridiculous." And I want to run far, far away *right* now. I cross my arms and take what I hope is a hidden deep breath.

I can still feel him goggling at me, so I peek up. He smiles in a way that makes me feel like I'm on a roller-coaster drop, and I gulp.

"So how you been these past nineteen-ish hours?" he says right into my face.

Ah-ha. "Have you been drinking, sir?"

"Naaaaahhh." He looks at the TV.

I poke him in the side, and he giggles like a preschooler. "All right, all right," he says. "Maybe a little."

Well, that sure explains a lot. And knocks some of the shine off, thank God.

"Just so you know, even if I weren't tipsy, I'd be glad you're here."

"Okay, Zan." But why am I so disappointed?

"I mean it, Danger." He drops his arm onto my shoulders and gives me a squeeze. "You really have become a bright spot for me. I'm over here a lot because home can get lonely, but you being here is making my little haven into a paradise." He shuts his eyes and smiles.

I stare at my knees. Kinda wish he wouldn't say these

types of things. Especially right now when I'm like over-stimulated and drowning in confusion.

And he smells really good.

I think he can tell I'm uncomfortable because he "stretches" and moves his arm away. "So we goin' ta *chuch* tomorrow?" he says. "Halleluuuuujah, praise tha *Lawd*!"

I shake my head but chuckle. "You're such a clown."

"And you're gorgeous" is his reply.

Nope! "Alrighty, I think that's enough tipsy sweet talk for the day." I pat his knee and put a good yard of space between us.

Then I grab the remote, raise the volume of the soccer game on the TV, and pray to the God whose house we're supposedly going to tomorrow (*ticket*, Rico . . . the *ticket*) that Jess comes out soon so we can leave.

A Word from Alexander Macklin's 1,200-Thread-Count Egyptian Cotton Sheets

We hate nights like these. Cold nights. Dry nights. Nights when our only physical contact is with one another.

Yes, when we do have Alexander between us, we often wind up sweat-soaked and twisted beyond recognition—he tosses about more than a skiff caught in a hurricane on the open ocean—but *that* is better than this . . . destitution. At least when he's here, he lives in this loneliness *with* us.

His mother hasn't come in to check on our well-being since she handed us off to the maid to be ironed and snapped, pulled too tight over the mattress corners, and tucked painfully down into the frame of Alexander's mahogany monstrosity of a sleigh bed.

We do wish she'd check on *him* more often.

While being transported to the laundry once, we overheard her tell the maid that Alexander reminds her "a bit too much" of the son she lost before he was born—but that's no fault of *our* boy's, now is it? And if Alexander's fevered dreams of his father pushing him off cliffs or locking him into cages or chasing him down with chains are any indication, things aren't exactly hunky-dory in *that* parent-child relationship either.

You didn't hear it from us, but he often dreams of freedom: convertible drives through the mountains wearing shirts with strange words—*Stanford, Notre Dame,* etc.—runs along open woodland trails at sunrise. . . .

As of late, there's a brown girl with large hair who makes a fairly frequent appearance at his side.

Anyway. It's nights like these—the empty ones—when we want him to come home so we can wrap him up tight and never let him go. If nothing else, it would keep *us* from feeling this alone.

He certainly doesn't like it. Why on earth would we?

-17-

Two-Bit Floozy

I wake with the scent of Macklin Magic still in my nostrils. It makes me smile, so I keep my eyes closed.

No clue how I got home, but I think this might've been the best I've slept in a really long time. Bed feels softer than it's ever felt, and I swear this pillow has arms . . .

And legs?

Oh God!

I squeeze my eyes tighter because . . . Yep. That is definitely an arm between my shoulder blades, a leg between my legs, and a chest beneath my cheek. Force one eye open and there's a chin.

Can't breathe now.

I shift to sit up.

His eyes open, and he smiles. "Mornin', sunshine."

Morning?

I look around. There's a pink halo around the edge of a window on the far side of the room.

"Shit!" I jump up from Finesse's couch. Still in my clothes from yesterday. "What time is it?" I say, rushing over to get my shoes on. "Where's Jessica?"

I look back at Zan who—*whoa*—looks downright delectable rubbing his sleepy eyes with his hair sticking up every which wa—

Focus, Rico!

He stretches, and the hem of his shirt lifts. "Jess left last night," he says in the midst of a yawn.

I stop dead. "She *what*?"

"She's got a midnight curfew, so she left at like quarter till." He yawns again.

I'm just like . . . standing here. Stunned. "She *left* me?"

Zan looks at me like I've lost it. "You said you wanted to stay."

"Huh?"

"We were watching a movie, and when she got up to leave, you said you wanted to stay. Bragged about not having a curfew and everything."

Okay, now he's just talking nonsense.

"You don't remember?" he says.

"No!"

Thinking back, thinking back . . . there was Ness and Jess's disappearance when we first got here, then Zan-the-Man all flirty with me on the couch. They came out, we played Scattergories (I won), then pizza and music and laughter and something fizzy that had kind of a bitter aftertaste—

"You spiked my drink?!"

Welp, he's wide-awake now! *"What?* No!"

"Well, how did—?"

"You *asked* for it." He shakes his head and puts his face in his hands. "Ness told you what he was drinking, and you asked for a cup of your own."

140

"Oh."

"You don't remember *anything*?"

I don't respond. Can't.

"Nothing at all?" he says, and as he does, his face morphs into that of a very sad baby elephant. Like if he had a trunk, it would be dragging on the floor right now.

My eyes narrow . . . and then go as wide as the tires on his Jeep.

Oh no.

"Did we . . . ?" My hand flies to my mouth. "Oh my God."

Confusion in the caterpillar brows now. "Huh?"

I scramble to get my Docs on. "I have to get out of here. What time is it? Crap, I'm *so* screwed!" *Ugh! No pun intended!*

"Rico, relax—"

"I was supposed to be at work at *six a.m.*, Zan!" Where the heck is my jacket? Bet that emergency phone of mine is on fire with missed calls. "I'm sure my mom and brother are freaking out. . . ." Oh right. It's upstairs in the Montgomery coat closet. Fantastic. "I can't even *remember* most of the night, and now you're telling me we hooked up—"

"Whoa." He lifts his hands. "I did *not* say that."

How the heck do I even get out of here? What if Ness's parents are sipping coffee over newspapers in the kitchen? I don't want them to see me leaving their house at this hour! I feel like such a stereotype . . . poor girl gets hammered and gives her cookies to some rich boy after crashing a party she shouldn't have even been at. Might as well have a red letter *T* for *tramp* tattooed on my cheek. "Well, that's what you implied with your sad face—"

"What?" Now he's pulling his shoes on.

"You think I was born yesterday? Why would you be upset about my memory lapse if we didn't hook up?"

He sighs and looks at the ceiling. Stands. "It makes me sad that you assume the worst of me, Danger—"

"Can we not do this right now?" Gotta be a clock around here somewhere . . .

6:47?!

I'm so dead.

Zan grabs his jacket from a chair in the corner I failed to notice. Mine is beneath it. He tosses it to me. I pull the phone out and check it—

Thirty-eight missed calls and twelve voice mails.

I try to listen to the first one, and the phone dies. I shove it into my back pocket.

I'm so so so so dead.

"Do you need to go to the bathroom or anything?" he says.

I jab my arms into my sleeves. "I'll go at the store."

"Fine." He walks over and buttons my coat for me. (*Is he serious? WE GOTTA GOOOO!*) Then he's taking my hand, interlacing our fingers, and pulling me down a short hallway to a back door.

The Montgomerys have a downward-sloping driveway that leads to a four-car garage at the rear of the house. That's why I didn't see Zan's Jeep yesterday: it was parked in the back.

As he zooms us through the neighborhood and out to the main road, a million and one questions are tumbling around in my head.

"Zan, did we hook up last night?"

"*No*, Rico."

"Tell me the truth."

"I am! Though why you don't believe me—"

"I just . . . need to hear you say it for real."

His jaw clenches. "We. Did. Not. Hook. Up."

"So what happened?"

He stops at the YMCA traffic light. "We talked. Laughed. Played frickin' *Twister*."

"Okay . . ."

"Then Jess wanted to watch *Final Destination*, which I'm pretty sure was a trick to get you and me closer together. But anyway . . . the movie started, and you got scared, so you curled up beside me on the couch."

The light goes green.

"Yes, you'd had a little to drink, but you seemed pretty lucid. If I'd known you wouldn't remember anything, I would've sent you home with Jess." He sighs. "I just thought . . ." Shakes his head. "Never mind."

"You thought what, Zan?"

"It doesn't matter."

"Maybe not to you, but it docs to me."

He keeps his eyes on the road. "I thought you wanted to stay with me, Rico."

And now I have no words.

No matter what he says, there's no way I buy that Zan Macklin *just* wanted to hang out with me. What do I even have to offer a guy like him? (Other than access to my secret places . . . which why would he even want *that*, considering all the gorgeous-rich-girl secret places he has access to?)

None of last night could've possibly been real.

We turn into the Gas 'n' Go, and he pulls right up to the door. "You want me to come in and explain to Mr. Zoughbi? I'm sure he and I can reach an agreement."

"No, it's fine," I say.

"You sure?"

Super not the time for this. "I said no, Zan. You can't sweet-talk my boss every time I have a problem."

"I was just trying to help—"

"I didn't *ask* for your help."

"Fine." He reaches across me and pushes the door open. "Have a nice day."

Okay. Deep breath.

"Look, I'm sorry, I just—" *can't figure out what else to say.* Too many thoughts/emotions/wishes/fears/questions swooping around and colliding in my head.

The connecting thread, though, is a sense of unworthiness. Being here, being with him with his nice clothes and rich scent in this nice car I could never afford because I work *here* at this fucking gas station for money that's gone before I ever get paid because we live way above our means in an overpriced, trash apartment in this stupid upper-middle-class area . . .

I hate all of it.

"Can I use your phone, please?" I cross my arms and sneer at the cracked pavement of the store parking lot. "I really need to call my mom, but mine is dead and I'd rather not use the one in the store."

He hands it over and shifts his attention out the window as I dial.

144

Part of me knows I should get out so he doesn't overhear the call, but I can't. He *was* there last night, so having my alibi beside me is kind of comforting (my life has become a mess of contradictions). If only I had the courage to slip my hand into his so he could hold it while I face the coming motherly rage inferno.

She answers on the first ring. Frantic. "Hello?"

Breeeeeathe. "Hey, Mama."

"Oh thank *God*! It's her, Jaxy!" she says, her voice muffling as she presumably covers the receiver. Then she's back. And loud. "Rico Reneé, where the hell have you been? We've been worried SICK!"

"I know. I'm sorry. Fell asleep at a friend's house."

"I called everyone I know, Jaxy spent the whole night crying. . . . And what about your job?"

"I'm at work now," I say. "I just wanted to call and let you know I'm okay."

"You bring your ass straight home when you get off. You owe your brother an apology *and* a goddamn afternoon."

"Yes, ma'am."

She hangs up.

"Guess we're not going to the church today?" Zan says.

I shake my head. Feel the urge to cry at the base of my throat. "I'm an hour late. I'll have to make it up, and I need to spend some time with my brother. He was upset last night."

"Next Sunday then?"

Part of me wants to explode. Really go off on him for thinking about the stupid *quest* or whatever he called it when my life is clearly in shambles.

145

But the other part? The other part knows I can't give up on that ticket. Especially not after basking in the glow of Jess's dreams coming true and being in Finesse's house, wrapped in the comfort of financial stability. Really *seeing* what money can buy.

There's a *lot* of it on that little slip of paper.

So.

"Yeah," I say. "Sounds good."

His shoulders relax. "Everything will be fine, okay, Rico?" I hand him his phone, and he catches my hand and tugs my middle finger.

I nod. "Okay."

But of course I don't believe him.

-18-

Victorious Faith

'm mostly right. About things being distinctly *not* fine.

Jax has a fever on and off the whole week, which is extremely stressful. When he hits 102° the night before my and Zander's rescheduled church visit, I bring up the public assistance thing again (solely for *his* sake), but Mama takes it personal and gets so upset, *her* stomach starts acting up.

I hate being at the apartment when they're sick because it becomes this black hole of despair. I'm also exhausted from working so much *and* trying to keep up with school/homework (failed that "We Didn't Start the Fire" test), so the store and school are suck cities too.

Which has caused my perception of Alexander Gustavo (Tuh.) Macklin to . . . morph.

It's strange and uncomfortable if I think about it too much (so I don't), but despite the mind-set I was in when he dropped me off at work, now anytime I think about waking up with our appendages entwined, I feel lighter. It's like for a moment I got to exist in another life. One where everything was taken care of and I could just *be*.

It's the same fairy-tale land I slip into anytime he's around

147

now. Which is more often than I would've expected. He sits next to me in history every day, and on Tuesday, he found my lunchtime getaway spot in the media center and decided to camp out there too. We don't talk any more than we did before (especially not in the media center; pretty sure the media specialist is a dragon in disguise). But the fact that he continues to show up and smile and occupy the same space and seem happy about it has given me this place I can escape to where nothing else exists.

It's disorienting, but what isn't these days?

As a matter of fact, when Zan pulls up in front of my apartment Sunday morning, I'm so relieved, I kinda wanna leap into his arms. He comes around to the passenger side of the Jeep, and it takes every bit of willpower I've got to resist wrapping myself around him and just . . . holding on.

It's terrifying.

He looks me over, top to toe. Since we're headed to church, beneath my borrowed-from-Mama's-closet wool coat, I'm wearing a plum pencil skirt and white button-down shirt, with actual high heels (also snatched from Mama's closet, lord help me).

It's like the sun is rising on his face as he takes me in. "Well, hot damn, Danger."

My cheeks combust, so I drop my chin. "Stop it."

He chuckles.

When I raise my head, he's still checking me out. Grinning.

"Geez, Macklin, have you no shame?" I pull my coat closed.

"Sorry." He shoves his hands in the pockets of what is

surely a Burberry trench. Rocks back on the heels of his mahogany leather wing tips. "It's just, uhh"—another sweep of the eyes from my head to my feet and back again—"hard to look away."

Tongue. Tied. And hot. Like *really* hot all of a sudden. I'd take off the coat, but I don't want him to see the sheer mass of junk in my trunk. It's occurring to me that he's probably noticed before, and now eye contact is impossible.

How do people *deal* with all these feelings?

"Come on." He pulls the door wide and helps me up.

I'm a little nervous he'll be able to tell how flustered I am once both doors are closed, but thankfully, he starts talking as soon as we're both buckled in. "So I looked up this church we're going to," he says. "Beau wasn't lying. It's big."

"Okay . . ."

"Just a heads-up. Picture's not great and we don't have a name," he says. "Not trying to be a Peter Pessimist, but we may have trouble finding someone who knows who she is."

"Oh." The fact that *that* fact didn't hit me as hard as it should've is telling. I peek at Zan. "How big is it?" I ask.

"Fourteen thousand members."

"Jesus."

"Precisely."

I smile. "Miracles happen in churches, right?" I reach out to pat his knee before I can think better of it.

The air in the car thickens, so I clear my throat and turn to look out the window. "Where is this place exactly?"

"It's got a Norcross address, believe it or not. Exactly seven-point-three miles from my house, so three-point-four from yours."

Not sure what's more shocking: that the church is so close, or that he knows the exact distance between our respective homes. "Didn't realize that many people in this town *go* to church."

"I'll take that to mean *you* don't?"

I shrug. "My mom does sometimes, but she doesn't make us come. I'm usually working."

"Gotcha."

"How 'bout you?"

"My family's Catholic. I go to Mass when my grandma makes me. Speaking of which, she's really looking forward to meeting you."

Huh? "Who?"

"My grandma."

"Your grandma . . . ?"

"Wants to meet you."

Now I'm staring at him.

"I might've mentioned you to her."

"Mmm . . . Okay . . ." *Why?* is what I don't say.

"She's super nosy, so she wanted to know all about you." He rubs the back of his neck. "So I told her. And now she wants to meet you."

I swallow and drop my eyes to my hands in my lap. What could he have said? *I've been hanging with this poor, sad brown girl who works in a gas station, smells like fake nacho cheese, and is obsessed with finding a missing lotto ticket?* "What'd you tell her?"

He snorts. "That's classified, Danger."

Punk.

I cross my arms. "You're annoying."

He laughs. "The fact that she wants to meet you should make it *clear* my report was full of praise."

"What's there to *praise*?"

"Oh, a *lot*." He looks me over again and winks.

Victorious Faith Chapel *is* big. And it looks nothing like a church. Well . . . nothing like I'd expect a church to look. There's no steeple, no stained glass, no bell tower (is that the same thing as a steeple?). What it *does* have is a two-story cross near the entrance to the parking lot, and a metal globe the size of our living room plopped in front of the main building. At least I *think* it's the main building . . . there are three and it's the biggest one.

"Man, they weren't lying about it being multicultural," Zan says.

He's right. It's like we've stepped into a UN summit. There are saris and dashikis and *hanbok* . . . even a guy in a kilt.

Also fascinating: there are tons of luxury cars in the parking lot, but also a slew of people crossing the street from the nearby bus stop. Just as we step into the globe-containing plaza, a small shuttle bus pulls up. HELPING HAND: AIDING ATLANTA'S HOMELESS SINCE 1991, it says on the side. When the people step off that bus dressed in the finest scraps of clothing they could come up with, I feel . . . conflicted.

Something I didn't tell Zan: the whole God thing's always been a little suspect to me. Before the radio in the truck stopped working, every time we'd get in, Mama would turn on what I called the Sermon Station, so I've heard all about how *good* God is and how much He *loves all His children.*

But for as long as I can remember, Mama has *prayed without ceasing,* and . . . well, I find it tough to believe this God character is so great when we continue to barely scrape by despite how hard Mama works *and* prays.

Seeing the mind-boggling difference between the Victorious Faith three-piece suits exiting Audis and Teslas and the attire cobbled together by the homeless bus people definitely isn't making me a believer. I mean, they're all going into the same building, aren't they? Why does the gulf between their respective *blessings* seem so wide?

Anyway.

Inside is even more intense. In addition to the ethnic garb, there are people standing around the perimeter of what I guess is the lobby holding various national flags.

And *everybody* is smiling.

"Freaky," I say.

Zander has apparently inhaled the Kool-Aid because he's not paying me any attention. Too busy looking around, beaming like a kid who just stumbled into Santa's workshop. "Is it like this *every* week?"

"Goodness no!" a frighteningly familiar voice rumbles from behind us.

We slowly turn around.

Oh God . . . I mean, *gosh.*

"I thought that was you two!"

It's the security guard from Checker Cab.

"Officer Kenny! Wow!" Because who could forget the

man? "Fancy meeting you here!" I look to Zan for help, but he's still smiling and tossing waves at random strangers.

"Welcome to VFC!" Kenny says. "So good to see y'all in the house of the Lord this morning!"

"Uhh . . ." *What to say?* "Good to be here!"

"You've chosen a fabulous Sunday to visit. Today is our Parade of Nations!"

"Parade of Nations?" Zan is utterly in awe.

"That's right! We've got ninety-three nations represented in our congregation. Most multicultural house of worship in Greater Atlanta!"

I don't think I've ever seen anyone as proud as Kenny is right now.

"Amazing," Zan says.

Trying really hard not to side-eye him.

"Glad you think so, young man." Kenny gives Zan's shoulder a shake, and Zan stumbles forward a good couple of feet.

Then Kenny looks at me. "Did you ever find your locket, young lady?"

And crap.

"Ummm . . ."

"That's why we're here," Zan says. (So he *is* still on planet Earth.) "We're trying to track down the woman who was in the cab *after* my friend here. Maybe you know her? Driver said he dropped her off here on Christmas Eve."

Well damn, Macklin.

"Really now?" Kenny replies.

"Mm-hmm. It was her first time here, apparently." He

pulls out the picture . . . if you can even call it that. More like a series of grayscale blobs on an 8.5x11-inch piece of paper with multiple creases from Zander's folds. "Sorry the photo isn't great. Retrieved it from some security footage at a convenience store. You can kinda see her, right?"

Kenny squints and rubs his chin as he looks at the paper. "We get a *lot* of visitors for the holiday services."

Trying not to panic. (Because I suddenly care?) "She was a little old black lady with a white Afro and light-up sweater—"

"You've seen her in person?" Kenny says.

Oops.

"Yes . . ." I look at Zan. "I work at the convenience store where we got the picture. The driver was dropping me off as he picked her up."

Kenny lifts an eyebrow. "She caught a taxi from a convenience store?"

Crap, crap, CRAP. "Yep." I gulp. "No clue how she got there."

He narrows his eyes and visually volleys back and forth between Zan and me. "What'd you say she looks like?"

This is going south super fast.

There's a giant clock over the entrance. Service starts in four minutes.

"Small frame, brown skin, large glasses, little white Afro . . ."

Kenny opens his mouth to say something else, but a petite lady with big, bright eyes and the most stylish tapered bob I've ever seen materializes at his side (thank *God*). "Who do we have here, Kenneth?"

154

Kenny smiles. "Pastor Darlene! This is . . ." He gestures for us to introduce ourselves.

"Gustavo Maxwell," Zander says, thrusting a hand forward. "Pleasure to meet you."

Gustavo Maxwell?

"And you?" She smiles at me.

I glance at Zan. "Oh. I'm . . . Reneé." I say. "Reneé . . . Banger."

Zan chokes and starts coughing.

"Oh my! Are you all right, young man?" Pastor Darlene says. Kenny smacks Zan on the back a little too hard and he stumbles forward again.

"Fine, fine," Zan says once he recovers. "Saliva went down the wrong pipe."

"Ah." Pastor Darlene blinks a few times and clasps her hands in front of her. "Well, welcome to Victorious!"

Good gracious, we are so busted.

"Thank you!" Too enthusiastic? Probably too enthusiastic.

"I'm glad you're here, Pastor," Kenny says. "These two are looking for a congregant . . . Older African American woman. Very small with large spectacles and a white Afro . . . that right, Ms. Banger?"

Zan chokes again.

I hate him I hate him I hate him.

"That's right," I say. "She was a first-timer on Christmas Eve." Please don't let her ask why we're looking because I cannot lie to a pastor twice.

"You'll have to speak with Ms. Maybelle," she says. "She's

155

our visitor coordinator . . . Don't think she's here this week, though."

Of *course* she isn't. Motherfu—lover!

"Ms. Maybelle?" Zan says.

And I'm thankful. I certainly can't speak right now.

"That's right. Ms. Maybelle Carver. Pleasure meeting you all. I'll see you inside." She winks and bounces off.

I'm pretty much a sizzling, sparking ball of nerves through the whole service and ride home, but once we're back outside my apartment, Zan tells me to wait so he can come around and "let me out." (Hmm.)

Once my feet are on the ground and the door is closed, he crosses his arms and leans against the Jeep. There's a wicked little glimmer in his eye. "So I was thinking," he says.

And that's it.

Why is my heart racing? "Do I get to *know* what you were thinking, or is it 'classified'?"

"Oh, shut up."

I laugh, and he blushes.

So my face gets all warm too.

"As I was saying, since the commencement of our quest, we've already broken the law, taken a road trip, slept together—literally—and gotten our Jesus on. As such, I really feel we've reached a point where it'd be wholly appropriate to part with a brief embrace."

Is he for real? "Oh."

"No pressure, obviously." His cheeks are re-reddening. "I just thought maybe—uhh . . ." He runs a hand through his hair.

"You want to hug me?"

He gulps. "Is that weird?"

"Well . . . I wouldn't say *weird*. . . ."

I don't know what to say.

I can feel him examining my face. "You find it hard to believe?"

"No, I just—" Can't look at him. BLAH! "Maybe a little?"

"Why?"

I shrug. Shove my hands into my pockets and dig my nails into my palms. He's hugged me before, and it was nice . . . but the first time was a front for Mr. Z, and the second he'd been drinking.

(Yes, I remember both.)

(This is so uncomfortable.)

"Just outside my realm of experience," I say. "We're not really huggers in my family unless it's like a special occasion."

"Oh."

"Yeah."

"I see. Well, we don't *have* to. . . ." He looks off into the distance and rocks back on his heels. Clears his throat. "Sorry. You have to get ready for work and everything, right?"

"Zan?"

He looks back at me. "Yeah?"

I step forward and spread my arms.

A Word from a Waffle House Saltshaker

've overheard my share of interesting conversations, but I must admit: when I heard *Macklin* spoken at my table tonight—everyone around here knows *that* name—the holes in my top perked right up. All started when the down-right dashing African American boy to my right ended a phone call and set his device at the foot of me, beaming like he was witnessing the first sunrise of his life. When the pretty blond girl with him saw his face, a smile split hers as well.

I couldn't look away.

Blondie: Zan?

Black Boy: Yep.

Blondie: Guessing the "outing" he refused to tell us about went well?

Black Boy: I've *never* heard him sound like that, Jess.

Blondie: How'd he sound?

Black Boy: Like he'd won the damn lotto or something. All giddy and shit.

Blondie: Stop.

Black Boy: I'm for real. Don't know what it is about her, babe, but she's really doing something for our boy. You know he's real skittish about this stuff.

Blondie: Still can't believe that trashbag stole his mom's bracelet.

Black Boy: Allegedly.

Blondie: Allegedly, my ass. First time you bring someone new into the house, something valuable goes missing? Gimme a break. And how much you wanna bet she *knew* the Macklins wouldn't press charges because it would cause a media frenzy? Every time I see her at school, I wanna punch her in the face—

Black Boy: Relax, Ronda Rousey. Point is, Zan's really into this one.

Blondie: Her name is *Rico*, Ness.

The black boy smiled.

Black Boy: So she's got you too then.

And the blond girl flushed the color of a freshly bloomed rose.

Blondie: What are you talking about?

Black Boy: Rico. You're sprung too. I can see it all over you. You wanna be BFFs and have slumber parties and shit—

Blondie: Technically it's b-*Fs*-f, but fine: yes.
I like her. She's *real*. And like . . . not-judgy.
Or snobbish.

There was a pause as Lucy deposited their food on the table. (I love that Lucy. Always gives me a good wipedown with a warm cloth before her shift is over.) Blondie picked me up—real warm hands though her cuticles were a little worse for the wear—shook me a few times over her smothered, covered, and chunked extra-crispy hash browns, set me down, took a bite, and shut her eyes as she hummed in ecstasy.

Black Boy: They really would be cute as hell
together.
Blondie: I hope he asks her out. Though if he does,
we'll have to watch her back. If there's one thing
I know for sure, the minute Zan Macklin has
a girlfriend, those snooty bitches at school are
gonna be salty.

-19-

PMS Basketball

And now I'm distracted.
Very distracted.

Like, just-closed-the-register-drawer-on-my-pinky distracted. *"Shit!"*

The soccer-mom customer snatches her vittles and beverages from the counter and rushes her three children out the door.

"Everything okay, Rico?" Mr. Z says from the doorway to his office.

"Mm-hmm. Nuss mass mah meen-he inuh weh-yeh-tuh—"

He comes out, clearly confused *and* concerned, and I take my finger outta my mouth. "Sorry." Good lord, this hurts.

His eyes drop to my hand and widen. "You're in need of a bandage. We have a first-aid kit just there beneath the counter."

Now I have to look (which I really didn't want to do).

Ugh. There's blood pooling beneath the nail and oozing out at the cuticle. Now I'm queasy. "I'm fine, I'm fine. I promise."

"Bandage." He points to the kit and disappears back into the office.

By the time I get the Band-Aid on, the store is empty. So now I'm stuck alone with my thoughts.

Of Zan.

Mama and Jax have both been relatively healthy, Mama's truck's running fine, and there are no outstanding bills to fret over. Which means it's easy to let the ticket drift into the background and just . . . *Zan*-out.

Zan . . . who decided that in addition to parting with an embrace, we must also *greet* with one.

None of them have been "brief."

Zan . . . who spent the last two days trying to convince me to let him be my chauffeur: pick me up for school every morning, take me home every afternoon, drive me to and from work, be the taxi for my and Jax's grocery runs.

Zan . . . who is slowly consuming my every thought, as well as creeping into my visions of the future: *Maybe it won't be so bad sticking around after graduation. Zan's sticking around too, after all. . . .*

Visions of the future that didn't exist a few months ago.

Thing is, the more interest he shows in me, the more awkward I feel. Like today in the media center, I looked up from the book I was reading to find him staring at me with this little smirk tugging at his mouth. I gulped and asked if there was something on my face, and he goes, "Danger, you have *the* coolest eyes I've ever seen."

The compliment caught me off guard.

"Are you kidding?" I squawked in response. "They're *weird*," and I lifted the book so he couldn't see me anymore.

It seems dangerous, this development of *something* inside me that's highly reactive to Zan Macklin. It makes me . . . want.

Except—and I'd never admit it to anyone because I feel stupid about it, but—I can't imagine our differences in background not mattering to the point where we could *really* be friends, let alone anything else.

I push the drawer closed—without my finger in it this time—just as the door chimes.

"Hiya, gorgeous!" Jess beams like the frickin' North Star as she bounces in.

Can't help but smile back. "Hey, Jess."

She props her elbows on the counter and sets her chin in her hands.

I look past her. "No Finesse? What is this, the apocalypse?"

She sighs.

"Sweet mother of Mary, you are pitiful."

"You hush your mouth."

I laugh. "You know it's true."

"Mm-hmm. You'll get there soon enough."

Boom. Just that quick, the lid on the box full of crap I'm trying *not* to think about is blown not only off, but up into the air and across the damn room. "Ha!" Totally forced laugh. "Doubtful."

"You'll see," she goes on, oblivious.

"I'll, uh . . . take your word for it."

And now I feel like an exposed nerve. This is the Jessica effect. Where being around Zan makes me *want* to dream, Jess exists as this itchy reminder of what life could look like if I did.

It's uncomfortable.

She nods and stands upright. "So how are you? I was in the area and figured you were here, so I decided to drop by."

The doorbell chimes again, and a group of pubescent boys pile in with the force of a freight train. The local middle school is named Pinckneyville, so the warm-ups they're wearing have PMS BASKETBALL emblazoned across the front.

They smell like damp gorillas who all have athlete's foot.

"Damn, girl!" the apparent ringleader says when he sees Jess. Voice cracks and everything.

"Oh God. Grow some pubic hair."

I snort. Despite not knowing each other, it's impossible not to like this girl.

As the PMS barbarians ransack the store—I see bags of chips flying through the air across two aisles—Jess goes on. "So how are things with Macklin?"

Ugh. I don't want to talk about this.

And yet, I obviously do. I *need* to talk about it, in fact. I *need* a friend to talk about it—about this *boy*—with. I'm frickin' seventeen years old.

I sigh. Look over her shiny blond hair, blushed cheeks, and brand-name clothes. Everything about Jessica Barlow seems perfect . . . until I remember her shower cap and secret cigaretting. Her chewed-to-nubs nails and scabbed-over cuticles.

164

Is she trustworthy, though? Her care for Zan seems genuine . . . and so does her interest in me.

And really, do I have any other options? It's not like *potential friends* are falling from the sky. . . .

"Jess, can I ask you something"—*look left, look right*—"in confidence?"

"Of course."

"Do you ever feel . . . *strange* around Finesse or your other friends?"

She starts nibbling at her thumbnail. "Depends on what you mean by *strange.*"

"Like . . . out of place?"

Our eyes meet, and she smiles. "All the time, Rico."

Just then, the funk of middle-school boy surges forward like a cloud of teargas. Jess barely steps aside in time to avoid being knocked over. I ring them up—holding my breath the whole time; $23.64 in soda and junk food—and the boy who can't take his eyes off Jess passes me a credit card.

Figures.

"I'll buy you a Sprite next time, beautiful." He winks at Jess as they grab their bags from the counter and turn to leave.

"Go get your Pull-Up changed, twerp!"

I laugh as the door shuts behind them.

"What was I saying?" she asks.

"Feeling out of place?"

"Ah, yes. That. So Ness and I have been together for a year and a half, right?"

News to me, but okay. "Yeah . . ."

She tucks her hair behind her ear. "Ask me how many times he's been inside my apartment."

"How many times has he—"

"Once. He's only talked to Mom twice, and one of those was over the phone."

Well dang. "Wow."

"Right. Side note, I've never shared any of this with anybody besides him. If it gets out, I *will* come after you."

I chuckle. "Duly noted."

"So when I first made the cheerleading squad in ninth grade, I got thrust into this mostly white, upper-middle-class wonderland. All the other girls had two parents and lived in nice houses with canopy beds and shit. Me? I wound up in therapy and on antianxiety meds."

Whoa. "Okay."

"As a little kid, anytime I would complain about *any-thing*, my mom would bring up 'the starving children in Africa,' so I wound up feeling shitty about not having as much as everyone else, and then on top of that, feeling guilty for feeling shitty."

My gaze drops to the counter as she basically reads my own life aloud to me.

"Halfway through freshman year, Micah—you know Micah Holloway? Tall, Blasian—"

"Physically perfect and filthy rich?" I say.

"Her feet are the stuff of nightmares, but don't tell anybody I told you that."

I laugh so hard, I almost choke.

"Anyway, she was supposed to come sleep over at the apartment we were living in then. The night before, I had a full-blown panic attack. Started seeing a shrink the next week. Still do a couple times a month now."

166

"But doesn't that get expensive?" I don't *mean* to say that aloud, but there it is.

Why does she look like I just asked if the sky was made of cupcakes? "It's covered by Medicaid."

"Oh."

Never woulda guessed Jessica Barlow was on public assistance.

I watch her realization dawn. "Wait . . . your fam doesn't get it?"

I shake my head.

"SNAP, either?"

"SNAP?"

She pulls a credit-looking card with a leafy background and a giant peach on the front from her purse. "To help cover food?"

Ah. "Nope," I say.

"Wow, you must be *way* better off than we are."

I open my mouth to tell her Mama won't apply, but the door chimes again just as Mr. Z steps out of the office. "Rico, there is a call for you."

"Umm . . ." Uh-oh . . . I've never gotten a call at work before. "Do you know who it is?"

He shakes his head. "They didn't say. I'll cover the floor while you take it, but make it quick."

My vision blurs.

"Whoa, Rico. You okay?" I feel a hand on my arm, and Jess comes back into focus.

"Sorry, I, uhh . . ." I look at the gaping door that feels like a step toward my doom. "I need to take this call."

"Sure thing. I'll grab a Gatorade or something so it

doesn't look like I'm loitering." As she walks off, I slip into the office, trying not to hyperventilate.

Pick up the phone. "Hello?"

"Agent Danger, this is Command."

Zan.

"I hate you," I say.

"Well, that's overly harsh. What'd I ever do to you?"

"I never get calls at work! I thought somebody *died* or something!"

He laughs. "Sorry. You won't give me your cell number, so this is the only place I knew I could catch you."

"Oh." *Why* am I light-headed? And sweating?

"I have news!" he says.

"You mean you're not calling to hear my voice? For shame."

Omg, I did NOT just say that. . . .

"Are you *flirting* with me, Danger?"

"*Pfffft.* No." Yes.

I can almost hear the mischief in his smile. "Liar."

"You gotta work on that egomania, Macklin."

"Oh hush, you."

I roll my eyes and smile. "So what's the news? I'm on the clock."

"I found Ms. Maybelle!"

"Ms. *who?*"

"Good God, what am I gonna do with you?"

"How 'bout tell me what you're talking about so I can get back to work?"

"Ms. Maybelle. The visitor coordinator from Victorious Faith?"

Oh! "Ah, yes. Her."

"I swear I care more about this quest than you do."

Mmmmm . . . "I've got a lot on my mind, all right?" *Mostly you.*

"When are you off?"

"Ten."

"Not today, goof. I mean what day this week."

Oh. "Thursday."

"Field triiiiiiip!"

"Nerd."

"You love it."

I roll my eyes again even though A) he can't see me, and B) fine, I kinda do. "You should really get over yourself."

He laughs.

Mr. Z sticks his head in and holds up two fingers. Guess I have two minutes*!*

"You know, you really could've told me this at school tomorrow," I say.

"Ah, I just wanted to hear your voice."

Roller-coaster drop. "You flirting with me, Macklin?"

"You bet your beautiful ass I am."

"Don't look at my ass."

"Oh, it's much too late for that, Danger. I'll be there to take you home at ten tonight. That okay?"

"Was that your way of asking?"

"In a manner of speaking, yes."

Hmph. "Try again."

"Rico, may I pick you up from work tonight, please?"

"Yes. You may."

"Excellent. Later, gator."
I hang up.
And stare at the phone.
Bite my lip and shake my head.
It's official: I'm distracted.
This is going to be a disaster.

-20-

Cookies

"So here's the deal," Zan says as we pull into the drive-way of a mint-green Victorian house the following Thursday. The sign on the mailbox reads THE REVEREND'S ROOST: CIRCA 1907. "Ms. Maybelle's grandfather-in-law built this house. It's part of the annual Historic Homes tour, and she agreed to let us visit because she thinks we're doing a school project on the history of Norcross."

"Got it."

"You ask her a few questions about her life and the house, then I'll bring up Victorious Faith and our mystery woman. If she remembers her, great! Hopefully we can get a name. If not—"

"We're shit out of luck and our quest is over." *You'll stop talking to me, and I'll go back to my miserable, meaningless life.*

He doesn't respond. Doesn't even look in my direction.

Which is . . . whatever. "All right, let's do this." I remove my seat belt and reach for the door handle.

"Wait." A set of fingertips grabs my elbow.

Whew, tingles. "What?"

"For one: let me get the door for you, please." He smiles.

171

It gives me a shiver. "And for two?"

"For two: in case this is the end, know it's been my highest pleasure questing with you, Danger."

Great. Confirmation that this could be the end. "Whatever." I go to open the door again.

"Wait, there's a *for three*!"

"Macklin!"

"Sorry, it's important."

Stab, stab, stab with my eyes.

"Just so you know," he goes on, "she thinks our names are Gustavo and Reneé."

Maybelle Carver is the second-cutest old lady I've ever seen. She answers the door in a nylon jogging suit (bright pink) with purple dumbbells in hand, and her shoulder-length silver hair is held off her face with a matching sweatband.

She beams when she sees us. "Well, *helloooooo!*" she says. "Gustavo and Reneé, I presume? Do come in, do come *in*!"

We do.

"Lucinda!" she hollers over her shoulder. "We have guests!"

A lady appears from who knows where. Jeans, T-shirt, sneakers. She smiles at us. "Coats?" she says, extending her hand, and we pass them to her before she disappears around a corner to the right.

I take in the *foyer* (that's what these areas just inside the front door of a big-ass house are called, right?), and though everything looks sort of antique and unassuming, I bet my britches this lady could bathe in hundred-dollar bills. She

172

claps and bounces on the toes of her white Reebok Classic high-tops, then busts a spin move and heads down a hallway to the left of a curved staircase.

Zan and I exchange a Look.

"Down here in the drawing room!" Maybelle chirps. Her pink-crowned head pokes out of an open doorway down on the left.

Along the walls are pictures that progress in age: from monotone photos of jolly-jowled white men, to a sepia photo of a couple in wedding garb, to a series of Polaroids spread across four frames, to what look like modern-day photos of three different white families with children. The hardwood floors creak and groan, and the air smells of dust and lemon furniture polish, but it just adds to the *old money* feel of the place.

The drawing room (snort) is jammed with gorgeous furniture that looks like it would fetch a fortune on eBay. There are a couple of winged-looking chairs, a long velvet couch, and a fancy-shmancy chaise lounger thing all arranged around a squat coffee table with bowed legs in the center of a massive rug—surely *Persian* or some such. There's an ornately framed mirror hanging over the mantel and a brilliant blaze roaring in the fireplace.

"Come, come," Maybelle says from one of the chairs. "Lucinda made tea and a sampling of cookies."

This is an understatement. There are three pots of tea and six varieties of home-baked cookies on the table. Zan and I take seats on the couch, then he pours each of us a cup and proceeds to pile a plate with cookies and offer it to me. "So Ms. Carver—"

"We can dispense with the formalities, dear." She winks. "Maybelle is fine."

"Oh, I couldn't possibly call you by your first name, ma'am. My father would have my head."

"A gentleman, eh?" Maybelle looks at me. "What a lucky girl you are! You know, it's wonderful to see you kids mixing things up these days!"

Zan coughs beside me. "Oh, we're not—"

"I had a liaison between my first and second marriage," she goes on. "Lionel was his name, and he was a black man. This was all before I found the Lord, mind you, but that Lionel *really* knew his way around a lady, if you catch my drift."

Jesus, Mary, Joseph, *and* Abraham.

"There was also Eduardo." She looks at Zan. "When you said your name was Gustavo, I expected you to look like him. Anyhow, *he* taught me a thing or two about *haciendo el amor.*"

Zan clears his throat, and I'm glad because I'm on the verge of spitting out my tea. "Sounds like you've had a fascinating life," he says.

"Oh yes. Very blessed! Now what may I do for you interracial lovebirds?"

Can I leave? I'd really like to leave now.

"Well, as I mentioned during our phone chat, Ms. Carver, Reneé and I are doing a project on the history of Norcross," Zan says. "I understand your late husband's grandfather was the first mayor?"

She nods once. "My *first* husband's grandfather, but yes. Yes, he was."

174

She even talks like a person who's never had a financial care in the world.

"Got it. And the first town hall was here in this house?"

She smiles and looks around the room. "Correct. As a matter of fact, you're sitting in the room where the city was named."

Okay, that's actually pretty cool.

"How long have you lived here?" Zan says.

"In the town? My whole life!" she replies. "I've ventured away here and there, but there's no staying gone. My friends and family are here, my church is here—"

"What church do you go to?" I blurt.

Zan pinches his lips together, but come on. Opportunity much?

"I've been a member of Victorious Faith Chapel since its inception fifteen years ago."

"Oh wow! You must be pretty plugged in there!"

I see Zan's jaw clench now, but (thankfully) Maybelle laughs. "You happen to be looking at the director of guest services!"

"Really?!" *Okay, maybe laying it on a little thick now, Rico . . .*

Maybelle doesn't seem to notice my theatrics. Just points to a massive wooden chest in a corner of the room. "The drawers of that cabinet contain visitor cards for the past three years," she says. "Not to toot my own horn, but since I took over, the guest-to-member conversion rate has increased eighteen percent." She smiles demurely and bats her eyelashes.

I gasp. "Za—I mean, Gustavo, this is fate!"

Zan is smiling, but I can tell he's not breathing.

"What do you mean, dear?" Maybelle says.

"Well . . . I work at a—consignment shop, and a lady brought in a bag of clothes the day before Christmas Eve. I found a . . . a *brooch* as I was sorting the clothes."

Zan sips his tea.

"The owner of the shop is also a jeweler, and when I showed it to him, he said it's probably worth a fortune. I know *I'd* be devastated if I lost such a treasure, so I've been trying to find the lady ever since."

"Oh my." Maybelle puts a hand over her heart, intensely moved, it seems.

"I remember asking about her Christmas plans, and she said she was going to visit your church for the Christmas Eve service . . . she'd never been before."

"Perhaps I met her then!" Maybelle says. "There were sixty-two guests who filled out cards that night. . . . Do you have her name?"

Zan looks at me with his eyes all alight.

"I never got her name, but I have a picture of her on me. I've been carrying it everywhere." I stand and pat my pockets, hoping Macklin takes a frickin' hint.

"I have it, actually," Zan says (thank God, who, if he's real, will likely smite us for all these lies we're telling). He shifts to pull the picture out of his back pocket and passes it to me. "You dropped it in the hallway."

"She was a tiny older black lady with little white Afro." I unfold the picture and pass it to Maybelle.

She furrows her brow, turns the photo to the right, and cocks her head to the left.

Then she smiles. "Christmas Eve, you say?"

"Yes."

Maybelle nods. "This is Ethel."

I look at Zan . . . who's already looking at me. "Ethel?" we say simultaneously.

"That's her name. I remember her quite clearly. The light-up sweater she had on was a little tacky, but she came up at the end of the service for prayer and I walked her out."

This rich old white lady *would* hate on Ethel's sweater.

Maybelle sighs and shakes her head then.

My mouth goes dry. "What's the matter?"

"She's one of the ones who got away," she says. "We tried to contact her but never got a response."

Uh-oh. "Do you think she, umm . . . ?" Based on the lack of color in Zan's face, I'd say he knows what I'm about to ask. "Do you think she passed?"

"Oh, I doubt that." Maybelle flicks the thought away. *(Whew!)* "We were probably just a bit too *hip* for her tastes. Women like Ethel tend to grow up Baptist, Holiness Pentecostal, or AME. Very traditional worship-wise—hymns and old Negro spirituals, that type of thing—and they rarely stray from the King James Version. You two familiar with the Gospel of Jesus Christ?"

Oh boy, here we go. . . .

"We're Catholic, ma'am," Zan says.

Maybelle fights so hard to hide her displeasure, I almost bust out laughing. "Oh" is all she says.

The air in the room goes a little sour, so I decide to just take the plunge. "Do you think you could give me Ethel's contact information? I'd really like to get her bracelet bac—"

"I thought you said *brooch*?"

And shit.

"Yes, yes, I'm sorry. Her brooch. Her . . . elephant brooch."

She eyes me for a few seconds, then sighs. "Unfortunately, it's against the VFC Code of Ethics to give out *anyone's* contact information without their express permission. If you'd like to leave *your* phone number, I can make an attempt at contacting her myself, but as I mentioned, no one was able to get ahold of her after her visit."

And scene.

She looks at her watch. "If the two of you would like a tour of the house for your project, now would be the time. I'll need to have my bath soon."

"That sounds like a fabulous idea, Ms. Carver," Zander says. "Thank you for offering."

"Right this way." She stands and heads toward the drawing room door.

We follow suit, and I jab him with a good glower—don't see a point in the façade now.

But he just winks at me. Which, despite the death of our quest, makes my insides go gooey. (Insult to injury, I tell you.)

When we get into the hallway, Zander pauses and puts a hand on his stomach. "Ahh . . . Ms. Carver, might I use your facilities?"

Maybelle looks a little grossed out (which is kind of funny), but she says, "Yes, of course. Second door on the left there," and she points down an adjacent hall.

"You lovelies can go ahead and begin the tour since I

know we're pressed for time," Zan says. "Tell me, was there *butter* in any of those cookies?"

Maybelle is clearly aghast. "Of course there was butter! They're *cookies*."

"Ah. Right. Definitely go ahead. This could take a whi—" His face goes blank. "Oh boy, gotta go now." And he pivots and rushes around the corner.

For a moment, Maybelle is rooted to the spot. Concerned about *Gustavo* ruining her plumbing, no doubt.

I touch her shoulder, and she startles. "Sorry," I say. "Shall we, ummm . . . do the tour?"

"Sure, sure," she says, glancing toward the hallway again. "My apologies. Right this way."

As we move through the different rooms she gives me a brief history of the house *and* the city—we see Lucinda rocking out with earbuds tucked into her ears as she vacuums the library—but the whole time, I'm thinking about Zan. Wondering if he's okay. Wondering if this is really the end. All I really catch is her mention of "birthing children" in the room where her first husband's grandfather "birthed a town," and on and on about this crown molding and that grade of mahogany for this bedroom floor.

By the time we get back downstairs, it's been a good twenty minutes, and there's still no sign of Zan. "I do hope your *friend* is all righ—" (Oh, so now we're just friends?)

"Whew!" comes a voice from the end of the hallway. Zan appears with a smile on his face, but it fades when he sees us. "Aw man, did I miss the whole tour?"

Maybelle looks him over from head to foot, disgusted

and not hiding it this time. Especially considering he's trailing a piece of toilet paper on his shoe. "I'm afraid you did, young man."

"Drat. You wouldn't have time to give me a quick run-through, would you?"

I feel my eyes widen, but I keep smiling.

"Sadly, no," she says. "You'll have to come back during the Christmas tour. Now if you two wouldn't mind, it's time for me to begin my evening routine. Lucinda!" she calls up the steps. "If you'll bring our guests their coats, please!"

Zan steps up to Maybelle. Takes her weathered hand. "Thank you so much for having us, Ms. Carver." He lifts the back of it to his lips.

I expect her to blush, considering her stories about *liaisons*, but instead, she snatches her hand away. Lucinda appears to the left (*where the heck did she come from?!*) with our coats draped over her arm, and Maybelle takes them, shoves them at us, and practically pushes us out the front door.

Once we're in the Jeep, I huff and cross my arms. "Well, that was rude."

Zan chuckles, then passes me a little card. At the top is the name Ethel Streeter, and while the phone number line is blank, there's a PO box listed on the address line.

My mouth drops. "No flippin' way . . ."

He grins. "Those cookies were delicious, weren't they?"

-21-

Happy Friggin' Birthday

For days, the Ethel Streeter visitor card is my constant companion. In fact, I take it out and look at it so often, I manage to memorize the PO address.

Except I can't seem to do anything with it. Every time I work up the courage to sit down at a computer for a quick Google search, my fingers freeze just before making contact with the keyboard.

I dunno what it is, but all of a sudden, the thought of pursuing a lead behind Zan's back feels . . . wrong.

Oddly enough, I also can't bring myself to loop him in.

He's constantly on my mind now. Even invades my dreams. In fact, I'm slowly waking from one where he's standing in front of me without clothing when he opens his mouth to speak and "Ricoooooo!" comes out in a voice that doesn't really sound like his own.

It's weird.

"Uhh . . . Macklin?"

He bends at the knee and leaps into the air. Comes down on top of me and knocks all the breath out of my body.

Eyes are open now.

Jax is climbing off me and running around the end of the bed to climb up and jump on me again.

"Ricoooooo!" he shouts. And then he leaps.

Oooof!

It's still dark outside.

"Jaxy, what the hell?" I toss him to the floor.

He hops up, unfazed. Climbs back to his starting position but begins jumping on my bed with me in it. "You said *hell*!"

"SO did YOU, dimWIT." *Gah!* "PLEASE stop JUMping ON my BED now!"

It's like he doesn't even hear me. "You were talking about *Zan-Zan* in your sleep."

Oh boy. "What?"

"Is he your *boyfriend* now?"

"No!" I roll over so he won't see the mortification all over my face.

"I bet you were having *wet dreams* about him."

Umm . . . I sit up. "What the heck do *you* know about wet dreams?"

He hops off the bed and rolls his eyes. "They're dreams where you're *doing it* with somebody, duh. Mason's big brother has them all the time and he pees out sticky stuff in the bed, so that's why they're called wet."

Heaven help me. I don't even know how to respond to that.

He grabs my arm and pulls. "Come *on*. Get up! We have

182

to make the special French toast for Mommy before she wakes up!"

"Huh?"

"The. French. TOAST. For Mommy!"

Oh crap. "What day is it?"

"Friday!" He throws his hands up like I'm the biggest idiot to ever exist.

"No, knucklehead. What *date*?"

"Two twenty-twoooooooo!"

Oh no, oh no, oh no.

It's Mama's birthday.

I totally forgot about it.

Jax can see it all over my face too. His little jaw slowly unhinges. "You *forgot*?"

And shit.

I jump up and scramble to pull my sweatpants back on (apparently kicked them off in the night when I was dreaming about *Zan-Zan* . . . ugh). "What are you waiting for?" I say to Jax. "Go get the eggs and milk"—*Do we even* have *eggs and milk?! God, I am a terrible daughter!*—"mixed up!"

He dashes off, and I try to figure out what to do. I've gotten Mama a birthday gift—and given it to her with breakfast—every year since before Jax was even born. Last year, she was dealing with some psoriasis on her hands, so Mr. Z helped me get this cream from Jordan that had Dead Sea minerals in it. Year before that, I got insoles for her shoes. When I come into the dining room empty-handed, it'll be dead obvious I forgot.

What the hell is wrong with me?

Jax and I get the apple-cinnamon French toast whipped

up, and I toss together an onion and cheese omelet and some bacon. *(When/where did we get bacon? It's like eight dollars a pack! This is why I do the shopping. . . .)* Then we set the table and both run off to get dressed.

When we get back, Mama is sitting in her spot, beaming. Jax has *his* gift in hand, and as he rushes over to her, I feel like the most imbecilic douche-jackass in history. Have I really gotten so wrapped up in this ticket hunt (and fine, in the irritating but admittedly hot rich boy hunting with me) that I forgot my friggin' mother's birthday?!

"Get over here, Rico," Mama says.

Time to face the music. "I, umm . . . I didn't really get you—"

"I have a surprise for you guys!" She cuts me off with a minute shake of the head.

Okay then . . .

"Ooh! A surprise!" Jax says. "What is it?"

She pinches his nose. "No school for you loves today because WE are going on a *trip*."

Um. "A trip?"

"That's right. As soon as we eat this delicious breakfast, we're hitting the road." She smiles up at me.

I've got so many emotions swirling right now, my face goes numb. Shock, confusion, disbelief . . .

Yet also a little bit of anticipation?

Hell, Jax looks like he's about to explode into a pile of Legos.

But then my focus shifts to the unsightly crack in the table. The hole in the upholstery of the one unoccupied chair. The grungy carpet beneath us and yellowed linoleum in the kitchen.

And the questions begin to roll: *Where the hell are we going?How are we getting there?Who's paying?What about work (mine and hers)?How many extra hours am I gonna have to pick up when we get back to make up what we'll miss?Why is she so inconsiderate?Doesn't she realize I can't just up and take off if I want to keep this job?That we NEED this income?What if things get super bad again?I bet she bought that bacon. . . . Why is she so hell-bent on spending money we don't freakin' have?*

And now I'm mad.

I part my lips to pour my anger all over the table, thick and sticky like spilled maple syrup—

"Rico?" Her shoulders slump. "Is everything okay?"

I just blink. Gape mouthed like a startled fish. Her eyes are . . . *open.* Guard down. Not sure I've seen her like this since the day she came into the shelter, knelt in front of me with tears in her eyes, and told me we were moving to our own apartment in a new town.

The fury drops off me in sheets.

Today's her thirty-eighth birthday.

And I forgot about it.

So I sit. I stuff my face (and feelings) with French toast.

"Get ready for the weekend of your young lives!" she says, her face glowing like she's bioluminescent.

I grab my glass of OJ and gulp, gulp, gulp. Then smile as I fight to keep it in my stomach.

———

Despite my panicked swirl of money-related emotions and my irritation with Mama over the *rashness* of this little jaunt we're on, I don't say a word once we hit the road.

Mama's oblivious. In the zone. Enjoying the open road as she bobs her head to the Michael Jackson satellite radio station she found while poking around the rental car's fancy dashboard.

I watch the trees blur by.

"Is Jaxy asleep?" she says, lowering the volume.

My sweet baby brother is stretched out across the leather backseat. "Yep," I say, peeking back at him. "Out cold."

"Good." She glances over at me. "I wanted to thank you."

"For what?"

Don't know that I've ever seen her this . . . *bashful* before. "For this trip," she says. "I've always wanted to take you and your brother to the beach, so I saved some of that money you gave me."

Oh. "You're welcome." I guess?

"I don't say it often, but I couldn't survive without you, Rico. And I don't mean that just in a financial sense. You set a great example for your brother, and having *you* around really keeps *me* going."

Where is this coming from?

"I know things can be strained between us, but I want you to know that I love you."

And now I'm about to cry? *Where is this coming from?* "I'm sorry I forgot your birthday" comes bubbling out of me. "I really didn't—"

"Stop." And now *she's* crying. "If anything, I should be

186

sorry." She wipes her eyes on her sleeve and sniffles. "Everything you said the night you gave me that money—"

"I thought you were gonna slap me."

Now she laughs.

"You're really somethin', kid."

I grab one of the napkins I shoved into the glove box when we got food and wipe my nose. "Can we stop now, please? This is a lot of emotion."

She smiles. "You're the greatest gift I've ever gotten, Rico."

GAH!

"I love you too, Mama."

My eyes do more leaking over the next couple of days than they have since the days of living in Granddaddy's van.

They leak when we get up to our two bedroom, ocean-view condo (that's bigger than our apartment and has better appliances), and Jax runs out to the balcony to shout "THIS IS AWESOOOOOOME!"

They leak when I'm standing by the shore as a wave crashes and I feel the ocean rush up over my feet for the first time.

They leak when I take my first bite of boiled king crab leg dipped in melted butter (so there *is* a God, then).

They leak when I stare up at the night sky and I see more stars than I knew existed.

They leak because I'm having a great time . . . but it's bittersweet. Every little luxury, while nice, is a reminder of what we don't have and can't really get. And despite my attempts to *enjoy myself,* as Mama keeps saying, my brain tallies every cent we spend here in Carillon Beach, Florida, and I can't help the waves of anxiety that crash over me.

As we set up on the sand the morning of our second impromptu vacation day and I gaze out over the water, I can't help but wonder what it's like to be Zan Macklin. To never have to worry if spending money on Friday will affect grocery shopping on Monday. Or if you'll make the rent. Or be able to pay the electricity bill so the power doesn't get cut off (again).

What's it like to hop up and go to the family doctor at the first sign of sickness? Eat whenever, whatever you're hungry for? Buy what your heart desires without the merest glance at the price tag?

How's it feel to take a vacation without being so jarred by the experience, you can't really have a good time? I hate that I feel a little resentful toward him because of how much I *know* he takes for granted.

It throws me back to our convo about Wally Winkle and how Zan had all this judgment to throw at the guy for *enjoying* his lotto winnings. I did manage to catch a bit of the first *JACKPOT!* episode on YouTube, and while, fine, he maybe did make some questionable choices (a twelve-bedroom mansion for him, his wife, and his dog does seem a bit excessive), one thing about Wally was abundantly clear: he's overwhelmingly grateful for his win.

"Rico, come help me build a sand castle for my robot!" Jax yells from way too close to the shore for the thing to last very long.

I look at the joy making the kid's wet-sand-colored skin

practically glow. Sigh and rise to my feet. Head up and shoulders back. Walk over to where he and Mama are already kneeling in the sand, and grab a bucket.

Try not to think about the thirty-five dollars Mama paid for the set of seven plastic pieces.

But then Jax wakes up at three in the morning with a fever.

103° this time.

There's ibuprofen and cold compresses and lots of blankets to keep the chills at bay. There's me singing "Smooth Criminal" to help him sleep, and Mama pacing back and forth with her hands over her stomach.

There's a vacation cut short. A sister in the backseat with her baby brother holding a sick bag.

There's Mama not stopping at an emergency clinic because she's scared it'll cost too much money.

A Word from Jaxon Daniel Danger's
Red Lego Robot

Jax doesn't feel very good. I'm all wet with sweat from where he's squeezing me in his hot palm, and it's making me nervous. He's a nicer kid than the last one who owned me—didn't let me out of his sight for the whole trip—and I know life is transient or whatever, but it'd be cool to keep him around.

I worry about that sister of his too. I bodyguard Jax from where he sets me on his nightstand before going to bed, and sis doesn't know it, but sometimes she cries in her sleep. She also sometimes wakes up sweaty and breathing super hard, thinking she's late for work. There was this one time she actually got out of bed, put her clothes on, and rushed out, only to come back like minutes later, drop down onto her bed, and shove her face in her pillow to cry.

She also doesn't know Jax was awake and saw the whole thing.

He was scared, and I kinda was too.

I think she has bad dreams, Rico does. For a while

she talked about some ticket she couldn't seem to find, and then she got into mumbling about someone named Zan.

Girls are weird.

At least this one loves her brother as much as I do.

-22-

The Doctor

Fever *breaks* breaks Sunday evening.

Stays broken Monday morning, but Jax's lymph nodes are so swollen, it hurts him to open his mouth.

Señora Alvarez is out of the country, and Mama has to go to work.

Guess who's staying home?

There's a part of me that wants to call Zan. As soon as we got home from Florida, I *did* look up that PO address and find that post office on a map, but—well, it's thirty miles away. And even if I could get to it, I wouldn't know what to do next.

Which means I need him again.

Also haven't talked to him in four days—a fact that *might* be clouding my judgment? Because . . . I miss him.

I don't know how people live like this.

I call Jess instead. Ask her to swing by and get my schedule so she can collect all my missed work for me.

Tuesday morning, the kid can open his mouth a little wider, but he's still struggling to swallow and can barely

192

move. Mama leaves for work, and I head to the kitchen to blend up a smoothie for him.

The phone rings.

I shut the blender off and grab the cordless. "Hello?"

"Chuck!" the person exclaims.

"Sorry. Wrong number."

"It's a Shakespearean term of endearment, Danger. Which you'd know if you weren't skipping out on school for the third day in a row."

It genuinely startles me when my knees give out, but once I'm on the floor, all the longing and fear and frustration and panic I've been trying to keep locked down for Mama and Jaxy's sake surges up to my eyeballs and pours out over my face. Like buckets and buckets of tears that shift from fury to joy to the deepest relief I've ever felt.

"Danger? You there?"

Pull it together, Rico! "Yeah. I'm here. What's up?"

"Well, hello to you too."

I smile. Put my head in my hand. "Hi, Zan."

"Mornin', sunshine."

"How are you?"

"A lot better than you from what I hear," he says.

Do I kill Jess or thank her? I guess I didn't tell her *not* to tell him anything. (Was that subconsciously deliberate?) "Probably."

"Can't talk long. Just wanted to tell you my sis-in-law's coming by to see my little buddy, so don't freak when a gorgeous Latina pops up at your front door in about an hour."

Can't even bring myself to ask any questions. "Okay."

"Also: I got a home address for our little old lady."

Whoa. "You did?" *How the hell*—

"I can neither confirm nor deny whether my methods were legal, but bottom line, mission accomplished. We'll talk more about it later."

Okay. So this is a nice surprise. "Sounds good, Macklin."

"Ani khoshev sheh ani ohev otach, Geveret Sakanah."

"What?"

"Ah, nothin' important. Just practicing a new language."

"And which language would tha—?"

"Bell's ringing. Talk later."

He hangs up.

At 8:28 a.m., there's a knock on the door.

Gorgeous Latina was an understatement.

"You must be Rico," the woman says with a smile befitting a whitening toothpaste commercial.

I shake the hand she extends, but I don't really have anything to say. Just looking at her makes me feel extremely insecure about my own . . . appearance. Massive, uncombed hair, ratty Malcolm X T-shirt, and holey sweatpants. Chipped toenail polish too.

"I'm Anna-Maria," she says. "Alejandro sent me—"

"Alejandro?"

"Sorry, sorry." She shakes her head. "Alexander. *Zan.*"

"Ah. Yes." *Alejandro?*

"He didn't say a whole lot when he called, but he mentioned your baby brother?"

That's when I notice the lettering on her black bag: ANNA-MARIA G. ROJAS-MACKLIN, MD.

Zan sent a *doctor*?

I don't even . . . Why is everything spinning?

"Are you all right?" Anna-Maria puts a hand on my shoulder. She smells imMACKulate. (I mean, why *not* give the Macklins their own adjective?)

"Yes, sorry," I say. "Come in." And I step aside so she can imbue our little domicile with magic just by entering.

When Jax—who's stretched out on the couch reading *Superfudge*—sees Anna-Maria, he literally drops the book.

Me too, kiddo.

"You must be Jaxon." Anna-Maria extends a hand as she approaches. "I'm Dr. Rojas-Macklin."

Jax just stares. I'm sure we look like starved orphans who have never known kindness.

"I can take your coat," I say, suddenly embarrassed. The place is a wreck, and it being the size of a shoe box makes the wreckedness that much more evident.

She smiles and hands it to me. PRADA, the tag says. Likely more valuable than Mama's actual truck.

I deposit it in the coat closet—my trench winds up on the floor since we don't have an extra hanger—and when I come back she's looking down at Jax. "Do you mind if I sit, young man?"

He shakes his head and pulls his knees up to his chest to make room.

"I've heard a lot of great things about you, Jaxon. *My* little brother—you know Zan, yes?"

He nods again.

"Well, Zan is one of *your* greatest admirers."

Jax grins all smugly and looks at me. I give him the

195

you-better-not-say-anything-inappropriate glare, and he turns back to Anna-Maria.

She continues, "I hear you're not feeling too well?" and he shakes his head no. "You mind if I check a few things? Maybe we can find the cause and get you on the road to feeling better?"

"Okay," Jax rasps.

God, he sounds awful.

Anna-Maria pulls a paper mask, a stethoscope, and a pair of gloves from her bag. "So there's something going on with that throat, but we'll listen to your heart first, all right? I'm going to slip this inside your shirt. It'll be a liiiiiittle cold."

His eyes go wide when the thing makes contact, but I can see he's trying to be tough.

"Okay, now breathe in deep for me."

He does.

She moves the thing. "Again . . ."

She does this a few more times. "Have you been coughing at all?"

There's another knock on the door, and my eyes snap up and lock on Jax. Who's looking at me like *Well, are ya gonna get it?*

This is all a bit overwhelming.

A feeling that quadruples when I open the door and find Zan-the-Man holding a box so full of gadgets, it looks like he robbed a Best Buy.

He waggles his caterpillars at me.

Though I'm rooted to the spot and can't speak, I totally go warm all over.

"Ya gonna invite me in, Danger? This box is heavier than it looks."

"Yes, of course, sorry." I step to the side.

He enters and closes the door. Leans to the left, so he can see past the "entryway" wall into the living room. "Jax, my man!"

Then Zan says, "¡Hola, vieja!" in an accent that sounds so natural, a chill shoots down the center of my chest.

"Te voy a golpear el trasero, pendejo," comes the reply from Anna-Maria.

Zan laughs.

She goes on: "¿Estás faltando las clases hoy, eh?"

"No le digas a mi papá."

"Las locuras que hacemos por amor . . ."

"Silencio, por favor."

Now she laughs.

Okay, so I took German for my foreign language requirement (I know nothing), but I certainly know the word *amor*. . . . Anyway, I'm no expert, of course, but Zan speaks Spanish like his brain's been soaking in it for years.

He sets the box on the floor and pulls me a foot to the right so we're hidden from Jax's and Anna-Maria's view. Squints up his eyes and puts the back of a hand against my forehead. Takes the other one and puts it up under my jaw.

"What are you doing?"

"Checking to see if you have a temperature."

"Everyone has a temperature, Macklin."

He rolls his eyes. "You know what I mean, Icey."

"Been a while since I've heard *that* one—"

And then my feet are leaving the ground. His arms are around my waist, and his face is buried in my neck. The eyebrows tickle a little. "Well then." No clue what to do with my arms.

"I missed you, Danger."

He murmurs this against the exposed skin just above my clavicle, and sweet mother of *everything*, is it hot in here. "I can see that."

He puts me down and I remember my attire. "Did you really just hug me?" I ask, sticking a finger through one of the holes in the hem of my shirt. "I look like hobo-Mufasa on steroids."

"No you don't, silly." He laughs and tries to tuck a part of my mane behind my ear. "Mufasa dies, you know? I was thinking more grown-up Simba."

"Oh my God, whatever!" Smack to the chest.

Are we flirting? We're totally flirting. In my busted apartment of all places.

He smiles, and boom: just like that, I'm teleported. There's no sick brother or overworked mother or missed days of work to worry about.

Only Zan-the-Man.

I really wish he would *stop*.

"Are you fluent in Spanish?" I say to break the (*very* loaded) silence.

"Yep."

"Impressive."

He shrugs. "Not really. Been speakin' it my whole life."

Hmm . . . I take a good look at the hella tan skin and

thick, dark hair. *Gustavo* comes to mind (as does the reminder that I know almost nothing about this idiot boy).

"Zan?"

"Danger?"

"Are you biracial?"

He grins. "You could say that, I guess."

I'm about to dig deeper, but then Anna-Maria comes
around the corner. She looks at the space between us—
well, the lack thereof—and there's that smile of hers again.
"Es muy hermosa, hermanito." She's talking to him but looking at me.

"Te lo dije. No te acuerdas porque ya eres vieja."

"Cállate la boca, imbécil."

Zan laughs and leans closer to me. "She just called me a
moron," he whispers loud enough for her to hear. "Can you
believe that?"

"Vete, llorón."

Zan winks, scoops up his box, and disappears around the
corner.

Once he's gone, Anna-Maria turns to me, all traces of
humor erased. "Rico, how long has Jaxon been sick?"

Crap.

"He's had a fever and sore throat off and on for a little
over two weeks," I say.

She nods. Which is . . . interesting? I was expecting
Two weeks, and he hasn't seen a doctor?! I'm calling DFACS!
"I swabbed his throat, and he did test positive for strep,
so I'll get some amoxicillin to you before the day is over,"
she says. "Just know that if it comes back, he may need his
tonsils removed."

Well, that would be a nightmare. Surgery involves hospitals. Hospitals involve lots of money. I vividly recall Mama once saying she'd "rather die than go to a hospital" during one of her colitis bouts.

I'm trying not to panic.

She looks over into the living room and smiles. "Joaquín and I started dating when Alejandr—*Zan*, excuse me, was five years old. For as long as I've known him, Zan's wanted a little brother."

I peek around the corner. Zan has set up an iPad on a pillow across Jax's lap and is helping him pick a movie to watch.

"Joaquín?" I ask.

"Zan's eldest brother. He was seventeen when Zan was born. There was another brother who passed away at fourteen in a dirt bike accident the year before Zan's birth, and then their sister, Tehlor, is twelve years Zan's senior. He was practically an only child."

"Oh." It's embarrassing that I knew *none* of this, yet Anna-Maria caught us practically canoodling not ten minutes ago.

"Looks like *your* brother is making his sibling dreams come true." She winks.

I retrieve her coat, and Zan and Jax wave to her as she goes out.

And it looks like she's right. Because when Anna-Maria drops by with the medicine four hours later, Zan is still here.

-23-

Circle Yes or No

He picks me up for school the next morning, and then drops me off at work after classes are over.

Same thing the next day.

And the next.

Saturday and Sunday, I work doubles, but he takes me to work, brings me lunch, *and* shows up to drive me home on both days.

And I go with it. I don't overthink (read: think at all) or question his motives (for the most part).

But then Monday, we're sitting side by side in history and I happen to glance in his direction. He's grinning at me.

Which makes everything I've been trying *not* to think about topple down on me with cold precision like massive hailstones:

> Zan's the reason Jax got the antibiotics we never would've known he needed.
> Zan's the reason I had actual *lunch* over the weekend.
> Zan's the reason I haven't set foot on a school or city bus in weeks.

201

Zan's (probably) the reason Mr. Z gave me a raise. Zan's the reason my brother's actually been happy at school because he can finally join conversations about the latest gadgets and video games and no longer feels like a "poor-kid pariah" (no clue where he learned *that* word).

The ($$$) amount I must *owe* Zan hits me with so much force, I can't breathe.

What the hell am I doing?!

As soon as the bell after last period rings, I dart out of the classroom so I can beat the crowds to the parking lot. There's no way in heaven OR hell I'm gonna be seen on Macklin's arm right now. If it weren't for the fact that we're going to the address attached to Ethel's PO box today, I'd go catch the school bus home to hide.

Hopefully he's smart enough to just come on out to the car.

Actually, looks like it's not gonna matter whether he's smart enough or not: I've been at the Jeep for all of forty-five seconds when I hear someone approaching from behind me. "Ya girl's already out here at the Tonka, dawg," a voice says.

When I turn around, Finesse is slipping his phone into his pocket. "Rico Suavico!"

I smile. "Hi, Finesse."

He opens his arms for a hug, and I step into them. (What is it with these guys and the hugging?) "What's good, baby girl?" he says.

How does one answer that question? Do I spout off a list of lies? "Uhh . . . most things?"

He laughs. "My folks've been askin' about you. You should come by the crib again sometime."

"You mean they don't think I'm some two-bit floozy for spending the night on your basement couch with Alexander Gustavo Macklin?" Whoops! Didn't mean for that to come out.

"You silly," he chuckles. "They don't even know about that. Jess never stops talkin' about you, so they're all intrigued and shit."

What the heck could she be saying?

As if he can see into my brain, Ness says, "You've really made an impression on her, you know? With the whole go-against-the-grain thing you got goin' on. Homegirl took me 'thrifting' last week cuz she said 'we need to stop being so conformist in our personal styles,' or something. Actually got this dope-ass jacket for like fifteen bucks." He tugs on the lapels of the brown leather bomber he's wearing.

I'm trying not to laugh. *Go-against-the-grain* thing? Yeah, okay.

"So my boy treating you good?" he says.

Oh God, can we not? "Uhh . . ." My eyes drop to the white line separating the parking spaces.

"You know he's hella into you, right? I don't think I've ever seen this dude so wrapped."

"Ah." *Stop it, Finesse! Really* don't need this right now.

"Don't tell him I told you this, but things were gettin' a little rough for my dude. Bunch of factory workers tried to sue his family and it turned out one of his dad's most trusted guys was at the center of the whole thing."

"Whoa."

"Right? Every time I look up, it's somebody new tryna scheme money off Z's family. He was legit losin' faith in humanity, but you've totally brought him back to life."

My. Face. Is. On. Fire.

Finesse's eyes shift over my shoulder and he smiles. I'm about to turn and see why when a pair of arms slips around my waist.

They're . . . not Zan's. Too skinny. And the chest—which is now pressed against my back—is too low and cushiony.

"We were just talking about you," Finesse says, and the arms release me. Space invader steps around me and into Ness's waiting embrace.

Jess. (Duh, Rico.)

"And what were you saying?" She pinches his nose.

"That you're the most gorgeous girl in the universe."

Oh barf.

And now they're kissing. I'm apparently no longer standing here. They're full-on . . . *wow* this is a lot—

"Geez, freakazoids, get a *room*." (Definitely know *that* voice.)

Now an arm I *do* recognize slides across the front of my shoulders, and I get pulled back against a delightful-smelling guy-chest.

I instinctively crane my neck to look up.

"Hi," Zan says.

Head spinning.

Finesse and Jessica break apart and as they look at us, this identical smirk quirks up the left side of both their mouths. (Gross.)

Meanwhile, Macklin releases me and goes to open the passenger door. "You ready to roll? Drive's about twenty-five minutes."

"Mm-hmm." I turn back to Ness and Jess. "Guess we'll catch you guys later."

Jess winks. "Don't do anything I wouldn't do."

This is all so very confusing.

I act like I don't see Zan's outstretched hand and climb in by myself.

Not sure if it's anticipation of what we'll find at the address or pure weirdness between us, but neither of us says much on the long drive over.

We've been on the highway for a solid twenty minutes when I peek over at him. His eyes are glued to the road.

And now I'm having a flashback of how that jawline felt against my collarbone when he scooped me up in that insane hug last Tuesday.

What do I *do* with all this? He can't possibly *really* like me, can he? All signs point to *yes, he can, dumbass*, but . . . we're too different.

Aren't we?

And if he *did* like me, he would say so, right?

"You're awfully quiet over there, Danger."

I clear my throat. "Look who's talking—well . . . not talking either."

205

He chuckles. "For real, though: Are you okay? You seem . . . different."

So he did notice (was I thinking he wouldn't?).

Question is, what do I tell him? "Different . . . how?"

He clears his throat. "You didn't wait for me after school."

Why does he sound wounded? And why is it infuriating me and making me want to hug him back to happiness simultaneously?

What is happening?!

"What's the number on that mailbox?" he says like he didn't just turn the air in the Jeep to emotional soup. We've pulled to a stop and he points to the house on the corner of the adjacent street. It's one story and buttercup yellow with white shutters, and there's a FOR LEASE sign with the name of a realty company sticking out of the immaculate front lawn.

"Looks like . . ." I squint. "Twenty-seven twenty-one."

"Hmm."

"Hmm?"

"That's the house linked to the PO box," he says.

"Oh."

During our brief moment of unintentional silence, the soupy air solidifies into something much heavier. I know he and I are thinking the same thing in this moment—if this is really Ethel Streeter's house, and it's for lease . . .

I mean, she *was* pretty old.

But what if she just like . . . retired to Florida or moved into one of those swingin' senior communities or something? It says *for lease*, not *for sale*, which means someone wants to maintain ownership of this place even if someone else is living in it.

Right?

"I'm gonna pull up a little closer so we can get the number off the sign," Zan says.

And now I sigh.

Which melts the smile right off Zan's face. "You okay?"

What do I tell him? That every curveball in this "quest" makes me wanna quit for the sake of avoiding more disappointment? That my family is going to be one hundred and eight dollars in the red on March 1 unless I manage to pick up twelve extra hours over the next three days? That I should've grabbed an extra shift *today* instead of coming here?

Do I tell him I feel like I currently owe him way more than I could repay in any near future?

Do I tell him I'm not even comfortable sitting next to him right now?

And yet I don't want to move.

All I know for sure: I can't go back.

"Get a little closer," I say. "I can't quite see it from here."

A ginormous smile erupts up into Zan's cheeks. "Rico?"

"Yeah?"

"I need to tell you something."

"Okay . . ."

He takes my hand and fixes me in that green-eyed stare. "I *really* like you," he says.

A Word from Ethel Streeter's House
(Because It Really Is Ethel Streeter's House)

I really am Ethel Streeter's house, by the way. She moved outta me and in with her son Bartholomew just a few weeks ago.

It's been lonely as all get-out without her here. And they recently "redeveloped" the area—you should see the monstrosity they tossed up next door mere months ago—so the black folk who have populated this neighborhood for as long as I can remember can't (or maybe *won't*) pay the exorbitant rent price Ethel's financial advisor suggested so she'd be "competing with the surrounding renovated homes also listed for lease."

Guessing I'll be occupied by some strange white people like the ones I see jogging with their mini-dogs in strollers soon.

Oh, and just so you're aware—Rico's currently thinking about this as we speak—that thing she's looking for? It's not anywhere inside me.

-24-

Brazen Bitch(es)

I really like you too, Zan.

I still cannot believe I said that. Out loud.

Now it's Friday and I'm standing in front of my bath-room mirror feeling like a friggin' idiot because I just poked myself in the eye with a mascara wand. And there are dark tears running down my cheeks.

Looks like I'm weeping dirt. *Rico Reneé Danger, Goddess of Filth—*

"Rico?" Mama opens the door.

Too late for me to splash water on my face to get rid of the mess, but you know what? That's fine. She should see the results of her failure to teach me these things, dammit.

"Hon—whoa," she says. There's a mocking glint in her eye. "Struggling a bit?"

"Not helping."

She looks me over. My hair is curled, and I'm wearing a low-back houndstooth pencil dress I stole from her closet with *tastefully* ripped black tights. Haven't decided on shoes yet, but no matter.

"So I just got called into work for a few hours," she says.

"Okay . . ."

She sighs. "Señora Alvarez can't babysit."

According to the watch staring up at me from beside the sink, Zan is gonna be here to pick me up in precisely twenty-one minutes.

This is *not* happening.

"You're telling me this *now*?"

That was the wrong thing to say. "Unless your little *date* is planning to pay our rent, I suggest you readjust your priorities," she snips.

"It's not a *date*. We're just going to a movi—"

"Great! You can take your brother with you then."

Is she for real?! "But, Mama—"

"Either that or call it off." She looks at her watch. "I have to go."

And then she's gone.

I shut the door and turn back to the mirror. Things have been decent between us of late—except on the topic of money and/or the means of acquiring it. The tears are flowing with verve now, which just makes me feel stupid and babyish. "Told you this was a dumb idea," I say to my reflection. "And look at you now. Idiot."

I *did* get a sinking feeling in my gut when, after acknowledging our mutual *really-like* for each other on Monday, Zan asked if I wanted to "hang out in a non-quest-or-transportation-related capacity." I said yes before I could stop myself, but here we are, now nineteen minutes before the commencement of our Plan, and everything's falling apart.

Story of my life.

I turn on the water and am prepping to wash my face—hope Zan's not *too* upset about the cancellation; I can give him a real reason this time at least—when the door opens again, and Mama reenters and shuts it behind her.

I grab a piece of distinctly *not*-Macklin toilet paper and wipe my face so she won't see that I'm crying.

After setting her purse on the counter and draping something black over the shower curtain rod, she spins me around, grabs me by the shoulders, and pushes me down onto the toilet lid.

Okay . . .

Her brows tug down and she takes my chin. Turns it left and right to examine my face, then bores holes in my pupils. "Close your eyes," she says.

And I do. Got no fight left in me.

I keep them shut over the next however many minutes as my face is wiped, poked, tweezed (ow!), dabbed with this, and dusted with that. I'm told to *lift my chin, look up, look down, suck my cheeks in, bat my lashes, pucker,* and *smile.* Then my hair is yanked and pulled and pinned.

Then: "Open."

A smile cracks her struggle-crusted face, and she nods once, returns all the brushes, tubes, and containers to her purse, grabs the thing from the curtain rod, unfolds it, and stretches it out to me.

It's a jacket. Deliciously worn black leather with various zippers, pockets, patches, and buttons.

"Is this your *motorcycle* jacket?"

Her gaze drops.

Back when Mama first started college, she owned a

211

Harley-Davidson her dad had given her, and was in an all-female biker crew called the Brazen Bitches. When I was small, she used to strut around in the jacket and (playfully?) lament the fact that she'd had to stop riding when I was born.

When my grandpa died, she got rid of the bike *and* the paraphernalia.

Or so I thought.

I take it, awe surely evident in my open mouth and raised brows, and she looks me over from head to toe and says, "Doc Martens." Then she grabs her purse and turns to leave again.

Few seconds later, I hear "Bye, Jaxy-Baby!" and then the front door shuts.

I look down at the jacket in my hands.

Almost start crying again, but then remember there's makeup all over my face now. Makeup I haven't seen yet.

I turn around to face the mirror.

And almost fall down.

I've always been blown away by people who can put on a crap-ton of makeup for the sake of making it look like they're not wearing any. That's exactly what Mama did to me. I know the stuff is *there* because I can feel it, but the effects are very subtle: my cheekbones are a little more defined, the fullness of my lips is well balanced with the rest of my face, my brows are super neat, and my eyes look a little bigger and brighter. She even managed to play *up* my different-colored eyeballs. Even *I* think they look pretty cool right now. Combined with the hair she wrangled into this crown-looking thing? I *feel* beautiful.

For maybe the first time ever?

And now I'm . . . befuddled. Especially when it hits me again that I'm holding Mama's jacket. Like how did she go from popping on me about "priorities" to doing my makeup and completing my outfit?

I slip the jacket on—

And then I hear, "She's in here," and Jax rounds the corner with Zan in tow.

"WAIT!" I slam the bathroom door.

"Well, that was *rude*," Jax yells.

UGHHHH! "I'll be out in just a minute! Can you, umm . . . wait in the living room?"

"Rico, you've been in there for *two hours*."

I'm gonna kill him.

"You can't put a time limit on beauty, my man," from Zan. "Come on. I'll whup you in a couple rounds of 2K on the Xbox while we wait."

Right. Because all those electronics Zan brought over here when Jax was sick last week? The kid got to *keep* them.

I shake my head and try to refocus.

I peek out into the bedroom. They're gone.

"C'mon, Rico, you can do this. Obviously can't cancel now, so woman the frick up!"

(This is gonna be a disaster, I just know it.)

Into the closet. Boots.

One last look in the mirror . . .

Okay, can't lie, I look like a total badass.

When I step out of the bedroom, the boys' heads turn in tandem. Zan's caterpillar brows (he does, in fact, get them threaded, according to Jess) sideways-crawl up to his hairline, but Jax is the one who speaks: "Well, hot damn, sister."

"Jax!"

He throws his hands up. "It's the only appropriate response!"

Zan still hasn't said a word.

He and I lock eyes, and it hits me *just* how much I want him to like how I look. Not sure I like the feeling.

Come to think of it, maybe that's what's been bothering me about this whole thing. This sense that I'm not only allowing myself to get distracted from what matters most (*a-hunnit-and-six MIL*) but also like . . . losing control of myself AND setting myself up for the kind of disappointment that can utterly decimate a person. That I'm deliberately handing another human being the power to destroy me if they're (*he's*) so inclined.

That I'm changing—caring more, putting forth more effort . . .

Wanting.

In truth, I've never really *liked* anyone before. For one, I've never believed anyone in this rich-ass town could be remotely interested in me; and for two, the only example I've ever had of a "person in love" is Mama. We see where all that emotion 'n' devotion got *her* (get it? Emotion 'N' Devotion = END).

So I've kept myself locked down.

But now?

Please say something, Macklin. . . .

He does: "You, umm . . ." He clears his throat and looks away. "You ready to go?"

214

And there it is.

My chin drops . . . maybe if I look closely enough at the floor, I'll be able to see that heart of mine dissolving into our matted excuse for carpet.

"Oh. Guess I am." *Could I sound any more pathetic?* "Jax has to come with us, by the way. Hope that's okay."

And if it isn't, door's right there, bucko. Feel free to let yourself out.

Jax huffs and rolls his eyes. "I *told* him already." He turns off the game and television, then comes over and stands in front of me. "Can we go now, please, Rico?"

That's when it hits me: I'll have to pay for his movie ticket. I set aside a little money from this week's paycheck so I could pay for *myself*, but it's not enough for Jax too.

See? Disaster.

Zan comes over and holds his keys out to Jax. "How 'bout you go on out to the Jeep and get it warmed up for us, little dude? You can even sit in the driver's seat."

"Cooooool!" Jax takes the keys and rushes out the door.

Which leaves me alone with Zan-the-(clearly unimpressed)-Man.

I reach to tuck my hair behind my ear, remember Mama doing it, and instantly feel like the world's biggest jackass. Stupid boots and tights and dress and jacket and makeup and hair.

"You might wanna go on out . . . not sure letting Jax start your truck is a good idea."

"Ah, he won't be able to start it at all." And then he's stepping closer. "Won't crank unless the clutch pedal is down."

Oh.

"Just didn't want the kid to hear me say how incredible you look."

Well then. I clear my throat. "Thanks."

While I stand there blushing and surely emitting the fragrance of girl-scared-witless like some freshly unfolded tulip, Zan looks me over from head to toe. *Reeeeeeeally* slowly.

Am I even wearing clothes right now, because it certainly does not feel like it, good*ness*.

His eyes finally reconnect with mine and he smiles as he raises my hand to his lips.

I have nothing at all to say.

No clue what movie we saw because the only thing I was conscious of during the entire one hundred and seventeen minutes was Zan Macklin's bare forearm against mine on our shared armrest.

Afterward wasn't much better: Zan insisted on buying Jax and me loaded sundaes from the adjacent gourmet ice cream shop—this was after he insisted on paying for our movie tickets *and* the extra-large popcorn and box of Tropical DOTS Jax wanted—and the whole time we were there, all I could focus on was his interaction with Jax. Whether or not *I* wind up "falling in love" (whatever that means) with the guy, it's obvious the baby brother I love more than my own life already *has*.

And it's clearly mutual. Zan looks at Jaxy like he designed the solar system.

None of this is helping.

Now we're pulling into the space next to Mama's truck

in front of the apartment, and I *really* don't want him to leave. I try to sneak a peek at him, but he's already staring at me.

We both smile.

How did I *get* here? From running to hide when he came into the store to goo-goo eyes in the front seat of the Tonka? That's not to mention the road trips and random people and visits to strange houses we—

OH!

"Oh my gosh, I almo—"

"I need to ask you something," he says at the exact same time.

We *both* blush and look away.

Absurd.

"You first," he says.

I look over my shoulder at Jax, who is passed out in the backseat.

"Mmmm . . . I should probably get him into the house. You mind waiting a few minutes? I'll come right back out."

Zan snorts. Kills the ignition. "You really think I'm gonna let your gorgeous self carry that sack of potatoes?"

Before I can object, he's out of the car, opening the back door, and carefully extracting my brother from his Jeeply den of slumber.

Unfortunately, when we reach the apartment, and I get the deadbolt unlocked, I try to turn the knob and discover that it's locked too. And there's no keyhole for the knob-lock on the outside.

So I'll have to knock.

Which, unless I can convince him to give me Jax and

head back to the Jeep (unlikely, though I certainly intend to try), means Stacia Danger is about to meet Alexander Macklin.

"I can handle it from here if you want to head back to the car. My mom's gonna have to come open the door since it's locked from the inside."

"Awesome!" He shifts Jax to his shoulder and knocks.

Minor freak-out

Mama opens the door, leans into the jamb, and crosses her arms. "So you're him, huh?"

Oh God.

"You didn't tell me he was a white boy, Rico."

OH. GOD. "Mama!"

"Alexander Macklin, ma'am." He extends a hand. "Pleasure to make your acquaintance."

Her eyebrows furrow and she turns to me. "Did he just say *Macklin*? As in Macklin Ente—"

"Yep. Can we bring Jax in?"

"Certainly explains the new *toys*—"

"I need to talk to Alexander alone for a minute."

Mama eyeballs the bejesus out of Zan, and his face creeps crimson. He'd left before she got home on the day he came to hang out with Jax post–doctor house call, and while Mama knew that the prescription came from "my friend Zan's sister-in-law," I never mentioned his last name.

This is exactly why.

"Here, give the kid to me," she says.

He does.

"You have until midnight, Rico." Looks back at Zan. "Mr. Macklin, it was nice to meet you." *Why does everybody*

218

Mister *him?* "Thank you for . . ." She looks him up and down and forces a smile. "Everything."

The door shuts.

"Okay then . . . ," Zan says.

"Don't mind her. Back to the car?"

"Sure."

We go. He helps me in as usual, and once his door is closed, he turns to me. "I had a really nice time tonight, Danger."

I smile. Sigh. "Me too, Zanny Zan."

"What'd you want to tell me?"

"Oh." See? Almost forgot again. It's that damn cologne, I swear. "I called the leasing agency for the house."

"The house?"

So he forgot too. That's kind of a relief. (More smiling.) "Ethel Streeter's house? Well, what *might* be her house."

"Oh, duh. Sorry. Been a little distracted." Throat clears. "What'd they say?"

"Well, the agent in charge is on vacation for the next two weeks, and they don't want to let anyone else show it, so I set us an appointment for Sunday the twenty-fourth. Is that okay?"

Now he's trying *not* to smile. And failing.

"Hopefully we can find out if Ethel *does* own the house, and maybe even where she currently lives."

"Looking forward to it, Danger."

We lapse into a few seconds of silence and I swallow. "You wanted to ask me something?"

"Right." He runs a hand through his hair. "So I have an older sister?"

Tehlor, Anna-Maria said. "Is that a question, Macklin?"

"Shut up. Point is she's getting married next weekend. Huge hullabaloo, super formal, yadda yadda. She's the only girl in the family, so my mom and grandma went all out, even more than her quince. Don't even wanna consider what they probably spent . . ."

In almost two months, I have never heard Zan Macklin ramble like this.

Also . . . her quince?

"Would you be willing to go with me?" he says.

Well, that certainly snaps me back to reality. "Say what now?"

"You can say no, obviously. It's just that Ness and Jess will both be there, so I thought it'd be cool if you came too." A pause and then: "Like . . . as my date."

I grin. "I guess Jax ruined *this* date, huh?" *Crap.* "I mean . . . not that you ever *said* this was a date . . . Sorry. Ignore me."

More cheesy, red-cheeked grinning from him.

This is a lot. "Sister's wedding" means *sister.* Parents. Family. That's not to mention stuff like attire, shoes, makeup.

He said it was "super formal." . . . Doesn't that mean fancy ball gown (that I can't afford)? I glance down at my boots. Obviously can't wear *these* guys—

"What do you think?" He's staring at me now. "Ness and Jess are both coming, and she would love to have you there. She told me."

Astonishingly difficult to hold eye contact when he looks so *hopeful* and said hope is directly linked to me. Because what is he really hoping for? And can I actually deliver?

He's used to the very best of everything. . . . I've never even had an unworn pair of shoes.

What would make him want to take *me*?

Why does he even like me?

What could he possibly see?

I have no goals. No plans. No real dreams. Literally nothing going for m—

There's a knock on the window, and I squawk like a tickled chicken.

The person on the other side is laughing her golden head off.

Zan shakes his head—smiling—and pushes the button to lower the glass so Jess can lean in.

"I'm a smidge disappointed these windows aren't foggy. Are you two actually *talking*?" She shakes her head. "For shame."

"Oh my God, Jess."

"Byyyyye!" And she waves and walks away.

"So?" Zan says as the window rises.

I gulp and stare at the back of Jessica's shrinking head.

I'm *allowed* to want this.

And hell, we can't do anything about the ticket for the next two weeks anyway. Might as well kill some time.

"I'd be honored to, Zan." *Honored, Rico? Really?*

"You would?"

"I mean, *honored* is kind of a strong word but—" Blah. "Whatever. Yes. I'd love to go with you to your sister's wedding."

Fireworks explode in his green eyes.

-25-

P.W.T.

Turns out my dress worries are moot.

Señora Alvarez's daughter owns a formal gown boutique called Belle's Basics. (Like from *Beauty and the Beast*? Mama rolled her eyes—which was better than the way she narrowed them suspiciously when I asked if I could go to the wedding—but I secretly love it.)

Long story short, Jax overhears me telling Mama about my invite; Mama, who after a *clear* moment of hesitation, says I can go provided I find "appropriate attire without touching bill money." Without telling us, Jax goes to Señora Alvarez about how *my-sister-got-invited-to-this-fancy-wedding-by-the-boy-she-loooooooves-and-I-really-want-her-to-go-but-she-doesn't-have-the-*"uh-pro-tee-ate uh-tired." That's what she tells us he said when she shows up to offer her daughter's assistance.

I pull a double on Tuesday so Jess and I can go to the dress store after school on Wednesday. After three solid hours of sheer chaos, both of us walk out with gorgeous gowns, shoes, *and* jewelry, completely on the house.

(Wild.)

When Saturday rolls around, Jess and I hop into her car at 7:03 a.m. and drive over to Finesse's house to get ready.

Thus commences the most amazing twelve-hour period of my life thus far.

The first six hours are one hundred and fifty percent thanks to Jessica Kirby Barlow. "Oh my God, I have to tell you . . . ," she says while we're sitting on the floor, waiting for our toenails to dry.

"What?"

"So my dad, right?" she says. "He's some married tech executive out in Silicon Valley with kids not much younger than my mom. I've known *that* since I was five, but yesterday I found out he sends Mom undocumented hush money every month so she'll keep quiet about my existence."

How does one respond to that?

"To think she's constantly riding my ass about 'contributing more,' when this whole time she's been getting paid by that douchebag," she goes on. "I swear, I can't *wait* to get out of here, Ree."

So now I have a nickname. It makes me smile.

Also makes me okay with saying: "My dad's married with kids too."

"Yeah?" She sets her chin in her hand. "Tell me more."

"I've never met him and probably never will. He lives in Spain."

"*Spain?*"

I nod. "My mom had a fling while studying abroad."

"Well damn."

"Right."

"So I take it you and your brother have different dads?"

223

"Yep. *His* dad, though single, was rich and shitty like yours." Oops. "I mean, not that your dad is *shitty*—sorry, that was presumptuous."

"Oh, he is absolutely shitty. Go on."

It's strange. I'm feeling things I've refused to acknowledge for a long time, but with Jess, it's almost like I can't help but open the cage. I tell her all about Jax's dad and getting kicked out and being homeless for a while.

"Holy shit" is her response.

I swallow. "My mom worked really hard and we eventually moved here, but it was kind of a dark time. I literally never talk about it."

"I had a sister who died as a baby," she says. "That's the reason we left Cali. Not even Ness knows."

Brief pause, then we both sigh. "Thank you," she says.

"For what?"

"I've been carrying that around for a long time. Felt good to like . . . release it into the ether."

I smile. "Same."

And it's true. I feel lighter now that someone knows we were homeless but isn't judging or repulsed or, worst of all, giving me pity-puppy eyes.

We smile at each other for a few seconds, having what I think is my first real *friendship* moment since . . . *ever*?

I take a deep breath. "Can I tell you something else?"

"Of course."

"I'm a little bit . . . in awe, I guess, of your and Ness's plans for the future."

"What do you mean?"

"Just that you're both going to college and have career goals and all that."

She frowns. "You don't?"

"Not really. My mom needs my help financially, so I don't really have much of a choice but to keep working."

"Hmm."

Is she judging me? I hope she's not judging me. "What does 'hmm' mean?"

Now she smiles. "Nothing bad. Just wondering what you'd do if you *did* have a choice."

I shrug and look away. Feeling very exposed right now. "I've honestly never thought about it."

"Well, maybe you should."

"Should what?"

Jess rolls her eyes. "*Think* about it, Rico. You say you have no choices, but that's not true. *Everyone* has choices. Are some of them hard? Yes. But if you want something bad enough . . ." Now *she* shrugs.

And I don't respond. Because what if she's right?

"You'll figure it out," she says, squeezing my shoulder. "For now, we have the wedding of the decade to get ready for."

"Right." Because I'm not letting this day be ruined. "Let's do it."

Over the next several hours, I pretend my other life doesn't exist. Jess puts that old 'NSYNC album on, and we dance. We sing. We sip cans of Aranciata Rossa Sanpellegrino, and we put hot curlers in each other's hair.

We eat pizza and then she teaches me how to put on

foundation and powder (found a bag with the right colors beside my bed this morning with an unsigned *Have fun!* note in Mama's handwriting), then how to make my eyelids sparkly and put mascara on without injuring my corneas.

Not once do I feel ashamed or embarrassed or afraid.

Apparently Ness *and* Zan are somehow involved in the wedding, so it's actually a really good thing I agreed to come—if I hadn't, Jess would've had to "brave the anxiety-inducing waters of expendable wealth" alone.

I know because she won't stop thanking me.

"I *seriously* appreciate you being here," she says for the umpteenth time today as we sit down on opposite sides of the expensive-looking desk in this bedroom full of *her* stuff. "You're like the friend I didn't know I needed."

It's the strangest thing. Never in a kabillionbajillionillion years would I have imagined prepping for Zan Macklin's sister's wedding inside Finesse Montgomery's house with Jessica Barlow . . . who is currently polishing my fingernails royal blue to contrast with the coral color of my "keyhole-back" (read: *backless*) mermaid gown.

In truth, I don't even know how to feel about it.

"So how did you and Finesse wind up together?" I ask, looking around.

"Ah, it was inevitable," she says. "When I moved here in sixth grade, I got assigned to the desk right in front of his. He used to sit and play with my hair."

Okay, that's adorable. "Seriously?"

"Mm-hmm. First day of school, I sat down in front of him, and within thirty seconds, he'd picked up my braid and said, 'Wow, it's like golden silk!'"

I laugh.

"Needless to say, once I turned around and saw how cute he was, I started wearing it loose. We totally lost our virginity to each other in tenth grade, but it took until the beginning of eleventh for us to get *together*, together," she says. "People can still be a little weird about the interracial thing."

You didn't tell me he was a white boy, Rico. "Yep." Though is Zan actually *white*? I still don't know. . . .

She starts the second coat of blue on my right hand. "I'd ask how things are going with Zan," she says, "but I have a feeling you're not sure yet?"

I don't respond. Because she's right. And I know that despite just sharing my deepest, darkest secret, confessing the more-than-partners-in-quest stuff I've been feeling toward Zan will make it that much more real. Not sure I want to deal with that yet.

Then again, I guess I did admit it to *him*. . . .

Why do I get such a strong feeling of impending doom when I start thinking about this?

Jess hasn't said anything else—guess she's waiting on me to respond. Man, I hope this doesn't come back to bite me in the ass. . . . "I mean, I definitely *like* him—"

"But money," she says without looking up from my hand.

"Huh?"

"It's the money thing, right?" She puts some quick-dry drops on each nail and then blows on my fingertips; it gives me a shiver. "Like you don't really feel worthy?"

I'm instantly hot. "That's one way to put it."

"I get it, dude. I really do. Will you do my right hand?"

She pulls a bottle of black polish from the desk drawer. "Remember how you asked me if I ever felt out of place around the people I hang out with?"

"Mm-hmm."

"That was one of the reasons it took so long for me and Ness to get together," she says. "I couldn't fathom somebody with *so much money* wanting anything to do with my P.W.T. ass."

"P.W.T.?"

"Poor white-trash."

"Ah."

Of course this makes perfect sense—hello, I'm living it (minus the white-trash part)—but it's jarring to hear it put so bluntly. "How'd you get past it?"

"I didn't," she says. "Probably never will. Even if we wind up married and I make more money than he does—and I plan to, thank you very much—it won't change the fact that when we visit his parents, we'll be coming *here*." She gestures around the room. "But visiting my mom will probably always involve some tiny apartment that reeks of booze and cigarette smoke."

"Jess, if this is supposed to be a pep talk, you're failing miserably."

She laughs. "It's true, though," she says. "I *still* feel weird when he buys me stuff or pays for me when we go out on dates. I just choose not to let it rule me, you know? I know like . . . *society* or whatever suggests otherwise, but my value as a human being has nothing to do with money."

This makes me giggle. "You sound like my mom's self-help books." *That don't seem to do much for her.*

"Three and a half years of therapy for this shit. Bottom line, Ness couldn't care less about the difference in our parents' bank accounts, so if it comes between us, it's on me."

I sigh.

She has a point, but still. Zan's on like a whole different level.

"It'd be pretty sad to miss out on a good thing because of a bunch of bullshit, wouldn't it?"

She lifts her hand and blows on her nails.

-26-

Eye of the Storm

To call Tehlor Macklin's wedding to Chadwick Montgomery *lavish* would be understated to the point of absurdity. I don't think I've ever seen so many fresh flowers or things that sparkle under one roof.

Finesse is a groomsman. *King,* as I hear multiple people refer to the groom, is his older cousin. But he (Ness) spends most of the ceremony sneaking glances at Jess, who looks beyond incredible in her low-cut maroon gown and elbow-length black gloves. Even *I'm* struggling not to stare at her.

Then there's Alexander Gustavo Macklin, looking every bit the million-dollar magnate his name implies, in his ultra-debonair charcoal tux. It's got the same bedazzling effect on his green eyes as Jess's smoky-eye/vamp-lip makeup has on her blue ones, and when he smiles at me from across the aisle where he's sitting with his family (*so* much money, good gracious), I thank whatever God is worshipped in this church for the fact that I'm already sitting.

I keep my focus forward during the entire exchange of nuptials, largely because I can *feel* him looking at me. I swear if we make eye contact, electricity is gonna shoot through the air between us. We'll both die instantly, and this whole place will burn to the ground.

After the *I do*s and the most intense kiss I think I've ever witnessed, Zan gets whisked out for pictures. We all hop in cars. I wind up in the backseat of the Montgomery Tesla SUV, squeezed between Jess and Finesse's little sister, who I swear at one point whispers, "I wish my brother would date someone like *you*, not Malibu Barbie."

I don't get to see Zan up close until we get to the reception site. And despite my being anxious and looking around for him with the focus of a bloodhound on a scent trail, he manages to sneak up on me. There's the familiar fragrance of his cologne, then the sudden warmth of a large hand on the small of my (exposed) back. Which triggers an explosion of . . . I honestly don't even know what to call it.

A couple years ago, Hurricane Irma ripped through Puerto Rico, and I became obsessed with destructive storms. The idea of something beyond human control having the power to wreak such havoc was utterly terrifying, so I latched on to the idea of an *eye*, that point of relative calm at the center.

That's what Zan's hand feels like. The eye of the storm. Every inch of skin outside of what he's touching is *raging* with sensations I've never experienced before.

When I turn around, he takes a step back, looking me over in that way that makes me feel like he's peeling my dress off with his eyes. Which isn't entirely unpleasant.

But still. "My face is up here, Macklin."

He coughs into his fist. "My bad."

There's an awkward pause where we're just staring at each other. So I break it: "You like my dress?"

He laughs. Rich and deep. Full of the Macklin Magic. A fidget spinner has appeared—*spin spin spin*—in his right hand. "I have zero doubt you know I like your dress, Danger. Who's the egomaniac now?"

"Shut up."

Spinner vanishes into a pocket, and he interlaces our fingers. Tugs. "Come on. There's somebody I want you to meet."

"Umm . . ."

"Shit, I'm doing it again." He lets my hand go. Takes a deep breath. "Lemme start over."

Man, do I wanna kiss him right now. (*Really, Rico?*)

"Rico, there's someone I'd like to introduce you to. Would you be interested in coming to meet her?"

Can't say no, of course. "Sure. Thank you for asking."

He smiles and extends an elbow this time. Once I take it, he leads me around and through what seem like piles of riches, jewels, and precious metals with opposable thumbs, and we approach the group of people surrounding an older, light-brown-skinned woman perched on a cushy chair like a queen on her throne.

The crowd parts for Zan (*pffft*), and when she sees him, she spreads her arms. "¡Nietito!"

He leans down and she kisses him once on each cheek.

"Lita, este es Rico," he says, dragging me forward (and he does have to *drag* because my feet feel cemented to the floor).

"Ohhhh! ¡Mucho gusto, mi amor!" She rises, and everyone

232

behind us starts whispering. "Come, come to Lita. I am *so* happy to meet you!" She wraps me in a hug—apparently, all Macklins smell otherworldly—and then tugs my face down to kiss me on both cheeks like she did Zan.

Then she pulls back. "You should be ashamed, Alejandro," she says to Zan while looking me over. "Your description of her beauty was mierda."

That word I know . . . and *man*, is every inch of my skin on fire.

Zan's is too. "Rico, this is my grandma—"

"Ay with the *grandma* thing." She waves the word away like some foul odor.

It unearths a smile from the deepest depths of my being, and she returns a matching one. I've never had a grandmother, but if Lita is the prototype, I can see what the fuss is about. Her presence is like a blanket with arms.

"Thank you so much for coming, mi'ja," she says, squeezing both of my hands. "You will visit our home for dinner and we will talk much more, okay?"

She kisses me again and returns to her seat before I can respond.

"Wow. She's like a celebrity," I say to Zan once we're out of earshot. I hear *Lady Consuela* multiple times from behind me.

Zan laughs. "Definitely the Macklin Matriarch," he says. "Kind of a sore spot for my mom, but it is what it is."

I really want to ask what country she's from, but if the answer is *this one*, I'll feel like an assho—

"Mexico."

"Huh?"

"My dad's half Mexican. That's where the Spanish comes from. Lita insisted we all be fluent."

"Ah."

"You'd be surprised how weird people get when they find out."

"Really?"

"Yep. It's like their prejudice boils up and cooks their brains. Come meet my parents."

Over the next ten minutes, I meet Mr. and Mrs. Macklin, the bride, the groom, four aunts, three uncles, seven cousins, Zan's brother Joaquín—big hug from Anna-Maria (who Zan tells me is also Mexican and came to America for school; stirs that *choices* thing right back up)—and a next-door neighbor girl who, despite my presence, gapes at Zan like he powers the spinning of the earth.

We don't spend any more than a few seconds with each person, but I definitely get a feel for Zan-the-Man's origins. There are a *lot* of huggers.

After the fancy passed hors d'oeuvres and expensive champagne (that I dutifully skip), we sit for a five-course dinner. I have quite the cheap palate, so the beluga caviar, foie gras, steak tartare, and veal Oscar aren't really my speed, but despite feeling like I'm in some kind of fairy-tale land, not once do I ever feel as out of place as I anticipated.

If I had to guess, I'd say it's because the baby brother of the bride rarely lets go of my hand.

A Word from Zan's Fidget Spinner

got a lot of play after that wedding. Once Alexander was back alone in his "bedroom" (which is almost the size of Rico's apartment, not that it matters), he couldn't sleep. He worked me for hours—staring up at the ceiling, rocking in his desk chair, pacing the oak floor.

Thinking.

About her.

How good she is to Jax. How hard she works.

How much better a person she is than he. He wishes he had her courage. Her resilience.

He thought about how soft and warm her skin is. Her perfect hands and beautiful eyes. Her question from all those weeks ago—*Is that what* you *want?*—spun inside his head at the same velocity I spun between his fingers.

He thought about the company and how he doesn't want to work there, let alone take it over.

But does he have a choice?

How would Dad react if he went to college instead? And what would Alexander do for money? Yeah, he'd been "working" for years . . . but being employed by your family's half-a-billion-dollar company was probably different from having a job with a real boss and all that.

Then there was the ticket. The search for Ethel Streeter. His growing suspicion they were headed for a dead end—no pun intended.

Should he just tell her? Come right out with it?

And then what?

He flicked me again.

Spin, spin, spin, spin, spin, spin . . .

-27-

Macklin'd

I don't even get time to process the evening and put my feet back on the ground because it turns out Lita is serious about the dinner thing: halfway through my shift the next day, I get a call at work from Zan telling me she wants me at this family dinner for the newlyweds before they head off on their monthlong honeymoon.

That dinner is tonight.

(Also: *month*long? Where the hell are they even going?!)

After calling to clear it with Mama—who sounds reluctant but eventually caves—I spend the next four hours stocking and restocking everything in sight—working on candy right now—in a futile attempt to keep my nerves in check.

The thirty-second intro-plus-hugs with Zan's whole fam in the thick of a wonderland wedding were one thing. I was all dolled up and actually kinda looked like I belonged there.

Today, though? I'm in ripped, bleach-spotted jeans, a faded—though nicely fitted—Batman T-shirt, a pair of glittery flats Mama scrounged from a thrift store near a ballet studio, and her Brazen Bitches biker jacket. My hair looks like a fist protruding from the crown of my head, and the only thing on my face is a series of dark spots from my last breakout—

"Ricoooo!"

"Oh my God!" I startle, and the box I'm carrying goes into the air.

Guess I can say I make it rain Skittles now.

"Sorry, honey. Didn't mean to startle ya." Hypershiny black shoes and navy dress pants appear in my peripheral. "Just wanted to say hello. Lovin' the Batman shirt!"

My eyes climb the suit and land on a smiling face.

Mr. Fifty hasn't shaved since the last time he was in here.

It's actually not a bad look. "Nice beard."

"Ya like it?" He runs a hand over it. "Thought I'd try something new."

In his other hand, he's got a Slim Jim, a Vitaminwater Zero, and a bag of salt 'n' vinegar pork rinds (yuck).

I smile. Like a real smile. It's kinda weird, but seeing Mr. Fifty today is . . . settling.

I gather the scattered Skittles bags and stand. "Come on up front and I'll ring those up for you."

($41.86 in change.)

The jitter reprieve lasts exactly thirty-eight minutes. Because at 3:54 p.m., when Zan saunters in looking every bit the son-of-a-millionaire he is, my angst rockets through the fluorescent-lighted ceiling again. He winks at me in passing as he goes to greet Mr. Z, and after getting a full report on the Macklin paper products he supplied, he waits

238

until I finish clocking out, takes my hand (the rest of me whips into hurricane frenzy), and pulls me outside.

I'm still figuring out how to breathe normally.

"Can we pop by my house so I can change?" I ask. That's when I realize there's no Tonka.

"Change for what? You look perfect."

"Uhh—"

"This is us today," he says as we approach an old two-door Honda. He opens the door for me, and the seat belt automatically slides forward on a track to let me inside. Once the door is shut, the thing moves back to its starting point, strapping me in *without* my consent.

I peek around. Thing's even got a cassette tape deck—I would've sworn Mama's truck was the last working vehicle on earth with one of those.

Once Zan is held in place by his own demon seat belt, he fastens the one that goes across the lap (which prompts me to do it too), then shoves the key in the ignition and tries to start the car. There a *whrrrrr-whrrrrr-whrrrr* sound, but no crank.

"Dammit," he says.

Something beneath the steering column gets pulled and there's a *pop* sound. Then he hops out and the hood goes up. After about twenty seconds, hood drops, he hops back in, turns the key again, and boom. *Put-put-putter,* but the engine's running.

I am so confused.

"Soooooo . . ."

"Took the Jeep in for regular maintenance—oil change, tires balanced and rotated, that type of thing, right?"

"Sure."

"They found *two* 50D nails in the sidewall of my front passenger tire. TWO!"

No clue what any of that means. Which doesn't help my Poor Girl Visiting Rich World jitters. "Okay . . ."

"The things are five and a half inches long and six millimeters in diameter!"

"Dang." Still clueless.

"Our mechanic thinks somebody did it on purpose. Anyway, those tires are special order, so it'll be Wednesday before a new one is in."

"What about the spare?" *You know, the one protruding from the back door?*

He shakes his head. "That's what I said, but my mom doesn't want me driving around without a spare, so even if we were to use that one, I'd have to wait until the new one comes in."

Ah. I see. "So this is your spare car." Because of course he would have a spare car—

"This is my dad's car."

"Ah, so it's *his* spare car, not yours. My bad."

"Try the one he drives every day. He doesn't have a spare."

I take it all in . . . the crank windows, the manual locks, the torn upholstery with the padding sticking out of it. "Nope. You're full of it."

He laughs. "Cross my heart. He's actually pretty proud of it. He's never spent more than two thousand dollars on a car, yet every car he's had has lasted at least a decade. He's on year eleven with this baby fella, and it was already sixteen years old when he bought it." He pats the dashboard.

"Parts can be hard to find, and Dad'll have to replace the spark plugs soon if he doesn't want to get rid of him, but Timothy Macklin will definitely rock this car till the wheels fall off. Literally."

Wow.

"Something very few know about my father: the guy does *not* like spending money."

Hope this isn't outta line. . . . "Your sister's wedding seemed pretty extravagant."

"That was all Mom and Lita. Dad had bloodshot eyes for two days after finding the bill for the flowers. Never in my life heard him yell *Mami* so loud."

I chuckle. "So what's your mom like?"

"She drives a fully loaded Maserati SUV."

Now I'm *really* laughing.

He shakes his head. "It's ridiculous. She's the company attorney, but she'd spend everything if he let her."

Wonder what that's like . . . the *limit* being a friggin' Maserati. "I still can't believe I'm going to your *house.*"

Whoops. That wasn't supposed to leave my head.

"Why not?"

"Oh come on, Macklin. Before a couple months ago, would *you* have expected the weirdo brown girl from history to wind up beside you in your dad's bucket?"

He laughs. "*Gorgeous* weirdo brown girl from history. Get it right."

"I'm serious!" And flustered now. Hate when he catches me off guard like that.

"Okay, touché." His head turns toward me in my peripheral. "Loving every minute, though—"

"Eyes on the road, fool."

More laughing from him—and smiling from me—but when we get to the next red light, he turns to me with a kind of serious look. "I've got a question for you, Danger."

Gulp. "Okay . . ."

"What if it were you?"

"Huh?"

"We've been looking for Ethel Streeter because you're convinced she has a winning lotto ticket, right? What if *you* had it? What would you do with the cash?"

Well, this is out of left field. "That's . . . random."

"Well, the longer we go without finding her, the more I think about it," he says. "I did the math: if the winner took the annuity option, after taxes they'd get roughly two-point-four million a year for thirty years. That's over two hundred grand a *month*, Rico. Only like three percent of American households see that *annually*."

"Okay . . ."

"Just interested to hear what you'd do with that kinda dough."

Why is he asking me this?

Actually, better question: Why does the thought of answering make me uncomfortable? It's not like I don't know. . . . My mind runs through a list every time Jax or Mama gets sick. Even wrote it down once. I'd obviously start by getting us some good health insurance. . . .

But I certainly can't tell *him* that.

"I'd probably buy us a new car and a decent house."

He nods. "Go on."

"I've never really thought beyond that," I say. "I guess I'd start a college fund for Jax. Maybe send him to Space Camp."

"Oh, is he into space? I had no idea."

I swallow again. I honestly don't know either, but every kid would jump at the chance to go to Space Camp, right? I didn't get to, so why not Jax? "Yeah."

"What about for you? College?"

"I mean, if I have that kind of annual income, I won't *need* college. Don't people go to earn the credentials that will land them higher-paying jobs?"

"Fair. So would you invest what you don't need to live? Save it? Give it to charity?"

"I told you I hadn't thought that far, Macklin. It's a waste of time. I don't have the ticket."

I'm annoyed.

And he can tell. Doesn't ask any more questions.

Unfortunately, after a few minutes, the silence is suffocating. So I break it. "What would you do?"

"Hmm?"

"If you had the ticket? What would you do?"

"Oh." His eyes narrow, and he gulps.

Which is weird. "I mean, you said yourself that *you* aren't rich, right? You have to work for your money just like the rest of us. So the ticket could be beneficial to you too."

A reminder I needed. I've been trying not to think about it, but right now? In *this* car with him asking me that question?

"So? What would you do?" I press. "Get your own place and move out? 'Invest,' as you say, so you never have to

work? Start your own line of Macklin fidget spinners?"
Man, am I on edge now. Wonder if he can tell.

He glances at me out of the corner of his eye. "You really wanna know?"

"Yep."

"I'd throw it away," he says. "That kind of money's a recipe for disaster."

I don't say anything after that.

Zan's old-school rap music is the only sound in the car for the rest of the ride—ironically, the song playing when we pull up to the wrought iron gate features a guy bragging about having no job or rent money but driving a Benz and wearing "gator boots" and ("pimped-out") Gucci suits.

And as we roll up the winding driveway, I'll admit that after the twenty-minute trip here in the geriatric Honda, I halfway expected us to pull up to something moderate.

Nope.

The house is astounding. Brick. Wide and deep and pillared.

A literal mansion.

Zan pulls into door four of the six-car garage, and I see not one, but *two* Maseratis—an SUV the size of my bedroom, and a convertible coupe. "Your mom has two cars?"

"Nope," he says, shutting off the ignition. "Convertible is Lita's. Come on."

I leave my jacket in the car—kinda doubt Catholic grandmas are into Brazen Bitches—and we approach the door that leads to the inside of the castl—I mean the *house*.

I try to keep my cool, but even more than Ness's, *this*

home reminds me of days exploring the empty shells of houses with Mama and letting my imagination run free. The moment we're out of the car and I see that the garage has a loft space (what is *up* there?), words start flying out before I can swallow them back: "Macklin, this *house*. How many bedrooms? How many baths? Is there an elevator?"

"Eight bedrooms, ten full baths, four half, no elevator." He sighs. "You really want me to go over all this?"

"Sorry." I take another look around the massive garage. "I've just never *seen* a house this size, let alone been inside one."

He stops walking and turns to face me. I'm still gawking around like a dweeb, so I smack right into him. When I look up, he grins down and reaches around to tug my hair loose from its knot. As the curls tumble down, he shakes them out, then rests his hands on my shoulders and traces my collarbones with his thumbs. *(Whoa.)*

"There are three kitchens, an indoor pool and racquetball court, a gym with sauna and steam room, and a wine cellar so stocked, we could get the senior class wasted. Lita lives in a four-bedroom house out back, and *my* 'room' is basically an apartment complete with living room and kitchenette. I've got more shit and space than I could ever need, but you know what? Sometimes I get so lonely, the distance from my bed to the door seems insurmountable." We lock eyes. "And not counting Ness, you're only the second person to ever come over."

I blink. A lot. "Really?"

"Yep. *True* friends can be hard to come by, Danger. I, uhh . . . can't say I let a lot of people in, if you get what I mean."

What's weird? I totally do get it.

"Something valuable went missing the last time I brought a 'friend' over."

My gaze falls to my faux-sparkly shoes. "I'm sorry."

"Don't be." He kisses my forehead. "I've got you now. Literally nothing else matters."

I don't even get a chance to process what he said because next thing I know, I'm stepping into a bright room and someone is yelling, "Zan and Rico are here, you guys!"

The Macklins in two R-words: raucous and #raciallyreconciled. I'm swept into a series of boisterous greetings and warm hugs, and in a blink, we're gathered around a ten-seat dinner table.

Lita sits at the head with Zan's parents to her right. Next to Zan's mom—Ms. Leigh-Ann—is his stunning sister, Tehlor, and beside *her* is her new husband—who is basically Finesse with a bald head and goatee. Zan takes the seat to Lita's left, so I end up sitting across from his mom, and Dr. Gorgeous—I mean Anna-Maria—sits next to me with big bro Joaquín to her left.

As soon as we're all settled in, Zan's dad, Mr. Tim—can't *believe* I'm sitting this close to *the* Timothy Macklin—clinks his fork against his glass.

The chatter instantly ceases.

"Let us join hands and bow our heads for the blessing," he says.

We do, and he begins: "Gracious and heavenly Father, we thank you for this food. That it will nourish our bodies and keep us whole."

"Sí, Papá," from Lita.

"We also thank you for the gift that is family, and the addition of our newest member, Chadwick."

"We love you, King!" from Zan's mom.

"We thank you, Lord, also, for the success of Macklin Enterprises, and we ask for a grandchild at your earliest convenience."

Joaquín coughs.

"And lastly, Lord, we thank you for our young Alejandro, and for the light that has recently graced his life, pulling him out of darkness—"

"Really, Dad?"

"No interrupting prayer, Alejandro," Lita says. "And don't embarrass the boy, Timoteo."

"Fine, fine. Amen," Mr. Tim finishes.

When I open my eyes, there's a timbre of unease in the air that wasn't there before, and everyone's sneaking glances in my direction.

Except for Zan.

That's when it hits me: Mr. Tim was talking about *me*.

Oh boy . . .

"So Rico Reneé!" Mr. Tim basically shouts once the first dish is going around the table. He totally rolls the *R*s. "A beautiful name for a beautiful girl!"

Tehlor looks at me and shakes her head like, *I'm so sorry.* "Don't hit on Jandro's girlfriend, Daddy."

"She's not my girlfriend."

"Well, she should be!" Lita says. "Just look at her! Such majesty and poise!"

247

"Hard worker too!" Mr. Tim says (yells). "Alexander tells me you work almost full-time in addition to your studies!"

"Mm-hmm." I shove a taquito in my mouth. This conversation is moving so fast, I can hardly keep up. Speaking of fast, Zan sure was swift with the *not my girlfriend* thing. Not that I *want* to be . . .

"I think that's outstanding!"

("Of course he does," Joaquín murmurs before there's a *thump* against the underside of the table and he mutters, "Ow!")

"My first job was in an ice cream parlor at fourteen, but my *second* was at a gas station like you, Rico. Nothing more inspiring than a youngster with your work ethic! Jandro, why didn't you bring this treasure home sooner? Better yet, why aren't you following her lead?"

"Not the time, Dad," from Zan (through clenched teeth). *Deep breath, Rico.*

Zan's mom reaches across the table and puts her hand on mine (holy bling bling, fingers *and* wrist edition). "We're really thrilled you're here, sweetheart!"

Okay, this I can handle. "Thank you, Ms. Leigh-Ann."

"Whattaya say we have a little *girl time* next weekend, huh? Summer ready-to-wear lines should be in at Neiman." She winks.

"Are you kidding me, Leigh? Look at this girl! She's much too hip for *Neiman*," says Mr. Tim.

Heaven help me.

"Certainly nothin' like that *other* girl—"

"Dad," from Zan.

Other girl?

"Well, shopping or no shopping, you will come with me to Mass, sí, mi'ja?" Now Lita's winking at me. "We must keep our spiritual house in order. Are you a believer?"

Oh boy. "Umm . . ."

"Let's maybe let her *eat*?" Joaquín says. (Thank you, Lita's God, who I maybe do believe in a little bit now.) "We did invite her to *dinner.*"

And so they do. Sort of.

The conversation continues to bounce around the table, changing direction, shape, and color—politics, sports, immigration reform, something about adding vitamin E and vanilla essential oil to a new toilet paper prototype. And it's fun to listen to.

But as course three (this mind-numbingly delicious six-layer salad) makes its way onto everyone's plates, I get pulled back in.

"So, Rico, where you headed to college next year?" Chadwick aka King aka bald-Ness-with-a-goatee asks me. "You're graduating with Finesse and Zander, right?"

Ugh. "I'm graduating, yes, but no college plans." Nervous tuck of the hair behind the ear.

"Really? Why not?"

"Ah, college isn't for everyone," Mr. Tim cuts in. "Right, Jandro?"

Zan doesn't respond, but the temperature in the room seems to drop instantly.

"It's by choice, though, right?" Joaquín says. "No one's forcing you to take over a family company?"

"Joaquín!" from Lita.

"I'm not *forcing* anybody to do anything, Quín. If Jan wants to go to college, he can go to college—"

"You'll just cut him off financially."

"Can we maybe discuss this some other time? We have a *guest*." Ms. Leigh-Ann's face is as red as the peppers in the salad.

"All I'm saying is it'd be a waste of four vital fiscal years of Jandro's life doing 'college' when his talents could land him a great starting salary with room for quick advancement at the company."

"Jesus, Dad. He's your *son*, not some Macklin employee—"

"Enough," Lita says with *enough* authority to stop a runaway train.

Silence falls, dense and damp. Or maybe that's just the sweat overflowing my pores right now. Part of me wants to nudge Zan for comfort, but from the heat rolling off him, I get the impression that's not a great idea.

So I eat.

We all do.

It's interesting feeling the tension pulse through the room. Every gulp of a beverage and clink of silverware against a plate feels loud enough to shatter an eardrum. And where things seemed warm when we came in, the room—the house, even—has gone very cold.

Zan's knee connects with mine beneath the table, and my head instantly fills with questions. Are the "other girl" Mr. Tim mentioned and the "friend" Zan talked about the same person? Not once has Ms. Leigh-Ann actually looked at Zan . . . is that a common thing? Lita seems cool and clearly rules the roost . . . but she also didn't contradict

250

Mr. Tim or speak up with regard to Zan making his own choices.

I press my knee into Zan's a bit more firmly. The circumstances are different, of course, but I *know* what it's like to have a parent who sees you as a business decision instead of a kid.

I wish I could hug him.

Dessert comes. Which is when Mr. Tim polishes off his fourth glass of wine and says: "You all see the latest episode of *JACKPOT!*? Looks like that Winkle guy really shit the bed—"

"*Timoteo!*"

"Lo siento, Mami." He crosses himself.

(Totally chuckle at that one.)

"I don't know how you watch that crap, Dad," Tehlor says.

"Ah, I only watch 'cause there's money involved." (Zan snorts and elbows me.) "Anyway, a fellow trucker is suing the guy. Says Winkle stole the ticket from him."

"Is that even legal?" I blurt before I can catch myself.

Mr. Tim shrugs. "It's this guy's word against Winkle's. Thing is, Winkle's run through so much of his winnings, he confessed he wouldn't have the cash to pay if he loses the suit."

"What a dumbass," Joaquín mumbles.

I can feel Zan looking at me.

Mr. Tim: "I've said it a thousand times, but it really is good that other winner never came forward."

"Amen!" from Lita, which surprises me (though it probably shouldn't).

"Giving that much money to someone who can't manage it is no better than sticking a needle of dope in their arm—"

I tune out after that.

-28-

Baby Mama Drama

Odd but true: on the way home after dinner, when I tell Zan I'm going to cancel our appointment with the leasing agent (fully intending to just go without him), his head whips around so fast, I'm surprised it doesn't fly off his shoulders and land in my lap.

"*Cancel* it?"

"Yes? It's pretty clear your whole family feels the ticket will ruin Ethel's life."

Also, I'm a mess of contradictions right now and need some space to sort things out in my head. Witnessing Zan's . . . isolation, I guess, makes me wanna hold him the way I hold Jax after particularly bad bullying days at his school, but I'm increasingly bothered by the sheer speed and force with which he declared to his whole family that I'm not his girlfriend. It's like whatever door I *thought* was opening between us has slammed shut, and the deeper the words sink in, the more locks I want to add to it.

That's not even to mention this *other girl*. Why didn't he mention her when we were talking about dating? Who even *is* she?

"We've come so far, though, Danger. Don't you wanna see it all the way through?"

"We just spent an *hour* listening to your dad talk about how awful the lottery is." *After you made it* crystal *clear I mean nothing to you.*

(Yes. It stung.)

"Ah, what does he know?"

"Zan, *four hours ago* you said the exact same thing. And don't think I didn't see you nodding while your family was talking."

"Watching me pretty closely there, huh?"

Not the time. "Don't change the subject!"

He laughs. "Look, Danger: we've made too much progress on this thing to give up. Don't cancel. We're not quitting."

Again my questions about his motives rear up and threaten to bite me in the face. Will he really be cut off if he chooses not to work for the company? Would he really have to start from zero?

And what if I cancel and he just reschedules? He could totally do that. He knows where the house is and would only have to go back there and grab the realtor's number from the yard sign.

Despite the mess swirling in my brain, one thing's clear: I don't want him continuing the search and finding the ticket without me.

So here we are in the Tonka a week later, staring at the green bungalow that houses Orion Realty Group.

"You ready?" Zan says, eyes all a-sparkle.

I force a smile.

He's not playing me, is he? Pretending to like me so I can lead him right to the jackpot? I've been thinking about it: even if his parents did cut him off, he's got scholarship offers and can totally get a job to support himself like the rest of the 99 percent. Most college students are broke anyway, from what I hear. It's a part of the experience.

I glance at him again and he's still staring at me. All gooey-eyed and excited.

What if he *is* playing me? What do I do?

"We're four minutes late, Danger. Should probably go in now."

"Oh."

I grab the door handle and push it wide. Slide down, shut the door behind me, lean back against it, and shut my eyes. Gotta get my head back on straight.

Something runs between my eyebrows and down over the tip of my nose. Taps twice. When I open my eyes, Zan is looking at me. Visually tracing over my face.

He stops at my mouth.

Time to go. "All right, let's do this."

I push off from the Jeep.

The interior of Orion Realty Group smells like Pine-Sol and potpourri. "Welcome to ORG," says a receptionist with skin the color of an Oompa Loompa. "How may I help you this morning?"

Unfortunately, I'm too busy trying to deduce the origin of her ochre hue—spray tan gone wrong, or flagrant lack of SPF coverage?—to answer. "Umm . . ."

"We have an appointment with Mr. Greg Andree about

a potential rental property," Zan says, coming to the rescue unsummoned (as usual).

She takes us in and furrows her drawn-on eyebrows. Picks up the phone on her desk, rotates away, and mumbles into it.

Zan slips an arm around my waist and pulls me close. When I look up at him—caught me off guard, won't lie—he mouths, "Just follow my lead."

Okay . . .

The guy who comes down the stairs is so bald, his head glistens, but he's got this swagger in his step that makes me think he spent his youth man-bunned and getting into trouble.

He stops short when he sees us, and that's when I notice how intense his eyes are. Very pale . . . green? Gray? Hazel? Legit can't tell. "Wow," he says. "You're Reneé?"

I nod and extend my hand. "Mm-hmm. And this is . . . umm . . ."

"Gustavo," Zan says, extending his and smiling. "Gustavo Maxwell."

"Pleasure to meet you. I'm Greg." He looks from Zan to me, me to Zan. "You two are *younger* than I was expecting."

Zan nods. "We're both eighteen. Graduate from high school in a couple of months."

"I see."

"Had a little too much fun after winter homecoming, if you catch my drift." Zan winks and pats my belly.

Wait . . .

Did he just—

He totally did.

255

I'm sure my eyes are as big as cue balls.

Mr. Andree, though? Just grins and lifts his chin. Nods a few times. "My eldest boy is twenty-two. I just turned forty last month. You do the math," he says.

I feel Zan exhale beside me, and it's all I can do to keep from spontaneously combusting. From *not-my-girlfriend* to *got-her-pregnant*? I feel a wildly inappropriate laugh bubbling beneath my rib cage. The absurdity of it all is almost enough to make my brain crack Humpty Dumpty style.

"Well, shall we get down to business then?" Mr. Andree goes on. "I know the nausea can hit ya like a lightning bolt."

"SO true," Zan says. "We'll be riding down the road and . . . blegh." He blows his cheeks out and puts a hand over his mouth.

I wanna punch him.

"Here are the specs for the property you called about, young lady." Mr. Andree passes me a sheet of paper from the folder he's carrying. "I'll drive you all over to see it, but you gotta promise you won't puke in my car."

God, do I hate Zan Macklin right now. "I promise, sir."

"*Greg* is fine. You're adults now." He pats Zan on the back.

Fury rising.

After saying goodbye to the orange receptionist, we make our way to the door. Once outside, he says, "That the only house you're interested in? Not to make any assumptions, but that neighborhood's a little pricey."

"Oh." Not sure how to respond to that. "Okay . . ."

"Tell ya what," he says, "let me show you-all some other properties first. I've got a few in mind that would be perfect for a young family just starting out. In slightly less geriatric areas too."

I avoid looking up at Zan, who at some point moved his arm from my waist to my shoulders. I've got my fingers all intertwined with the hand dangling near my boob. No clue when that happened. Or why I'm not snatching away in abject fury over his baby mama lie.

Why doesn't anything make sense?

"What do you think?" he says. "Wanna check out some other spots?"

I really want to say no, but I guess if nothing else, it'll give me time to come up with a plan. I officially need to take this hunt back into my own hands. "Sounds good to us, Greg."

"Awesome."

As Greg rounds the corner to a gravel lot, I hold Zan back. "Hey, are you really eighteen? Cuz I'm not."

He smiles. "Mm-hmm. Turned eighteen the day before Christmas."

Car is a joke.

"Wow," Zan says from the passenger seat once we're on the road. "This is quite the vehicle."

"Platinum Cadillac Escalade ESV, my friend. Not real great on gas mileage, but she's my baby." He pats the dashboard. "A man's gotta reward himself for his successes. Speaking of which, you guys got jobs and everything? I know you said you're still in high school."

"We both work part-time, but between the three of us, work won't be necessary for the next few years, Greg.

Grandparents dropped me a pretty little trust fund." He nudges Greg with an elbow. (Gross.)

"Ahh," Greg says. "Gotcha. Probably shoulda guessed based on those threads you're rockin'. That's what, Calvin Klein?"

"Ralph Lauren," Zan says.

Not the least bit pregnant, but definitely want to vomit.

"You're a lucky young lady." Greg looks at me in the rearview. "Rare to find a teen dad who not only wants to take care of his kid, but has the means."

Yeah, this lie is *so* much worse than our other ones. Wouldn't surprise me if we stepped out of the car and got struck by lightning.

"So you got a budget in mind then?" Greg asks Zan.

"Trying to keep it under three K."

"A *month*?"

"Yeah. Is that too low?"

"No, no." Greg clears his throat and signals to change lanes. Wonder if Zan notices the course correction. "We can work with that. . . ."

And work with it, we do. Over the next two hours we visit a three-bedroom condo in the most expensive part of Atlanta (overkill), a loft in Midtown (not at all child-friendly), a penthouse downtown (is he serious?!), and an "apartment" within a larger Victorian house in some historic district.

Now we're walking into a cute little two-bedroom cottage in Decatur.

"The best thing about this place is it's got an open floor plan and no stairs, so if you're here long enough for your kid to reach the crawling stage, you'll be able to forgo the baby gates," Greg says. "Have a look-see. I'm gonna step outside for a sec."

"Okay, this kitchen is adorable," Zan says, looking around. In addition to the modern appliances, there's a potbelly stove in the corner. It's got the perfect-sized table and chairs near the wide window, and a breakfast bar that overlooks the little living room.

And fine: it is adorable.

I'm so confused, I really could puke.

It's like my brain's being pulled in two directions: on the one hand, fake future-home-hunting with Zan Macklin is kinda thrilling. As he takes my left hand so we can walk around this place like we've done at the others, I'm reminded of how invigorating the sense of *possibility* can be.

But then there's that right hand. The one Zan's *not* holding. The one that's been clenched in a loose fist since the moment he put his hand on my stomach. As nice as the near-constant contact and undivided attention I've experienced today have the *potential* to be, right now, all I can think about is how it's a giant façade.

Despite the fact that we've been acting like a couple all day, that Greg Andree is under the impression I'm carrying Zan's spawn, the hard truth remains: I'm not his girlfriend.

It's just that the longer he treats me like I am, the angrier I get.

"My sister would have a field day decorating this place," he says as we peek into one of the two bedrooms. "It'd be a good spot for us even without a kid." He steps behind me and wraps both arms around my shoulders.

259

Which . . . "A good spot for *us*, huh?"

"Totally. It's a nice area, two bedrooms, and a great location. We'll be near enough to our families to drop in, but far enough away that they can't drive us insane. Out of all the places we've seen, it's the best option."

The best opt—There's no way he's serious. Couldn't possibly be.

If this whole thing's a joke, it's officially *not* funny anymore.

I pull his arms off and turn around to face him. "Are you really suggesting we *move in* together, Macklin?"

He shrugs. "Ness and Jess are. Maybe it's a good idea for us too. We are both sticking around after graduation."

Tomorrow's headline: TEEN GIRL SPONTANEOUSLY COMBUSTS FROM OVERWHELMING DOSES OF BEWILDERMENT

"'Ness and Jess' have been a couple for two years, Zan. And as you made *clear* to your family, I'm not your girl—"

"You two get a good look around?" Greg appears in the living room, and that's the end of that.

I (low-key furiously) take Zan's hand so our "Realtor" doesn't think there's trouble in paradise. We haven't actually gotten the info we need.

"We did, Greg," Zan says. "This place is great. Probably number one at this point. Where to next?"

Nope. We're done here. "Greg, what do you know about the owner of this place?" I say.

Zan looks confused, so I give him the *I got this* smile he gave me back when we visited Checker Cab (feels like an eon ago that we were there).

Greg opens the file in his hand and flips through a few pages. "Dutch guy," he says. "This is one of four properties ORG manages for him, and the other three are happily tenanted."

I nod. "What about the Druid Hills house? I know we haven't seen it yet, but is the owner American?" God, I sound like a xenophobe.

Greg goes back to his file, and I can feel Macklin eyeing me. "Guessing by the name, yes, that owner is American."

"What is it, if you don't mind my asking?"

"Name on the deed is Ethel Streeter."

Bingo. (And thank Lita's God.)

Zan clears his throat. "Does your file say anything about her? Do people think she's a good landlady?"

He smiles. "Tenants who lease through us don't usually interact with property owners. That's kinda why we exist."

"But she's *alive*?" I say.

"I mean, I'd assume so, since her name is on the deed—"

"When's the last time you had contact with her?"

Zan squeezes my hand. Yes, I'm coming on too strong now, but we're so freakin' close, and I wanna get out of here. Hearing all this with him beside me is making me itch.

Greg's gaze shifts between us, but then drops to my midsection. He sighs. Goes back to his file. "Our interactions are with her asset manager at Dover Financial—"

"Shit! That's the company *we* use!" Zan exclaims.

Greg and I both look at him. "Sorry, Greg. You were saying?"

"Not much else to say." Greg shuts his file. "Would you like to head to that property now?"

Zan turns to me, his expression that of a kid who just found a treasure map.

Ain't happenin'.

I put a hand on my belly. "Actually . . . I'm feeling kinda sick all of a sudden."

"Oh, sweetheart," Greg says, face softening.

God, if you're real, withhold the fire and brimstone, please.

"Let's get you all back to the office. We'll talk en route." As Greg makes his way to the door, Zan's face fills with questions.

I rise to my tiptoes to plant a kiss on his cheek. "Guess *that* mystery is solved, huh?"

I squeeze his biceps and walk out.

A Word from the Potbelly Stove That Made the Kitchen in the Decatur House So Adorable

My home—and it is *my* home since I'm the only thing in here that hasn't been "renovated"—was built in 1934. And for the most part, I've been used for my intended purpose—heat. But when a young couple purchased the house in 1987, the husband told his wife I didn't work so he'd have a place to stash the gambling winnings she didn't know about.

Guy had a hell of a lucky streak.

That luck peaked in 1992 when he purchased a winning lotto ticket in South Carolina worth three hundred fourteen thousand dollars.

South Carolina permitted winners to claim big prizes anonymously, so he cashed in his ticket one weekend while his wife was away on a trip with friends, put the money in a black canvas duffel, and stuffed it inside me with the rest of his secret savings.

His wife, though, wasn't so lucky: she returned home despondent over the three hundred dollars she'd lost gambling in the casinos.

He began to watch her like a hawk. Would hold his

breath every time she stood close to me for longer than a few seconds.

One stormy night, he woke up, and she was missing from bed. He found her in the kitchen, just staring at me.

Like she knew.

As soon as she left for work the following day, he pulled all the money out to count it.

It was three hundred dollars short.

Or so he thought. In truth, he'd counted incorrectly. But since he was already convinced his wife had something to hide . . .

Well.

-29-

Mr. Dover

The next day, as soon as he sits down beside me in history, I pass Zan the note I prepped so I won't lose my nerve:

You talk to your people at the financial place?

Good morning to you too, Rico.

MORNIN' SUNSHINE! So, did you?

Somebody's testy today . . .

Macklin!

OK, OK! Yes. I did.

And?

He said we could drop by this afternoon.

Excellent! Right after school?

Yeah, if that works for you . . .

I'll meet you in the lot.

He scribbles something else and passes it back, but I don't read it. It's either a question I won't wanna answer or something ooey gooey that'll distract me, and I gotta keep my head in the game.

I didn't sleep last night. Too much swirling around in my chest. Rage over some guy I don't know thinking I'm gonna be a teen mom when I've never been kissed (nor had a boyfriend). Confusion over Zan's . . . well, over Zan in general. *("I really like you." "She's not my girlfriend." "Had a little too much fun after winter homecoming . . ." "This would be a good spot for us.")*

What's he even after?

Anyway: definitely need his help with what I hope is the final obstacle. Guessing the son of this financial firm's (surely) biggest client will (likely) be able to get any info he requests. My plan is once we've acquired Ethel's contact info, I'll "set up a time for *us* to reach out," but do it alone beforehand.

Just gotta dodge Zan's questions/affections long enough to get through this next thing.

By the time we step out of the elevator on the twenty-second floor of the steel and glass skyscraper that houses

Dover Financial, I am utterly exhausted. Turns out evasive maneuvering takes a lot out of a girl.

But we're almost there.

Down the hallway . . .

And there's the door.

Zan knocks.

"Come on in, Jandro" comes from the other side.

Zan pushes the door wide and moves to the side so I can enter first, and I get my best smile in place—

It crashes to the floor.

"Ricooooo!"

I'm either dreaming, or dead.

"You! Here!" he goes on. "In *my* workplace for once!"

Yep: dead. Definitely dead.

The name on the plaque beside the office door reads JOHN DOVER, MBA, CPA, CFP. But the guy sitting behind the desk, cheesin' like the Cheshire Cat?

Mr. Fifty.

"You two know each other?" Zan asks, looking as dumbfounded as I feel.

"You bet we do! Rico's my favorite employee at the Gas 'n' Go in Norcross! What a small world we live in!"

"You can say that again," I mutter.

Mr. Fifty—*Dover*—points to Zan. "You *dating* this guy?"

"Nope. Just friends." I step into the office in front of Zan. Look around. Might as well use my advantage. "Nice digs!"

"Well, thank you, Rico." He rocks back in his chair. "If I'd known *you* were coming, I'da ordered refreshments! Come in, come in! Have a seat."

This is gonna be easier than I thought.

I take the chair on the right, and when Zan sits down, I can totally *feel* the . . . *furywildermustration* would probably be the best way to describe it. It's coming off him in thumping waves that I bet match his heartbeat.

Probably best to get this over with as quickly as possible.

"So what can I do for you, Mr. Macklin?" Mr. Dover says to Zan.

Zan's lips part but—

"I'm the one who needed to speak with you, Mr. Dover," I say.

Zan looks at me. (Can't even read his face at this point.)

Dover does too.

"So you know how my store sold that winning Mighty Millions ticket on Christmas Eve?"

"Yep. Took me weeks to forgive you for not selling it to me." He wags his finger. "Anyone ever come forward with the big winner?"

"Nope," I say. "That's actually why we're here."

His eyebrows lift, and he leans back in his chair. "Do tell."

"After you left, I sold two tickets to an older black lady. She gave one to me—"

"You didn't tell me that," Zan says.

"It wasn't the winner."

"Okay, but sti—"

"So it wasn't important." I focus back on Mr. Dover. "My boss said he sold a bunch, but this is the thing: the winner included the numbers that make up my birth date. Which was on the ticket the lady *didn't* give me."

"Whoa."

"I know, right? Also: I can't imagine anyone else not coming forward. *I* only sold three, and since the one I sold you and the one I kept were both duds, the third one had to be—"

"The winner," Mr. Dover says.

"Exactly."

"Hmm." He rubs his chin.

"Zan and I have been trying to find the lady. My guess is she stuck it in her pocket or down in her purse and forgot about it."

"That's a heck of a thing to forget. . . ."

"She mentioned some memory problems."

"Really?"

"Yeah. In reference to something else, but still."

"Ah," he says.

"Anyway, the latest piece of the puzzle led us to you: apparently your company manages her assets. Her name is Ethel Streeter. We're just trying to get some kind of contact info for her."

"Streeter, huh?"

"Yes, sir."

"That's a fairly new client. Just started with them last month." He narrows his eyes, clasps his hands over his mid-section, and looks between Zan and me. Sighs and leans forward.

Ah, crap.

"Now, Rico, you know you're my favorite. . . ."

Crap, crap, *crap!*

"I've been working with the Macklins since before this guy was even born, so good move bringing him here with you."

Here goes . . .

"But I can't actually give out client information."

Even knowing that was coming, I deflate like a machete-poked bouncy castle.

But then . . .

"However. If one or both of you happened to slip over into the third drawer of that file cabinet in the corner and take a peek at the *first page only* of the file marked *Streeter* while in possession of a Post-it and ink pen while my back is turned . . . Well, there's not a whole lot I could do about that, is there?" He rotates his chair away from us to face the window.

Now I look at Zan. And he's looking at me. Neither of us moves.

After a few seconds, Mr. Dover goes, "Man, isn't it a lovely day? In about *one minute*, I'm gonna turn back around and finish my work so I can get out of here."

Zan and I both leap into action: he rushes over to the cabinet while I grab a stack of Post-its and a pen from Mr. Dover's desk. By the time he gets the file out and open, I'm standing next to him, ready to write.

As he whispers the address and phone number of Bartholomew and Ethel Streeter, I scribble as fast as I can. Then he shuts the folder, jams it back into the drawer, and pushes it closed while I shove the Post-it into my pocket (jackpot!), and we fly back to our chairs and drop down into them just as Mr. Dover rotates back around.

It's a little ridiculous, but I can't stop smiling.

————

I smile on the way down in the elevator.

I smile out the door.

I smile as I take Zan's hand and climb into the Jeep.

He's in. Door closed. Car cranked. I'm still smiling.

"Why didn't you tell me about the other ticket, Rico?"

Smile's gone.

"It wasn't important, Zan."

He doesn't respond.

So I go on. "What *is* important is this Post-it in my pocket. We got Ethel's contact info!" I smile as I say this, but his face is stone-times-infinity.

"We." He snorts. "You mean *you*. I might as well have not even come."

What is he, nine? "What crawled up your ass?"

"I mean, for one, we get to Mr. D's office, and you act like I'm not even there."

"And for two?"

"For two, it seems like ever since that day we—" He stops. Shakes his head. "You know what? Forget it."

And for a moment, that's all.

But then he sighs. Like tractor-tire heavily.

Which makes *me* nervous.

God, this is ridiculous.

I cross my arms and stare out the window. "Is there a *for three*?"

A beat, and then: "Kinda bummed that you were with-holding information."

"That doesn't count as *information*, Zan!"

"Yeah, well, it would've been good to know."

Now I snort. "I can think of a couple things you haven't told *me* that would've been 'good to know,'" I say. "You don't see my panties in a wad over it." Whoops!

Guess the lid's off.

"What are you talking about?"

"You know what? Don't even worry about it. As you made abundantly clear to your whole family, I'm not your girlfriend. Though I *am* good enough to be your baby mama, and depending on who you ask, that's better than nothing. Can we go now?"

"You're not my—" He shakes his head like some stuff inside it has been knocked out of place. "What does any of that have to do with anything?"

"Nothing, Macklin. Forget it." *Please forget it and forget this whole hunt too. Forget you even know me.*

"No, I'm not gonna 'forget it.' *You're* the one who just told Mr. D we're not dating—"

"We *aren't.*"

"So what's the problem?"

Well, *that* hurts way more than I would've expected. Worst part is I don't fully get why. This has all been so confusing.

All I know is there are tears on my cheeks before I feel the pricks at the corners of my eyes.

Glad *I'm* the one with Ethel's info.

"Can you take me home now, please? I gotta get Jax from the babysitter's."

No response. So I turn to make sure he heard me.

"You're crying," he says.

No shit, Sherlock. "I'll survive. *You* wouldn't know, but

272

being 'too *broke* to pay attention,' as my mother likes to say, makes you tough."

I hear him take a deep breath.

"Seriously, can we please just go?"

"Rico?"

"What, Zan?"

"Ask the question."

"*What* question?"

"The one you most want the answer to."

In an instant, about a jillion and one start swirling in my head: WhyAreYouHere?DoYouREALLYLikeMe?WhyAre YouHelpingMe?AreYouTryingToGetTheTicketForYourself? WhyDoYouLookAtMeTheWayYouDo?You'veSureBeen TreatingMeLikeAGirlfriend.IsAnyOfThatReal?IsItReally PossibleThatAGuyLikeYOUIsReallyIntoMe?WhatDoI EvenHaveToOfferYou?WereYouSeriousAboutUsMovingIn Together?What'sWithTheFidgetSpinners?AreYouUsing Me?WhatDoYouWantFromMe?WhatDoYouWantFor YOU?

What comes out: "Zan, what *am* I to you?"

-30-

Right on Time

Rico.

That was his answer: "You're Rico."

"But what does that *mean*, Zan?" I ask on the phone later that night. Didn't have the courage to while we were in the car.

"I don't know how to explain it."

"Try."

Heavy sigh then. "I've never met anybody like you, Danger," he says. "You make me question everything."

Huh? "I make *you* question everything?"

"Yeah. It's like my whole life I've been in this hallway lined with doors, but the only one I've been told I can open is directly in front of me. And I never really questioned that. It was just easier not to. Path of least resistance. And I guess, just like in real life, when you stare at one thing long enough, everything around it fades away—after a while, it seemed like there *were* no other options.

"But hanging out with you makes me feel . . . called to task, I guess. You seem to really see me, so I literally *can't* just go with the flow anymore. There's always this *What would Rico think?* in the back of my head now. You work hard, and you do so much for your family. Meanwhile, I'm just like . . . sitting here, whining because I can't do what I want?"

No idea what to say to that. Or how to feel about it. Like cool, he's seeing his privilege or whatever, but the fact that *I* was some kind of catalyst is . . . uncomfortable for some reason. Part of me wants to bring up the whole *girlfriend/* fake pregnancy thing again just to change the subject.

"It's like I have to take action," he continues. "Actually *think* about what I'm doing . . . and why."

"Do you really wanna work for your dad?"

A pause, then: "No. I don't."

"So why don't you just *not*, Zan? You *do* have other options. Scholarship offers and all that? Don't take this the wrong way, but the average person wouldn't—couldn't—just pretend those don't exist."

"There you go again," he says with a chuckle.

"It's a valid point!"

"I know, I know." Another sigh. "The truth? I signed a contract with my dad when I made varsity as a sophomore: I could play to my heart's content provided that when the senior season ended, I'd forget about football and get serious about the company. Violating said contract equals forfeiting any and all financial support from my parents for the rest of my life."

"Whoa. That's . . . intense."

"Tell me about it. The wildest part is I honestly *don't* love football enough to play in college. Hell, if I were more into it, I probably *would* have taken one of the scholarships."

"So what do you want to do? Like, in life."

"I don't really know. And I've avoided thinking about it because—well, the company. I'd probably have to try a bunch of stuff before I figured it out. And I'd be lying if I said *not* knowing doesn't scare the shit out of me."

I *don't* say *"Welcome to the real world, pal!"* Though, man oh man, do I want to. "So whatcha gonna do?"

"I knew you would ask that."

"So?"

But he doesn't get a chance to answer because I hear Mama come in. "Actually, hold that thought. I gotta run."

"Yeah, yeah, fine."

"I'll see you tomorrow."

"Cool."

I hang up just as Mama pokes her head in the door. "Jaxy has a fever?"

"Huh?"

Her eyes drop to the phone—with my hand still on it—and narrow. "You're surely not back here on the phone while your brother's curled up on the couch alone with a fever. . . ."

All the air leaves the room. "A fever?"

"Yes. A fever. When's the last time you checked on him?"

"Umm . . ."

And then her face morphs. From concern to puzzlement to rage. And I expect her to detonate—totally brace for it—but then every part of her seems to sag with disappointment. "Oh, Rico." She looks like she might cry. Which is so much worse than anger.

She leaves the room without another word, and the weight

of my miserable life drops on me with the force of a collapsing house.

There's a hole in my sock. I'm stretched out on a children's comforter on a twin bed. The blinds over the window are broken, and there's a crack in the drywall above Jax's bed. Which is in the same room as mine.

I've been on this "quest" for months, and none of these things have changed.

They probably never will.

"Rico, I need help!" Mama shouts.

And just like that, the final walls come crashing down.

Within a couple of hours, I'm sitting in the ER in front of a pretty, brown-skinned triage nurse with a sleeping Jax curled up in my lap. Mama stayed in the waiting room.

"How long has he been asleep?" the nurse asks.

The question startles me. How long *has* he been asleep? "I'm . . . I'm not sure. I haven't been keeping track."

"Okay," she says. "I'm going to wake him up now, all right?"

I nod.

She rubs her knuckles over the center of Jax's chest a bit too hard for my liking, and he whimpers. "Jax, sweetheart?" she says. "I need you to wake up for me, okay?"

He groans and snuggles deeper into me.

She does the knuckle thing again, and he literally growls, but his eyes do open. "Attaboy," she says while pulling out the corded thermometer wand and sticking it inside the attached box to get a cover on it.

"Who are you?" Jax says.

"I'm Nurse Bolar, honey. We're gonna get you feeling better. I need you to open your mouth and lift your tongue for me."

Jax does as he's told and the nurse gets his temperature—it was 105° before we left the house; no clue what it is now.

As soon as she pulls the thing out of his mouth, his head drops back against my shoulder and he's asleep again.

"How long has he been lethargic like this?" She slips a kid-sized blood pressure cuff on his arm and clamps a little gray thing on his index finger.

"Few hours?" I say. "He fell asleep heavy in the car on the way over here."

"And what's the complaint besides the fever?"

"Well, he was with a babysitter until I got home at seven-thirty, and when I first saw him, he said he had a bit of a headache and his neck was sore. But I didn't check for a fever then."

"Hmm." She presses a button on the machine Jax is now attached to, and the cuff tightens on his arm. "Have you noticed any rashes?"

"No . . ."

"He been sick recently?"

"He had strep a month ago. . . ."

"Received treatment?"

I nod. "Amoxicillin."

"He on any medication now?"

"No."

"Allergic to any?"

"Not that I know of . . ."

"You or your mother been sick at all?"

This is starting to feel like an interrogation. "No."

"And he hasn't had any issues since the strep?"

"Not that I know of."

"Okay." She reads the monitor and scribbles a bunch of stuff down on a chart.

I decide to tell the rest. "He'd been sick a few times before the strep."

The nurse looks up at me.

"He wasn't seen by a doctor the other times, but the pediatrician who came to see him for the strep did say something about the possibility of needing his tonsils out."

She pulls the cuff and finger clamper thingy off. "And what were the sympto—"

Jax starts convulsing in my arms. His eyes roll back in his head, drool spills out of his mouth onto my collarbone, and my lap is suddenly very warm and very wet.

I'm frozen.

"I need help up here NOW!" the triage nurse says, leaping to her feet. And then Jax is swept away from me in a whirlwind of different-colored scrubs.

They move Jax to a room in the PICU. He and Mama are out cold, but I couldn't sleep if my life depended on it. All the doctors and nurses have left, but all I see when I close my eyes is the massive needle the doctor stuck in Jaxy's back to draw out some spinal fluid.

They think he has bacterial meningitis.

Mama and I were told we got here right on time, but there's a part of me that can't shake the guilt of not acting sooner. When he told me about his headache and sore neck, I chalked it up to a combo of staying up too late and sleeping on the couch in an awkward position. I probably would've investigated his complaints more thoroughly if I hadn't been in such a rush to call Zan.

If I'd been focused on the right things, I would've been a better sister.

It all seems so trivial looking back. Macklin and I talked for over an hour about *choices*, but all I can think about *now*, looking at the bags and tubes and monitors attached to my baby brother, is how much this is gonna cost and how we have no money to pay for it.

It brings all the fears I keep buried up to the surface:

Fear of being judged.

Pitied.

People finding out how little I have, and looking down on me, or making fun of me behind my back.

And even *that's* frivolous when held up against the scariest thing of all: something bad happening to Mama or Jax, and me not being able to do anything about it.

Having no choices.

Listening to the beep of the heart monitor and watching Mama twitch in her sleep, there are a couple of things I know for sure right now:

1. I'm not telling anyone about Jax. His sickness will require fourteen days of IV antibiotics, and after that, they'll remove his tonsils. Which means he'll be here at least three and a half weeks. Next week is spring break—Jess is going on a cruise with Ness's family, and Zan will be at some work conference with his dad—so no problems there. But

I'll have to find a way to keep it under wraps *this* week and once everyone returns.

The other thing I know? This situation could sink us. Mama already called out of both jobs today, and unless I skip school tomorrow to sleep (which there's no way she'll let me do), I'm going to have to call out as well. That's two hundred and ten dollars gone from the budget. And there will obviously be more days like this one in the coming weeks. One of the doctors mentioned some program that'll supposedly help with the medical costs—if we get in—but still: if we don't work, we can't pay the regular bills.

Which would lead to—

No. I can't go there right now. Time to focus.

I reach into my back pocket and pull out the semi-crumpled and slightly smeared yellow square of paper.

I gotta find Ethel Streeter and that ticket.

-31-

Bartholomew

t's another five (excruciating) days before I manage to get all my ducks in a row: Zan got on the Macklin Enterprises private jet this morning under the impression that when he gets back to town a week from now, we'll visit the address we got from Mr. Dover; Mama is at the hospital with Jax under the impression that I'm headed to work a "bonus shift" I lied to her about; and I am in Mama's truck currently headed to 754 East Rockland Place in Lawrenceville, Georgia.

And I didn't call first.

I feel pretty terrible about all of it. The tonic-clonic seizure (with urination) Jax had in my lap has played in my mind on a loop from the moment I wake up in the mornings until I collapse into bed at night. In the shower, on the bus, while restocking Coke products, during the brief encounters I had with Zan this past week, I thought about that seizure and how close I got to losing my brother.

I feel terrible for lying to Zan about why I was working all week and didn't "have the free time" to make the trip to Ethel's before he left town.

But that guilt is countered by mental images of the liquid antibiotics dripping from bags into Jax's veins.

It's countered by the new lines on Mama's face as she misses more and more work.

The accumulating bills, regular AND hospital—and who knows how much the latter will be.

The lack of insurance to cover *any* of it.

Needless to say, my head is all over the place during the drive. I've been going over the possibilities just as often as I think about all the other stuff. What I'm *hoping* is that Ethel will remember me, and when I mention the ticket, she'll instantly remember where she put it. She'll retrieve it, we'll check the numbers and see that it's the winner, and she'll be so happy, she'll offer me some kind of reward for working so hard to find her.

If she doesn't offer a reward, I'll flat-out pull her aside and tell her about my situation. I'll ask if maybe she can lend me some money I can put toward keeping us afloat and paying some of Jax's medical bills, and I'll spend however long it takes doing whatever she wants to work it off (indentured servitude, essentially). While in theory, it could take years to earn back the kind of money I'm thinking, I figure she's old and will die before that point (no offense). Hopefully, I'll be such a good friend to her by then, she'll leave whatever remains to me in her will like you sometimes hear about old people doing on the news. (Or is it in movies? Whatever, doesn't matter.)

These are the only two possible outcomes in my mind, and I'm clinging to them like my life—*our* life: mine and Mama's and Jax's—depends on it.

Because it does.

Any alternative—

I can't think about alternatives. Alternatives lead to despair. Despair leads to the very dark place that's been sneaking up on me in the middle of the night. It's that time when I'm dangling somewhere between asleep and awake, and the lack of a body in Jax's bed presses down on me so hard, I feel like I'm suffocating. I can't go to Mama because she's either at the hospital or working a night shift. And even if she weren't, every time she looks at me, her eyes are all sad. Like she's still disappointed I didn't check Jaxy's temperature sooner.

Probably could go to Jess, but she might go to Zan.

And I can't go to Zan even in a secondary way (even though we've talked, even briefly, every night he's been away). He *cannot* know about any of this.

So there are no alternatives.

I look at the empty passenger seat beside me and sigh. Remember all the times I've occupied that spot in the Jeep. One half of an investigative team.

And now here I am alone.

I'd be lying if I said I didn't wish Zan were here.

Looking back, it was nice not having to be the driver.

And then I'm pulling into the left driveway of a duplex.

I'm so focused on the contrast between the blue shutters and the rust-colored bricks, the noise of me instinctively yanking up the parking brake sounds like machine-gun fire. And I jump.

Gotta pull it together.

I get out. Shut the car door.

One foot in front of the other.

I'm on the walkway now. It's lined with brightly colored flowers just like I imagine an older woman's house would be.

Up the three stairs, and at the door.

I want to throw up.

There's the doorbell.

I can't get my arm to lift.

Okay. This is what I came here for. I can do this.

I take a huge breath and push the bell.

Like nine days pass in the span of a few seconds.

Dead bolt clicks.

Knob turns. . . .

And the door swings open to reveal a short, dark-brown-skinned man with a little Afro and hair shooting out of his ears.

I think my heart actually stops.

He draws back, then shakes his head like there's something loose inside it and blinks a few times. "You look like my niece." He pushes his glasses up on his nose and clasps his hands over his plaid-covered paunch. "Whatcha sellin'?" he says.

"Oh. Umm . . ." I look at his face. He seems younger than Ethel. Couldn't be her husband . . . At least I don't think.

"Now don't get all shy on me," he says. "I'll support ya if ya pitch it right. Go on now."

"Oh, um. I'm not selling anything, sir."

"Okay then . . ."

"I'm actually looking for an Ethel Streeter?"

When his eyes drop, I know it's all over.

While Zander and I were searching high and low, Ethel Streeter was dying of stage five chronic kidney disease. Her son Bartholomew was completely emotionless as he told me how his mother hid the disease from him until it was too late, and then wouldn't accept the kidney he offered her. They merged their assets just a couple weeks before she passed, and he's currently in the process of getting her name off all the deeds. Most of her stuff—which previously filled the house Zan and I tried to visit in Druid Hills—is sitting in a Public Storage unit awaiting the estate sale he has planned for "after the legal stuff is in order."

I decline the iced tea he offers me, and within ten minutes, I'm back in the truck.

Stopping. Going. Stopping again. Trees blur by. Nothing registers.

I'm just . . . here.

And then I'm at the Gas 'n' Go. Even though I requested off today.

To go see Ethel.

Who's *no longer with us*, as Bartholomew put it.

By some miracle, I manage to get out and go inside.

"Rico? I thought you weren't coming in," Mr. Z says when he sees me from his perch behind the counter.

"My plans . . . changed," I say. "Can I still work?"

"Of course you can, dear. Clock in at will."

"Thanks, Mr. Z."

"Oh! Before I forget: when you next speak to your friend Mr. Macklin, do tell him we receive high praise on the quilted with aloe vera!"

Ugh.

"Will do, sir!" Whether before or after I break the news about Ethel, though . . .

I can feel the dark place creeping up behind me. I'll fight it off for as long as I can, but with no hope to cling to now—

I sigh.

Jax is still in the hospital.

And so is Mama. Which means no work for her today.

The fate of my family wraps around me like a weighted blanket.

Gulp the tears and panic away. Six-hour shift to get through.

Breaking down is not an option.

Another Word from the Right Ticket

This isn't over, dear reader.

I am still here. I am still waiting.

I will *not* be snuffed away into oblivion as if I never existed. Permitted to *expire* with my glorious one-hundred-and-six-million-dollar face smashed up against some lowly business card in this appallingly stale-smelling billfold.

I haven't seen the light since my purchase, but I hear conversations and music and strange spoken narratives (*audiobooks*, I heard them called?), and *money* is a frequent topic of discussion. It seems you humans would do just about anything for it.

She. Should. Not. Give. Up.

I will haunt her dreams until she finds me.

I'M WORTH SO MUCH MORE THAN THIS!

-32-

The Breakdown

The phone rings, and I startle so intensely, I fall off the bed. Once my heart rate comes down from the-brink-of-death, I hit the light on the side of my watch and pick up the phone as the numbers force their way into my brain. 11:58 p.m.

"Hello?"

"Ms. Danger?"

"Umm . . ." I rub my eyes. "Which one?"

I hear some papers shuffle. "I have a Stacia on file?"

"Oh. She's not here."

More eye rubbing. It's starting to register that a phone call at almost midnight is odd. And kind of scary, current circumstances considered.

"She's working a night shift," I say. "Is there something I can help you with? I'm her daughter."

"Is there a Mr. Rico available?"

"No, there's no Mr.—" Wait . . . "I think you might be talking about me. I'm Rico."

Silence except for more shuffling. Then: "You're Rico Danger?"

"Yes . . ."

"How old are you?"

What the heck? "I'm seventeen. Why?"

"Hold, please."

There's a rubbing sound, and then I can hear muffled voices like the caller is covering the receiver with her hand.

Then: "You're the elder sister of Jaxon Daniel Danger?"

Awake now.

"Yes. Is something wrong?"

"Is there a way we can get in contact with your mother, sweetie?"

Oh, so I'm sweetie *now?* "Not very easily, ma'am. As I mentioned, she's at work." This is getting frustrating. "Is there something wrong with my brother?"

She sighs. "He had a rough day today," she says. "Ms. Danger was here for a few hours this afternoon, but she left when Jaxon fell asleep. He's been inconsolable since he woke up and couldn't find her."

I shake my head. *Why* does she never listen to me when I tell her how important it is to say goodbye to him?

I *should* be at the hospital, but Mama insisted I sleep at home: spring break's over. Gotta go to school tomorrow. "I'll be there as soon as I can," I say before I have a clue what I'm saying.

"I'm sure your brother would appreciate the visit. We'll tell him you're on the way." She hangs up.

And crap.

Crap crap crapper crappy *crappola.*

It's two minutes past midnight. Buses stopped running two hours ago. No cash to call a cab.

No cash to do anything.

No cash.

Rent.

Electricity.

Water.

Food.

Gas and maintenance for the truck.

Spinal tap.

Antibiotics.

Extended hospital stay.

Down, down, down. Sinking down, down, down.

It's too much. I can't do it. I can't do anything about any of this. It's hopeless. I'm trapped. There's no getting out—

Phone rings again.

"Hello?"

"Rico?"

Jax.

Can't breathe.

"Rico, are you there?"

I force myself to stare at his empty bed. "Yeah, Jaxy, I'm here. Are you okay?"

"The nurses said you're coming . . . are you really coming, Rico?"

Crying now. "Yes, I'm coming, Jaxy. It might be a little while before I get there, but I'm coming."

"How are you gonna get here, Rico?"

God, this is so unfair.

Don't sniffle.

"You don't worry about that, baby boy. I'll be there as soon as I can, okay?"

"Umm . . . can you maybe bring my iPad? I've watched all the movies they have here."

Smiling now. My sweet, sweet Jaxy-Boy. "Sure, bud. I'll bring it."

"Okay, I'll see you soon?"

"You will. Very soon."

"K, bye!"

"Bye, Jax."

He hangs up.

I call Jess.

No answer.

I call again.

Nothing.

Again.

Nope.

I set the phone down.

Stare at it.

I can't do it.

I can't call him.

Zan-the-Man.

Yes, he got home this morning and politely asked if he could take me to lunch (which was huge . . . Zan of old would've just popped up at my job).

(I said no.)

Yes, I told him I'm excited to see him.

And I am.

But not under these circumstances.

1. He'll feel betrayed; I know how much he digs
   Jax, and I kept this from him. Not to mention

I'll have to eventually admit I went looking for
Ethel without him.

2. I don't want him rescuing me. Not right
now.

3. The thought of owing *him* something on
top of everything else? Seriously can't even
stomach it.

I can't call him.
I can't.
I sigh and look at the phone.
"Are you really coming, Rico?"
Guess this isn't really about me anymore, is it?
Zan picks up on the first ring. "Rico?" He groans. "Every-
thing okay?"
I close my eyes. Take a deep breath. "Not really."
"Why? What's the matter?" He's wide-awake now. "Any-
thing I can do?"
The first tear burns my cheek going down. "Yeah," I say.
"I need you."

We ride to the hospital without speaking. No music. No
handholding. No contact whatsoever.
As a matter of fact, after the end of our brief phone call,
neither of us says a word until we get to the door of Jax's
room.
"Wait," Zan says, catching my wrist as I reach for the
push lever.
I stop. Look at him over my shoulder.
"I should've . . . ," he goes on. Eyes to the floor, then back

to me. "Is it okay if I come in?" He shakes his head. "I don't wanna intrude."

And now my heart is a bubbling puddle of muck on the floor.

I hug him. Just rise up to my tiptoes and wrap my arms around his neck.

"Uhh. Okay . . . ," he says.

(This makes me smile.)

Once I release him, I take his hand, then I push Jax's door open and pull Zan into the room with me.

You'd think I brought in *the* actual Santa Claus.

"Oh my God!" Jax says, looking from me to Zan and Zan to me. "Oh my God! You brought *Z-man*?"

Zan smiles, and Jax puts his face in his hands. "This is better than I could've dreamed!"

Zan laughs and ruffles Jax's hair. "I missed you too, little dude," he says. "You cool with me dropping by every once in a while?"

"Am I ever!"

I smile and pull Jax's iPad (from Zan) out of my bag and sit it on the rolly tray-table thing. Zan grabs a chair from across the room and sits it right beside Jax's bed.

"They treatin' you all right in here, my man?"

Jax's face falls. "I guess. I'm ready to go home," he says, "but it's gonna be another week and a half at least. Trying not to get *too* depressed about it."

Zan sneaks a glance at me—I've grabbed a blanket and retreated to the couch built into the windowed wall—then turns back to Jax. "Depressed, huh?"

"It's a real thing, you know? Kid depression. There's a mind doctor guy who comes in twice a week to make sure I'm not getting too sad."

I sit up straight. "Does Mama know about this?"

"Mm-hmm," he says. "She was here last time he came."

Bothers me a little that *I* didn't know. I'm not his mom obviously, but still.

Zan changes the subject. "So what other cool stuff have you learned in here?"

Jax launches into a series of animated explanations: spinal taps, how his IVs work, what strain of bacteria caused his meningitis, which nurse is the "hottest"—he gets some side-eye from me on this one. After a while I tune out and let them talk.

Then Zan's shaking me awake. "Sorry to bug you," he says. "He's out cold. Probably for the night."

I look over at Jax, then back at Zan. Can't help but smile—despite the cloud of secrets, lies, and unanswered questions hanging over us. "Thanks for coming, Zan."

For a few seconds he just stares at me in that way he does that makes me freakin' nutballs. Especially right now when desire and obligation are occupying the same physical space. Cuz, *man*, what I wouldn't do to just escape with him. "You wanna grab a bite to eat?" he says.

Clock: 2:27 a.m.

Brother: freaked the last time he woke up and the person who'd been here was gone. Mama will be here in four and a half hours, and Zan's probably right about Jax being out for a while, but I'm not sure I wanna risk it.

My hesitation is . . . obvious.

"We'll leave him a note with my cell number at the nurses' station in case he wakes up."

Mmmm . . .

He squats and takes my hands. Looks me in the eye. "You need a break, Rico. Hour, hour and a half."

I sigh.

And nod.

We don't make it to the Waffle House.

We don't even make it out of the parking lot.

As soon as we're both in the Jeep, Zan asks me how I'm doing, and I lose every iota of my shit.

Stuff just comes oozing out: how terrified I was when my brother almost died in my arms; how I feel like everything's my fault because I didn't investigate his symptoms; how tired I am from carrying the constant fear that this month, there won't be enough money; how I went to the Streeters' and had to leave all hope on their doorstep; how I feel like I'm falling into a black hole and there won't be any getting out of it.

Zan listens. I can tell he's got a million and one things going through his mind because he chews his lip and keeps looking down at his wallet. But he doesn't say a word—even when I get to the Ethel part—and I'm thankful. Just holds my hand and rubs circles on my palm. Drapes an arm across my shoulders and draws me in to him. The more I cry, the closer we get until I'm curled in his khaki'd lap like a toddler, sobbing into the neck of his perfectly pressed polo.

"Zan?"

"Yeah?"

He's rubbing my arm up and down. It feels really good. Calming. "Do you *ever* dress down?"

Silence.

I lift my head so I can see his face.

His jaw is clenched.

"Was that offensive?" I say.

He clears his throat. (Maybe it *was* offensive?) "The truth?"

Uhhh . . . "Yes?"

"I don't want you to think I'm a slob."

Hold on. "Are you saying you dress the way you do to impress *me*?"

"Potentially?"

I laugh. So hard I start crying again, but from laughter.

"Stop laughing at me."

I laugh more. "Macklin, you could show up in a moth-eaten T-shirt and holey long johns and I'd be impressed just because you came." I snuggle into him again.

"Oh."

We settle into a calm silence. He was right about me needing a break, and I'm glad he's here to share it with me.

"Hey, Rico?"

"Mm-hmm?"

"Don't take this the wrong way, but you should probably get off my lap now."

"Huh?" My head snaps up.

He's *bright* red.

Oh.

I scramble off and over the gearstick back to the passenger seat. Not because I'm like *scared* of it, just because . . . Ugh, this is so embarrassing. "I should probably get back upstairs." ***Nervously tucks hair behind ears*** "You should head home and get some rest. School tomorrow."

"I'm going to get you some food," he says. "Then I'll go home."

"You don't have to do that."

"Trust me. I do. Lita was in this hospital for a hip replacement last year. Eat the food here, and *you* might wind up connected to tubes and a drip bag."

I laugh again. So thankful for him right now. Wish I could work up the courage to tell him. . . .

"Guessing I won't see you at school?" he says.

"Oh, I'll be there. I'm off work tomorrow, so I'll be able to go home and crash afterward."

"Will Jax be alone here? Should I come by and see him after I take you home to rest?"

"Zan." You'd think I'd be used to this from him by now, and yet.

"Sorry, sorry. *May* I take you to and from school tomorrow, and then come hang out with Jax so he won't be alone? Please?"

This guy.

Who isn't my boyfriend.

(Nope, not over that.) "I'd appreciate the rides, but our mom will be here until six. And then I'll come back. So he won't be alone."

He nods. "Well, I meant what I said to Jax about visiting. Just let me know when's a good time. You can even give

298

your mom my number and tell her to call me if she needs a break."

Fat chance, but super sweet of him to offer.

"Hey, Zan?"

"Yeah?"

"Can I tell you something?"

"Of course."

We lock eyes, and I count to three.

"Thank you."

-33-

Hear Ye, Hear Ye

School. Work. Hospital. Home.
　　　Hospital. School. Home. Work.
Hospital home. School work.
And on.
And on.
And on.

After Zan offers about a dozen times, and Jax literally *begs* her, Mama decides to work Zan into the "Bedside Buddy" rotation. I even catch her smiling when he shows up a couple of times.

Zan pulls Ness, and sometimes Jess, into the mix by arranging rides for me so I won't have to take the bus and can "maximize my time."

Two days pass.
Three.
Four.
A week.

I come, Mama goes. Mama comes, Zan goes. Zan comes, I go (after some maybe overextended embracing).

A rhythm is established, and all is well. . . .

Until the day before Jax is scheduled to get his tonsils out.

It's a Saturday. Jess picks me up from work right at one p.m. She's acting weird, but it's Jess. She's probably high on orgasms or something. (Is that a thing?) She blasts Cardi B on the way to the hospital—lip-synching and gyrating in her seat the whole time—and when I get out, she winks and blows me a kiss.

Definitely the orgasms. (Do she and Ness ever have *conversations*?)

But then Mama's more cheery than usual too. She and Jax are playing Uno when I get upstairs, but she positively beams when she sees me.

I stop just inside the door. Baffled.

"Oh look, my darling *Rico* is here!" she twitters like a drunken songbird.

"Umm . . . hi?"

Jax snorts.

"You're right on time!" She turns to Jax. "Uno and out, kid."

"Aww, man, not *again*!"

"Better luck next time." And she ruffles his hair before rising to grab her bag.

This would all be well and good if not for the big kiss she gives me on her way out the door. My mama is not a kisser. Yes, provided everything goes according to plan with the tonsillectomy, Jax will be discharged two days from now. But there's still the issue of looming unpayable bills, including an impending one from this hospital.

Hardly anything to be cheerful about.

"See ya laaaater," she says, and she does a little shimmy as she leaves the room.

I don't even—

Whatever. Never mind.

I sit. Pull out the book I've been reading.

Open.

"You should probably get a nap," Jax says from across the room.

"Why would I need a nap?"

"Z-man will be here before you know it."

Quick watch check. "*Z-man* isn't scheduled to arrive for six hours and forty-three minutes."

Jax shrugs. "Okay."

Again: What. Ev. Er.

I open my book. I will read and forget where I am: classic escapism.

Except then I *do* fall asleep. Zan strokes my cheek with the back of his index finger to wake me up the way he always does when I fall asleep here. (Have I been out *that* long?)

I reach up, grab said finger, and kiss it the way I've been doing lately.

"So is this what goes on in front of the kid when I'm not here?"

I sit up straight, eyes wide.

> **Zan:** blushing. (As usual.)
> **Mama:** garment bag draped over an arm,
>   eyebrow raised.
> **Ness:** trying not to laugh.
> **Jess:** looking like she's about to explode
>   from excitement.

302

When I sit up, Jess starts clapping and squealing. *That's* when I notice her twirly swirly hairdo.

"What the fu—"

"*RICO!*" Mama turns redder than I knew possible for her. What. Is. Happening?

"Come, come." Jess comes over and grabs my hand. "Lots to do, little time. We need to be fashionably late, of course, but if we get *too* fashionable, no one will see us come in—"

"*What?*"

Jess looks at Zan—who's got this ultra-smug grin on his face—and then back at me. "You really don't know why we're here?"

"Can't say I got the memo."

"Okay . . ." She looks at Zan again. Panicked? "But you know what's *happening* tonight, so you can surely put two and two together."

I just stare.

"Pay up, Barlow." Zan sticks out his hand.

"No way." Jess shakes her head. "There is absolutely no way she doesn't know."

"I told you she wouldn't have a clue. Now pay up."

Jess's brows furrow. "I mean, I know you're a little anti-social. . . ." She cocks her head. "You *really* don't know?"

"I know this is getting annoying," I say.

That makes Jax laugh. With all the brouhaha, I forgot we're in his hospital room.

"You *will* pay me," Zan says.

"Whatever." She crosses her arms and glares at me like *I* did something wrong.

So confused.

Zan goes on: "Mr. Montgomery, if you will, please?"

Finesse reaches into his back pocket and pulls out a rolled-up paper—actually, based on the color of the thing, *parchment* is probably more accurate—tied with a red ribbon.

From his front pocket, he produces a kazoo. Of *all* things. *Dun dunnadun dun-dun-dun DUUUUUUN!* he toots. Ribbon comes off. Parchment unrolled. "Lady Rico Reneé Danger, art thou present?"

Uhh . . . "Yes?"

"Superb." He clears his throat and lifts the parchment to read. "Hear ye, hear ye: the illustrious and dashingly handsome Sir Alexander Gustavo of House Macklin hath traveled far, wide, high, and deep, over mountains, through valleys, and into and out of the churning belly of a volcano, for the sake of presenting thou, O beautiful and brazen Lady Rico Reneé of House Danger, with a most heartfelt and positively irresistible proposition. Hast thou the ear to hear?" Parchment lowered.

What did he even just say? "I hast?" Wait . . . "Hath? Hasteth?" Zan buries his mouth in his shoulder the way he does when he's trying not to laugh at me. "Whatever. I have an ear. Two actually. Now *what* is going on?" And why am I so nervous?

"Sir Zanny Zan, if you will, please?"

Zan steps forward and takes a knee in front of me. Jess squeals again, bouncing on her toes. Mama rolls her eyes but is totally smiling too. "You kids are ridiculous."

"Lady Danger," Zan begins, "for the duration of the quarter-year previous, thou hast been unto me the likeness of the brightest sun on the clearest day."

"Oh brother," from Jax.

Mama cuts him a look that could wither all the foliage in the room.

Zan goes on. "As I was saying, there is none more pure of heart, mind, nor beauty in all this vast and treacherous wilderness known as life."

"Oh my God, Zan."

He smiles. "Your right hand, please."

I raise an eyebrow and warily extend my hand. When Zan takes it, Jess whispers, "I still can't believe she doesn't know."

Ness snorts.

Zan holds my hand in both of his and smiles up at me, eyes sparkling like pale emeralds. "Rico Danger," he says, "wouldst thou grant me the honor of permission to escort thee to the promenade?"

"Escort me to the *what*?"

Jess: "Blessed mother of God, Rico. He's asking you to prom."

"Prom?"

"*Yes!* As in our *senior prom*. The thing *everyone*'s been talking about for the past two months."

"You're asking me to *prom*?"

"Yep," Zan says.

"And it starts in like five hours, so we should maybe get a move on—"

"Jess, *chill*," from Ness.

"Sorry."

He's asking me to prom?

"I knew you wouldn't be into it, which is why I didn't ask you a month ago," says Zan. "But let's be honest: it's been a rough few weeks, and we *both* need to have some fun."

I bite my lip and look down at my hands.

"He's right," Mama says. "You're not allowed to be *here* tonight, and Señora Alvarez is house-sitting to make sure you don't go home. Prom's as good a place to be as any. I've got your dress right here."

"And it's *amazing*," Jess says. "I helped pick it out."

"From Belle's Basics?"

"Nope. Nordstrom." And she smiles like she just shared the best news ever.

Belle's Basics *might've* meant free. Nordstrom, though?

I look at the garment bag, and then up into Mama's eyes. A terrifying storm cloud forms overhead—or so it feels. "Mama, may I have a word with you outside?"

She nods.

We go.

I'm boiling now. (Which sucks because I'm supposed to be ecstatic.) "You have to take that dress back," I say. "We can't afford it. Especially right now."

"Don't do this, Rico."

"Do what? Actually *consider* how much debt we're about to be in? What about work?"

"That's none of your concern."

"But, Ma—"

"I *get* it, Rico. Money is tight." There are tears in her eyes, and I'm floored. "Life is hard and endlessly unfair, but it's

306

also *short*, and you need this, honey." She holds out the bag. "Please. This one time, let me give it to you."

I hate her. And this. I hate being in this position. I hate that she put me here just like she put me in this stupid, over-priced town where I can't "get a good education" because I'm always *working*. I hate that I didn't realize my own prom was tonight. And I hate that if I go, I'm basically saying it's *fine* that she spent money on this stupid dress instead of putting it toward bills. Rent. Gas. Something linked to keeping us all alive.

I hate that I'm seventeen years old and on the brink of tears because for the first time in my life, I have actual friends, and two of them are about to move away.

I hate that I still feel inadequate and unworthy anytime I look at Zan.

I hate that I even let him get close to me.

I hate that I tried to find that stupid ticket. Maybe if I hadn't, none of this other stuff would've ever happened: Jax wouldn't be in the hospital because he wouldn't be sick. Mama wouldn't be standing here offering me a dress we can't afford because nobody would've asked me to prom. I'd still be invisible, the way I *liked* it.

"Please, Rico." She's crying in earnest.

(*"But did you really like it, Rico?"* The dress calls to me from within the bag. I wonder what it looks like. . . .)

I stare into the face of a woman who really is trying her best. All things considered, she probably needs this as much as—if not more than—I do.

Because, fine: I do need it.

I sigh. "Okay."

"Okay?"

"Okay."

She hands me the dress and pulls me into a hug. "I love you so much, honey."

"I love you too."

Blah, too much emotion.

We go back in.

"So how 'bout it, Rico?" from Ness. "You rollin' with us, or chillin' in the hospital lobby tonight?"

I look around the room at the expectant faces of the people who obviously care for me way more than I give them credit for.

And I burst into tears.

A Word from the Dress

They dance.
   And dance.
And dance, dance, dance.

Even when Rico's legs strain against my satin lining, burning like she dipped them in Hades's river of fire, they dance.

And dance.

And dance.

I'm the murky blurple of a dark night and bedazzled all over with tiny Swarovski crystals. So with the low lights and the dark walls and the little strings of light twinkling as they dangle from the ceiling, Rico feels like she's twirling within a night sky.

And then there's Alexander Macklin. His arm around Rico's waist. His hands on her hips (and sometimes her thighs). His chest and stomach against her back and shoulders.

Those arms tighten around her and me from behind, and he leans down to set his chin on her bare shoulder.

She slides a hand around the back of his neck up into his hair, and continues moving her hips.

"I need you to be my girlfriend," he says right into her ear.

"What?" she counters. My lining is damp now because she's instantly sweating way more.

"Rico Danger, will you please be my girlfriend?"

Rico stops. Removes his arms. Turns around. Looks over his face. "Why now?"

"Huh?"

She wipes her damp palms against me at the outer thighs (I crinkle in a cringe). He wouldn't know it, but her heart is racing. "The girlfriend thing."

People are staring now.

"Oh. I mean . . . If you don't want to—"

"That's not it at all. I just . . . I dunno." Questions churn in her belly. *Is this what I* want? *What would it even mean?* "I wanna know why."

And then he smiles. "You've changed everything for me, Rico."

They stare into each other's eyes.

"Does it ruin the moment if I say I need to think about it?" she says.

And he laughs. Loud. It ripples over me, and the tiny hairs on Rico's neck and arms rise to attention.

He closes the space between him and us. Slips those arms back around our waists. "Take however long you need, m'lady."

"You are such a cornball."

And maybe it's the music. Maybe it's the crystal-strung

ceiling and the scent of perfume-masked sweat in the air.
Maybe it's me . . . maybe it's his tux. Maybe it's the dancing.

He takes her face in his hands.

Looks at her eyes.

Her nose.

Her lips.

"Rico, may I kiss you, please?" he says.

Rico nods.

Their mouths meet and the world explodes.

-34-

Breaking and Exiting

Zan has no idea where we're going, and I can tell he's nervous.

Nervous, I'm sure, because I'm lit as a live wire.

He keeps sneaking peeks at me out of the corner of his eye when he thinks I'm not looking. I turn and smile at him when he does it again.

"Something I can help you with, sir?"

He narrows his eyes. "Something's off with you."

Crap. He noticed.

"You sure everything's okay?"

"Yup!" I lie.

There's a pause. Heavy. "You're really not gonna tell me where we're headed?" he says.

"Nope. Hang a left at the next light."

He sighs. The knuckles of his left hand go white as he clenches the steering wheel.

"So how's the J-Dude? Goes back to school tomorrow, right?"

I nod. "He's anxious since he missed so much. Completed a lot of makeup work, but it's hard for him, you know?"

"I can only imagine. Anything I can do to help?"

"You've done plenty, Zan. We're all really grateful."

"Okay!"

"Take the next right."

"Aye, aye."

My eyes latch on to the clock on Zan's dash: 3:28.

I swear the universe hates me. I've seen that number everywhere the past week. License plates, billboards, the HOW AM I DRIVING? sticker from the back of a Home Depot semi . . . Everywhere, reminders of what I snuck and looked at while Mama's back was turned seven days ago.

$328,002.76. That's the cost of a monthlong hospital stay for an uninsured kid with meningitis who needed a tonsillectomy. *328* has become a massive, angry black elephant with poison-tipped tusks, glaring at me everywhere I turn. (Perhaps this is retribution?)

I gulp. Look back out my window. "Left at the stop sign, and then right into the first parking lot you see."

"You sure do know these directions well, Danger." Laced with suspicion.

"I *might* have scouted the place a few times." The bus stop catches my eye as we pass. "It's right here."

Zan slows and turns into the driveway. Clears his throat. "Public Storage?"

"Yep!" I wiggle my eyebrows at him and point to the gate that'll take us to the outdoor units. "Code is 5613."

"Okay . . ." He punches it in and the gate opens.

"When you get to the end of the aisle, take a left."

He does. My heart beats faster as we breeze along the rows of garagelike orange doors. "Third aisle on the left."

"Hate to break it to you, but that's a tight squeeze for the Tonka. I drive down there, we won't be able to open the doors," he says.

"Okay. Park here then. We'll walk the rest of the way."

Jeep stopped, parking brake up, engine cut, seat belts off.

I take his hand once we're out and pull him into the row. We walk for thirty seconds or so. "Here," I say, rotating to face an orange door on the left. It's no wider than the front door of our apartment. "Unit six-oh-three."

"Awesome."

Standing here with him makes me feel electrified. I look up. Surely beaming. "This is Ethel Streeter's storage unit," I say.

"Ah. Cool, I guess?"

"Remember how I told you her son said all her stuff had been put in storage? Well, I called last week to ask about the estate sale, and he said it'd be at least another month before it happens."

His caterpillars creep together. "Okay . . ."

"I think it's some kinda sign that her unit's at *this* location."

"How do you even know that?"

"I made up a lie about needing to store something, and he 'recommended' this place and said her stuff was here. My mom's got a unit here too with some of my granddad's stuff in it. Took a bit of digging to get the right unit number for Ethel, but here we are, right? The final barrier!"

Why does he look so baffled?

"All her stuff is still inside, Zan," I say. "Jackets, pants, purses—"

"You can't possibly know that, Rico."

"But it makes sense, doesn't it? Her son said *all* her stuff was being held in storage." I face the door again. "The ticket could totally be in there, you know? All that separates us is this silly orange thing!"

His eyebrows tug even lower. Which I didn't think was possible. "Okay, hold on," he says, taking a deep breath like he's trying to stay patient or something.

It sets me on edge.

"For one," he says, "pretty sure going into someone's storage unit without their permission is trespassing. For two: how would you even get in there? It's locked." He gestures toward the heavy padlock with his chin.

I smile and remove a hairpin from my bun. "I'm pretty sure I can pick it."

He pulls his hand from mine then. Steps back. "I don't think that's a good idea, Rico."

"What?"

"I mean, you said the estate sale is in a month, right? We can be the first customers."

I shake my head. Primarily to express disagreement, but also to keep from crying. "It's too risky," I say. "If he pushes the sale back, we could miss the cutoff for claiming the prize."

He sighs and drops his head. "Rico, we can't break into a stranger's storage unit—"

"She's hardly a *stranger*," I say. "We searched for this woman for months."

"So now we have a right to go through her stuff? It's breaking and entering."

What's his *problem*? "Why are you making it sound so criminal? We're looking for a *lottery ticket*, not committing burglary."

He sighs then. "God, I thought we were done with this." Runs his hands down his face.

Exasperated. And patronizing.

I know the look *and* the feeling: it's the same one I used to give Jax when he'd get pushy about us buying something at the store he knew we couldn't afford (Chocolate Chip Cookie Dough Ben & Jerry's, anyone?).

Something inside me snaps. "You don't get it, do you?"

He doesn't respond.

"God, what am I saying? Of *course* you don't get it."

"What are you talking about, Rico?"

"*Need*, Zan. You've never lacked anything, so you don't know what it's like to be in NEED."

His lips pinch shut.

"Is it that hard to understand?" I say. "My family NEEDS that money."

"Okay, bu—"

"Jax's hospital bill was over three hundred thousand dollars. Yeah, there are programs to help, but my mom will still have to file for bankruptcy. We were *struggling* to make ends meet before, so there's no way we can work out of a hole that deep."

"What about your insurance?"

"We don't *have* insurance, Zan."

All the color drains from his face.

"I get that this whole thing's been a game for you, but for *me*, it's the difference between having somewhere to live and being homeless."

"That's a little extreme, Rico."

I sigh. "It's not, Macklin. We're behind on the rent. Totally missed it last month with Jax in the hospital, four days *late* and going to miss it this month too. Mama missed March too." She was short *because she took us on that stupid trip*. "We got an eviction notice two days ago. My mom lost one of her jobs because she was spending so much time at the hospital."

Also lost fifteen pounds, some of her hair, and a decent portion of her will to go on.

When he finally opens his mouth to speak again, I'm expecting him to ask why I didn't tell him. Righteous indignation of Alexander Gustavo Macklin, prince rescuer of the damsel in distress.

But he doesn't. "Is that what this has been about since the beginning?"

"What?"

"Helping your mom." He looks at me. "You pulled me into this under the guise of doing a good deed for an old lady. Has it always been about getting what *you* need?"

Not sure what to say to that. I guess in the beginning, it was about Ethel, but if I said I never thought about what could be in it for me, I'd be lying. How *would* I have felt if we'd found her, and she'd thanked us, collected her winnings, and ridden off into the sunset without looking back?

Does it even matter now?

"A lot has changed since we started this. Whatever my

317

initial motives were or weren't, Ethel Streeter is gone. That ticket can't do her any good now, but it *can* help me and my family. I've lived in a shelter before, and I'm *not* going back. If you don't want to help, you're free to go." I roll the hairpin between my fingertips and stare down at the lock.

In my peripheral, I see him reach into his pocket, and I can't resist looking to see what he's taking out.

His wallet.

Unbelievable.

"I'm not taking your money, Zan. That's not how this works. Don't insult me by offering."

He ignores me, opens it, and reaches into the slot that holds cash.

I look away. "I'm serious. I swear if you offer, I'll never speak to you again."

What he sticks into my line of sight, though, isn't green. It's white.

It's got watermarks of peaches, and a peach-colored strip running down its left side. There are words and numbers—slightly faded—printed on it in black ink.

Six numbers to be exact.

17
06
46
01
29
07

Same ones I memorized months ago.

I can't move.

"Take it," he says.

There is absolutely no way.

"Zan, why do you have that?"

"I'm really asking myself the same question."

Smartass.

"How did you get it?"

He doesn't answer so I look up. (Old habits die hard.)

"I bought it," he says.

He's still holding it out, so I zoom in on it again. "I don't understand."

"As I mentioned when we were house-hunting, I turned eighteen on Christmas Eve. I'm actually surprised you didn't pick up on it then. That I could have it."

No words.

"I wanted to commemorate my birthday by buying something I couldn't have gotten the day before. Couldn't bring myself to purchase cigarettes or get a tattoo. So I bought a lottery ticket."

No. Words.

"Mr. Z sold it to me while you were hiding in the bathroom. Honestly forgot about the thing until that day you pulled me aside in the cafeteria. I went home and checked the numbers before I met you at the park."

Can't breathe now.

"Are you gonna take it?"

"You've had it *this whole time*?"

He sighs. Runs a hand through his hair. "Yeah. I have."

Stay calm, Rico. "What were you gonna do if we found Ethel Streeter?"

"I was gonna give it to her," he says. "If she was really in need and seemed like she could handle it—"

"*Excuse* me?"

There's that confused face again. "You're excused?"

ASS. HOLE. "Who the hell do you think you are?"

"Huh?"

"If she 'seemed like she could handle it'? What gives you the right to decide what somebody else can handle?"

"Last I checked, I'm the rightful owner of this ticket," he says. "Pretty sure I can do whatever the hell I want with it."

I look him in the eye. "You lied to me."

"What?"

"You lied," I say. "I asked what you'd do if you had it, and you said you'd throw it away. You lied."

He doesn't respond, but his jaw flexes and his eyes narrow. . . .

"As a matter of fact, why do you still have it, Zan? We've known Ethel's dead for weeks. Why didn't you 'throw it away' as soon as we found out?"

His bottom lip disappears between his teeth. Which makes me that much more furious.

"You weren't even gonna tell me, were you? Were you planning to just hold on to it as a hundred-and-six-million-dollar keepsake? Maybe use it as a bookmark to remind yourself of the luck you have but don't need? Would you frame it eventually? Hang it in that CEO's office you'll eventually occup—"

"Did it occur to you that *I* could use this money?"

320

And there it is. My suspicions made real. "Anyone could 'use' the money, Zan."

"That's not what I mean, and you know it. I'll admit it: no. I *don't* know what it's like to be poor or to 'lack' what I need, as you put it. But I *do* know what it's like to not have choices. To have someone else decide the course of your whole life."

I'm shaking my head. "That's not true, Zan."

"What do you mean, it's 'not true'? I don't see anyone telling *you* that you have to take over the family business."

"You can say no."

"What?"

"NO, Zan. The word NO. You can say it. You can go to college. Get a *regular* job like the rest of us. No one's *making* you stay with your parents' company. No one's *making* you 'climb the ranks' until you can take it over. YOU are making those decisions. If *anybody on earth* has 'choices,' it's YOU."

He doesn't respond.

"That's the problem with you rich people. You think the way you live is *normal*. Like, great, you worked at Daddy's company and made enough money to buy yourself a nice car, but you have no *idea* what it's like to have to work to keep a roof over your head or clothes on your back or food in your stomach. My family is on the brink of losing *all* of those things, and *this whole time*, you've had that ticket. Were you gonna cash it in behind my back? Get yourself some *choices*? Some financial freedom? A way off a path you don't wanna take, but are anyway because you're too used to your lavish life to *really* start from the bottom?"

"Gimme a break, Rico. It's not exactly like you were honest this whole time. You were hiding stuff too. What were *you* gonna do if we found Ethel? *Steal* the ticket from her like you're about to break into her storage unit?"

It takes everything in me not to punch him in the face. I turn around and start walking in the opposite direction from where we parked.

"Where are you going?" he calls out after me.

"I'm going home. Well . . . what's 'home' for now. Don't follow me."

"Rico, wait. I didn't mean that stuff, I was ju—"

"Don't even worry about it, Zan," I call over my shoulder. "Not like you would've before!"

I hate him.

I hate him I hate him I hate him. I hate his stupid cologne and fancy clothes and ridiculous car and absurdly large house. All his money and privilege and *stuff.*

"At least take the ticket," he shouts. "We both know you need it—"

"Don't need it from you."

"You're gonna get kicked out of your place—"

"None of your concern, Zan!"

"I'll give it to your mom, then."

"Yeah, she certainly 'can't handle it.' Throw it away like you said you would."

"You're really gonna let your family wind up on the street over this?"

That son-of-a-bitch. What was I *thinking* getting involved with him? "Enjoy your winnings, mighty millionaire! Maybe they'll give *you* a TV show too!"

322

I exit the pedestrian gate and walk to the bus stop. Getting out of the storage area requires the same code as getting in, and since I doubt he was paying attention when I gave it to him, I should be safe until the bus comes—

But then he pulls up.

Knowing him, I expect some version of *This is all very silly and not worth the destruction of our relationship; please get in the car so I can drive you home.*

But that's not what he says at all.

"You know what your problem is, Danger? You're too proud. Everything you need—everything you were *searching* for—was right in front of you. All you had to do was take it."

I can't even blink, let alone speak.

"Just wait," he says, rubbing the organic pink Himalayan sea salt from his fancy-ass dining room table into the wound. "It's gonna bite you in the ass." The window rolls up, and he speeds off and out of sight.

I sit. Stare at the lines in the road. His words land on my skin and seep in. As the truth of them fills me, I break.

At least he's not around to see it.

A Word from Alexander Gustavo Macklin

wanted to tell her. I really did.

But the more time went by, the more I liked her, and the more I realized that if I told her, she'd be pissed at me for keeping it from her for so long.

Did I ever think about just cashing it in? Of course. Numerous times. But I knew the search would be over then, and I didn't know how to like . . . keep her. As awful as she'd say that sounds.

She's so different from other girls, Rico is. At no point did it seem like she actually *wanted* anything from me. Which was confusing. Because while I thought that's what I was looking for—a girl who wasn't *after* anything—it was also frustrating. A girl who doesn't want or need anything is a girl who can walk away.

It's what I both love(d) and hate(d) about her. Her independence. Every time I brushed up against it, I was reminded of my *de*pendence. Because everything she said was true. My options *are* endless, even without Dad's money. I've just been scared to face them.

Which means Rico Danger and I have something in

common. Because no matter what she says or what kind of *responsibility* she tries to hide behind, she also has more options than she wants to admit and is afraid to step out too.

She also has no idea what she wants. We're two peas in a snuggly little pod, her and me.

At least we were. . . .

Anyway, guess it's time to *make* some of those *choices* she and I talked about.

First up: what to do with this ticket.

Happy Friggin' Birthday (Again)

graduate from high school.

School, work, home becomes *work, work, home* because I get a second job at Belle's Basics.

Ness and Jess move to Athens a week and a half before my birthday, but I don't go to their farewell party because I've successfully avoided *Zan-the-Man* for a month and eleven days. The happy lovebirds stop by the Gas 'n' Go on their way out, thankfully. I keep my composure, but I'm sad to see them go.

I take over the payments for a larger storage unit, and Mama manages to get everything moved before apartment management can toss it all on the street. We don't wind up in a shelter, thanks to Señora Alvarez, who insists that we move in with her. (Mama agreed.)

Time rolls.

I call out of both jobs on the lotto ticket redemption deadline day and spend the entire thing curled up in bed, mulling over stuff I usually avoid thinking about. As I look around the bedroom I share with Mama and Jax, there's a part of me that regrets not taking the ticket from Zan.

Where would we be now if I had? Certainly not living on the charity of a neighbor, who knows how many tens (hundreds?) of thousands of dollars in debt. Probably in a nice new house, not too big. Not too small. Nice backyard. Maybe a swing set for Jax. Maybe a pool if we'd splurged.

Things that'll never be.

On my eighteenth birthday, I have to be at the Gas 'n' Go at six in the morning, and when I get off, I go straight to Belle's Basics. Fourteen-hour workday. I maybe lied to Mama about what time I had to be in so she and Jax wouldn't wake up early to make me breakfast.

Goal is to forget it's my birthday at all.

And it's working for the most part. A few hours into my shift, I've restocked the cooler and aligned all the labels on the cold beverages; I've rearranged the candy bar section so that the Mars products are on the left and the Hershey on the right; I've shifted the chips in the chip endcap around so they make a rainbow from top to bottom; I've moved the chewing gum so the center six read, 5 EXTRA ECLIPSE ORBIT JUICY FRUIT TRIDENT.

I'm in the middle of cleaning the bathrooms (though I refuse to refill the Macklin toilet paper and *moist towelette* dispensers) when there's a knock on the door and Mr. Zoughbi sticks his head in.

"Rico Danger."

But why does he look mad? "Hi, Mr. Z."

"I am very upset with you, young lady."

Uhhh . . . "Come again, sir?"

"Why did you not tell me today is your birthday?"

Oh.

"And you are here cleaning toilets? No, no. This will not do." He shakes his finger at me.

"Sorry, sir." (What else can I say?)

"You come out this instant," he says. "There is a visitor for you, and you must leave at once."

A visitor? Couldn't be Zan . . . Mr. Z would've definitely said his name.

Maybe it's Mama? I don't think Mr. Z knows what she looks like, so it could totally be her. I anticipated getting reamed out this evening, but if she's here to see me now, she's definitely late to work. Which means she'll be *double* pissed.

I'd really rather scrub the toilet.

"You know, I'm almost finished in—"

"Out! This instant! You are taking the day off! With pay!"

I sigh and drop the scrub brush in the bucket. Peel off my rubber gloves and hang my head as I exit the bathroom. This is going to be tortur—

"Ricoooooo!"

My head lifts. "Mr. Dover?"

"In the flesh! Happy birthday, honey!" He presses something into my palm and closes my fingers around it.

I force a smile. "Thanks—"

Wait . . .

"How'd you know it's my birthday?"

His whole face lights up. "We got a lot to talk about, kid. Your wonderful boss says you're free to go, right? Care to join me for breakfast?"

What the hell? "Umm . . . sure?"

"Flying Biscuit okay?"

I stare at the green pocket square in his suit jacket. "I guess . . ."

"Great! Grab your stuff and let's roll. I'll meet you outside."

"Okay."

"Blue Mercedes!" The door chimes as he walks out.

For a minute I just stand there. Trying to . . . well, I don't know. I go to untie my apron, and the thing in my hand crinkles.

I open my palm to see what it is.

And I smile for the first time all morning.

Of course.

It's a fifty-dollar bill.

During the seven-minute drive over, Mr. Dover won't stop grinning. It freaks me out a little.

Once we're inside and seated, he says, "Order whatever you like, but I suggest the shrimp and grits. They're to die for." Like us being at breakfast together is the most natural thing on earth.

What is happening?

I've never been *inside* this restaurant before, and the server appears before I get a chance to look at the other food options, so I take his advice. As she takes my menu and walks away, Mr. Dover sips his coffee. I can't help but watch his every move.

"So," he says, setting the cup down. "Did you catch me on television the other night?"

"You were on television?"

"You mean you missed it? Awww, come on, Rico! A guy only gets one TV debut!"

"Sorry."

He laughs.

"Makes sense, though. If you'd seen me on TV, you'd probably guess why we're sitting here."

"I would?"

"Mm-hmm."

We lapse into silence. Another sip of coffee.

"Soooo . . . are you gonna tell me?" I ask.

He laughs. "I like you, kid. Straight to business. I can appreciate that."

"Thanks, I guess?"

He opens his briefcase and pulls out a small stack of papers.

"So here's the deal," he says. "If you hadn't missed my TV debut, you would've seen me on the news holding a giant check for one hundred and six million buckaroos."

I stop breathing.

"A little over a month ago, someone came to my office with that lost lotto ticket you were looking for. Long story short, said person created a pair of trusts and donated the ticket to fund them," he continues.

"The grantor has asked to remain anonymous, but Dover Financial was appointed trustee, and you, Rico Danger, were named one of the beneficiaries. In layman's terms, that means I manage the trust, but the money gets paid to you."

Still not breathing. Can't.

"According to the terms, at no point during the next thirty years will you have any control over your flow of income. The deed specifies that the Georgia Lottery will pay taxed and annuitized funds directly to the trust, and those monies will be distributed as follows: a fixed amount will be paid into an account of your choosing for immediate access on the first of each month. A portion has been allotted to cover outstanding medical debt acquired by a Jaxon Daniel Danger, and the rest has been split three ways: there's a 529 college savings plan with this same Jaxon Daniel Danger listed as beneficiary, a second 529 with *you*, Rico Reneé Danger, listed as beneficiary, and a high-interest savings account that you'll have access to on your forty-eighth birthday."

Cannot. Breathe.

"The 529s can be used solely to cover college or university tuition costs. Use of the monthly funds will be at your discretion, but as the assigned advisor for the trust itself, I am available to discuss any options you'd be interested in exploring: investments, charitable giving, major purchases, I'm your guy." He winks.

Do I pass out now?

"Should you choose to decline the monthly payments entirely, those monies will be shifted into the savings account," he says. "Was all of that clear?"

"Umm . . . sort of?"

He chuckles. "What part didn't you understand?"

Any of it? "So the medical bills—"

"Covered."

"And taxes . . . ?"

"Taken care of. All I need is a signature and an account number for the immediate-access payments."

He flips to a signature page and lays a pen beside it. "Please read through the documentation before you sign."

I look at the papers.

Pick them up and try to read them.

They blur out of focus.

Eyes shift to the pen.

His face.

I can't take this money.

The papers.

From the sound of it, though, I also can't *not* take this money.

His face.

I *have* to take this money.

The pen.

I didn't *earn* this money.

The papers.

We *really* need this money.

How much is it even gonna *be* per month? And what do I do with it for real? Give it to Mama? Put an apartment in *my* name? I am eighteen now. . . .

Medical bills were taken care of, sounds like. But there are other bills. Gotta get some solid health insurance. Savings is already covered. . . . But what about an emergency fund? Mr. Dover mentioned investments and charitable giving as well. . . .

The papers.

His face.

The papers.

The pen.

The server sets a plate of hot shrimp and grits down in front of me.

"Go ahead and eat," he says.

I exhale.

-36-

Jackpot

The first "immediate-access" payment hits my account six days later: $8,333.33.

Which makes the whole thing real.

I buy Mama—who mysteriously wound up with a job at Macklin—a laptop, and she meets with Mr. Dover to learn how to use the budgeting software he *advised* me to buy. (They hit it off a little more than I'm expressly comfortable with, but what can I do?)

Then I transfer most of the monthly payout to her account. I do set a chunk aside for one particular dream (a girl's gotta do *somethin'* for herself every once in a while), and the rest goes to a charity that helps needy families with unexpected medical expenses.

This is my plan for every month.

As soon as I'm awake and showered on day seven, I pull on the cute sundress and sandals Mama got me for my birthday. Once dressed, I run out to the truck I got permission to borrow. And then I head out, surprising myself by remembering the way to a place I've only ever visited once before.

The truck's been leaking oil (which Mama can now afford to get *fixed*!—and now that I don't have to help with rent and bills, I can save my income and eventually get myself a car too), so I park at the edge of the driveway and walk up to the access control panel outside the gate. My hands are sweating so much, my finger totally slips off the *Call* button.

A woman answers. "May I help you?"

"Oh. Umm . . . This is the Macklin residence, right?"

"Yes."

Whew!

"This is Rico Danger. I'm at the gate."

"Okay . . ."

Panic. *Who am I even talking to?*

"Is Zan—Alexander, I mean, home?"

"He doesn't live here" comes through the little speaker.

My face falls. "But you just said this is the Macklin residence."

"Yes."

"How does Zan not live here?"

"He moved away."

"Moved away?"

"He has his own house now."

Which of course makes sense—Mr. Dover did let it "slip" that only half the total value of the lotto ticket would flow into the trust part with *my* name on it. He wasn't allowed to disclose the name of the beneficiary for the *other* trust, but come on.

The fact that he's not where I thought he'd be makes me feel like I'm falling, though. And not in a good way. "Do you have an address?" I ask.

"No."

Maybe I should've called *here* first. Was trying to surprise him, but clearly that's a bust. I could call him from my new cell phone, but I doubt he'd answer an unknown number. "Can I . . . maybe come in and use the phone?"

"You should go now."

"Wait! Is someone else home? Mr. Tim or Ms. Leigh-Ann or Lita?"

"Not here. Goodbye before I call police."

There's a *click*, and the line goes dead.

That certainly didn't go the way I expec—

Wait.

He has his own house. . . .

I smile. Sure he does.

Well played, Zan-the-Man. Well played.

Tracking Greg Andree down is pretty easy.

I honestly expect him to read me the riot act because he obviously knows Zan's real name *and* the fact that we lied about me being pregnant.

He doesn't.

Just hands me an envelope with my (real) name on it. Inside there's a piece of paper with the address, and a key hanging from a keychain that says HOME SWEET HOME.

When I get to the Decatur cottage, the Tonka's in the driveway.

I contemplate ringing the doorbell, but then I look at the envelope again. It's in Zan's handwriting.

I take a deep breath and insert the key. The door creaks as I push it open and step inside.

The interior air smells like clean laundry and warm apple pie. I'm tempted to call out to see if he's here, but instead I make my way down the hall to the back of the house.

When I get to the living area, he's sitting in a rocking chair.

I stop dead, and he looks me over that way he does.

I gulp and look away. "It, uhh . . . it smells really good in here," I say.

"I made an apple pie." He nods toward the breakfast bar. There's a pie there.

Huh. "I didn't know you could bake."

"Learn something new every day." He clasps his hands over his midsection. Grins and looks me over again. "That's a pretty dress."

"Thanks. Birthday gift."

"Ah, yes. Happy belated."

"Thanks." Eyes on my green toenails. "I got *your* gift, by the way. . . ."

"My gift?"

My head lifts. "From Mr. Dover?"

"Huh?" There's that baffled look I know so well.

For a second, I panic. Had to be him, right? He's the one who had the ticket. . . . "You know. The *trust*?"

He raises a caterpillar (they've been trimmed, it seems), lifts his chin, and looks down his nose. "I have no idea what you're talking about, Danger. Completely forgot you had a birthday."

I roll my eyes. And smile.

"You look beautiful."

"So do you."

He snorts.

"I mean . . ." *Pull it together, Rico!* "It's really nice to see you, Zan."

He smiles. "Just so you know, that room over there is still yours if you want it. I know we had our little tiff, but offer stands for you to move in. There's a no-sneaking-into-Zan's-room-to-watch-him-sleep rule, though. And you have to pay rent. It's every man for himself round these parts."

I glance at the open bedroom door. Furniture inside looks amazing, but . . . "I can't, Zan."

Another smile, this one sadder. "I figured you'd say that."

"Maybe we can start over? As friends?"

"That's cool. You'll only have a year to get to know me, though. I'm headed to Stanford next fall."

Sure wasn't expecting that. "Wow."

He nods.

"Congratulations, I guess?"

"Thank you. Any college plans for you?"

My eyes fall to my feet. "I'm thinking about it."

"What else are you thinking about?"

"Huh?" Head lifts.

"Got any other plans? Sky's the limit, right?"

Now I really smile. Glance up at the ceiling. Despite the fact that I'm not touching those monthly payouts—dignity won't let me—I guess he's right.

Definitely using that college money, though. Eventually.

We lapse into silence, and my gaze is drawn back to the pie. Almost smells better than he does. "You really made that?"

"I did."

So much to learn.

"Hey, Rico?"

"Yeah?"

"I'm glad you came by."

"Me too."

He smiles.

I smile.

"Hey, Zan?"

"Yeah?"

"Can I have a hug?"

"A *friendly* one?" He wiggles the eyebrows.

I laugh. "Something like that."

He stands and spreads his arms.

I step into them, and the Macklin Magic washes over me.

"Zan? Can I tell you something?"

"Of course," he says.

"I'm gonna go to Space Camp."

Author's Note

In the fall of 2015, the Powerball lottery jackpot rolled past the $656 million U.S. record set in 2012—and kept climbing.

Seeing the number on the billboards rise triggered vivid childhood memories of overhearing adult family members discussing "the things we could do with that kinda money" and stops at gas stations so those same family members could spend their last couple bucks to "play these numbers." While I've never known the kind of poverty that meant we didn't have food on the table, money was always pretty tight. And growing up in the poorer part of an area where many of my classmates drove Benz/BMW/Audis to school made my relative poverty feel . . . well, shameful.

Seeing that 2015 Powerball jackpot rise reignited old anxieties—of hearing "We can't afford that," and feeling my chest tighten at the thought of my classmates finding out how little I had. It also triggered a heap of new questions: How does relative poverty affect a kid? What were the lives of my rich-seeming classmates actually like? How different are the experiences of teens whose parents have plenty from those whose folks barely scrape by?

What would it have been like to win the lottery?

Thus was born Rico Danger (pronounced DON-gur, thank you very much). A girl—suspiciously similar to me in appearance—who works in a gas station where a winning lottery ticket worth a buttload of money is sold. And as I wrote through her desperation and her unexpected collision with wealth in the form of a cute boy, one major fact emerged: there's a whole lot more to people than how much—or how little—is in their bank accounts.

Nic

Acknowledgments

So this is the thing: sometimes you write a whole book, but so much time passes between when you wrote it and when it gets published—four literal years, in this case— that you sort of can't remember *everyone* involved who you need to thank. I was not on my toes enough to keep a list like I should've (And no, I haven't learned my lesson so don't even ask.)

All that to say this particular list of acknowledgments is likely to be lacking. Apologies in advance. If you feel you contributed to this book and don't see your name listed, by all means write me an angry email. I will grit my teeth and take it.

Here goes:

Nic Stone's Very Much Inexhaustive List of People She Remembers Helping with This Book:

1. Mom and Dad. No you, no me. No me, no book. Duh.
2. Phoebe Yeh (obviously). We went through a lot of *ideas* for this one. The footnotes were a no go.

Thank you for pushing me until I landed on the inanimate objects, and being super into it once I did. And speaking of inanimate objects . . .

3. Amy Sarig "A.S." King. The pagoda in *Please Ignore Vera Dietz* is the literal reason this book is full of POV chapters from inanimate objects. That book is everything, and you are the G.O.A.T.

4. Elizabeth Stranahan. You just put up with so much and have to read so much dreck, and you send me such excellent boxes of books, and I really appreciate you, Lizzy.

5. Rena Rossner. You read even the earliest, most boring iterations of this thing. Bless you.

6. Nigel Livingstone. Other half and baby daddy of the year.

7. Octavia Roberts. While *Overnight Millionaire* was a perfectly okay title, *Jackpot* is infinitely better. Thank you.

8. Dede Nesbitt and Tanya Rogers. Also tried-and-true friends who read this thing when it was super boring. (Remember when I thought I should write a "straightforward" novel? Who the hell was I kidding, am I right?)

9. Ashley Woodfolk. YOU read this when I was super hating on it. That makes you a true friend. And when I told you to stop reading it because I was fixing it, you did. **heart-eye emojis**

10. Tehlor Kinney. Not only did you read this when it was super boring, but you let me steal your name. Thank you.

11. Greg Andree. You also let me steal your name.

12. Jay Dover. Not only did you let me steal your name, but you keep me financially responsible with your fiscal wisdom. Sometimes middle school

homies grow up and like, *adult* together. Who'da thunk?

13. Casey Reed Joiner. Another middle school forever love of my life and my very own pseudo Jessica Barlow. I love you.

14. Dean Maria Martin. Your Spanish assistance was invaluable, and so are you. #educatorsrule

15. Liz Acevedo. Also, thank *you* for answering my ignorant Spanish questions. And for just being an all-around badass. I wanna be like you when I grow up.

16. Dhonielle Clayton, Tiff Jackson, and Angie Thomas. No explanation necessary.

17. Lauryn Mascarenaz. For your early read and feedback. And for telling me you loved it when I was super insecure about the whole shebang.

18. Jarred Amato. The dopest. Period.

19. Joey Tam, I'm pretty sure your critique is literally what pulled this whole thing together in my head.

20. Kristin Schulz. #workwife4life, you have no idea how much you liking this thing has helped me chill. For real.

21. Random House fam: Kathy, Auntie Barbs, Auntie Judith, Aunt Felicia, John (NEMESIS!), Dominique, Syd, Adrienne, Angela, Jules, Christine, Alison, Lisa M. . . . (This is when I start forgetting people. SORRY!)

Anyway, anyway: with all of you by my side, *I* clearly hit the jackpot.

UNWAVERING.
UNCOMPROMISING.
UNFORGETTABLE.

Don't miss the sensational follow-up to #1 *New York Times* bestseller and William C. Morris Award finalist *Dear Martin.*

#1 *NEW YORK TIMES* BESTSELLING AUTHOR OF *DEAR MARTIN*

Dear Justyce

a novel

NIC STONE

PART
ONE

The End

Snapshot:

Two Boys on
a Brand-New
Playground
(2010)

It didn't take much for Quan to decide he was leaving this time. He feels a little bit bad, yeah: knowing Dasia and Gabe are still in the house makes his stomach hurt the way it always does when he finds himself faced with grown-people problems he can't fix. But Quan's only nine. Running away *alone* is hard enough. Trying to bring a four-year-old sister and a two-year-old brother just isn't gonna work.

He's glad spring has sprung early. Didn't have time to grab a jacket as he fled. He's pretty sure there was too much commotion for anybody to notice, but he takes a few unnecessary turns en route to his destination in case Olaf— that's what Quan calls his mama's "duck-ass boyfriend" (which is what Quan's *dad* calls the guy)—*did* notice Quan's exit.

What Quan is sure of? He couldn't stay there. Not with dude yelling and throwing things the way he was. Quan knows what comes next, and he couldn't watch again. It was hard enough seeing the aftermath bloom in the funny-looking bluey-purple blotches that made Mama's arms and legs look like someone had tossed water balloons full of paint all over her. He couldn't really do anything anyway. Though Olaf (Dwight is the guy's *actual* name) isn't *too*, too big, he's a whole heck of a lot stronger than Quan. The one time Quan did try to intervene, he wound up with his own funky-colored blotch. Across his lower back from where he hit the dining room table when dude literally threw Quan across the room.

Hiding that bruise from Daddy was nearly impossible. And Quan *had* to hide it because he knew if Daddy found out what really happened when Olaf/Dwight came around . . . well, it wouldn't be good.

So. He made sure Dasia and Gabe were safe in the closet. That was the most he could do.

As Wynwood Heights Park looms up on his left, Quan lifts the hem of his shirt to wipe his face. It's the fourth time he's done it, so there's a wet spot now. He wonders if there will be any dry spots left by the time he gets the tears to stop. Good thing there's no one around to see. He'd never hear the end of it.

He bounces on his toes as his feet touch down on the springy stuff the new playground is built on. There's a sign that says it's ground-up old tires, that the play structures are made from "recycled water bottles and other discarded plastics," and that the entire area is "green," but as Dasia pointed out the last time Mama brought them all here, whoever built the thing didn't know their colors because everything is red, yellow, and blue.

The thought of his sass-mouthed little sister brings fresh tears to Quan's eyes.

He makes a beeline for the rocket ship. It sits off in a

corner separate from everything else, tip pointed at the sky like it could blast off at any moment. Inside the cylindrical base, there are buttons to push and dials to turn and a ladder that leads up to an "observation deck" with a little window. It's Quan's favorite spot in the world—though he'd never admit that to anyone.

When he gets inside, he's so relieved, he collapses against the rounded wall and lets his body slide to the floor like chocolate ice cream down the side of a cone on a hot summer day. His head drops back, and he shuts his eyes and lets the tears flow freely.

But then there's a sound above him. A cough.

The moonlight through the deck window makes the face of the boy staring down at Quan look kinda ghostly. In fact, the longer dude stares without speaking, the more Quan wonders if maybe he *is* a ghost.

"Uhhh . . . hello?"

Dude doesn't reply.

Now Quan is starting to get creeped out. Which makes him mad. This is supposed to be the one place in the world he can *relax*. Where he's not looking over his shoulder or being extra cautious. Where he can close his eyes and count down from ten and imagine shooting into space, far, far away from everything and everyone.

"Yo, why you lookin' at me like that?" Quan spits, each word sharp-tipped and laced with the venom of his rage.

"Oh, umm . . ." The other boy's eyes drop to his hands.

He picks at the skin around his thumbs. Something Quan does sometimes that gets him yelled at.

Hmm.

The boy goes on: "I'm sorry. I just . . . I wasn't expecting anybody else to come in here."

"Oh."

The boys are quiet for a minute and then: "I'm Justyce, by the way."

Justyce. Quan's heard that name before . . . "You that smart kid they was talking about on the morning announcements at school? Won some contest or something?"

Justyce again doesn't reply.

"Hellooooo?" Quan says.

"You gonna make fun of me now?"

"Huh?"

Now Justyce looks out the observation window. Quan wonders what he's seeing.

"I wish they would've never made that announcement. Winning an academic bowl isn't 'cool.' Everybody just makes fun of me."

Quan shrugs. "Maybe they just jealous cuz they ain't never won nothin'."

Silence falls over the boys again, but this time, it's not so uncomfortable. In fact, the longer Quan sits there with Justyce above him, the better he feels. Kinda nice not being *totally* alone. Which makes him wonder . . .

"You're a fifth grader, right? You not gonna get in trouble for being out this late?"

"Oh, I will," Justyce says.

It makes Quan laugh.

"I snuck out," Justyce continues. "But it's not the first time, and I'm sure it won't be the last. I think my mama knows I'll always come back."

"Wish *I* didn't have to go back . . ." It slips out, and at first Quan regrets it. But then he realizes his chest is a little looser. This one time at Daddy's house, Quan watched a movie about this big ship that hit an iceberg and sunk, and there was this one scene where the main lady was being tied into this thing that went around her stomach and laced up the back like a sneaker. He later learned it was called a *corset*, but that's what comes into Quan's head when he thinks about his life. "My mom's boyfriend is a asshole," he continues.

The laces loosen a little more.

"He's my little brother and sister's dad, so like I *kinda* get why my mama keeps dealing with him . . ." Little looser. "But I hate him. Every time he come around, he mad about somethin', and he takes it out on my mom."

"Sounds familiar," Justyce says.

"And I be wanting to stick around for my brother and sister but—wait." Quan looks up at Justyce, whose chin is now propped in his hand.

All eyes (and ears) on Quan.

"What'd you say?" Quan asks.

"Hmm?"

"Just a second ago."

"Oh. I said that sounds familiar."

"Whatchu mean?"

Justyce sighs. "My dad was in the military and went to Afghanistan. Ever since he came back, he's been . . . different. He drinks a lot and sometimes has these 'episodes,' my mom calls them. Out of nowhere he'll start yelling and throwing stuff." Now Justyce isn't looking at Quan anymore. "He hits her sometimes." Justyce swipes at his eyes.

Quan stands up. "You ever come here during the day?"

"Occasionally." Jus sniffles. "Sorry for crying."

"Man, whatever. Now I see how you won that 'academic' thingy."

"Huh?"

"What kinda fifth grader says *occasionally*?" Quan shakes his head. "I'm gonna head home and check on my brother and sister," he says. "You should go check on your mom."

The boys meet eyes, and understanding passes between them.

"I'll see you around." Quan ducks and slips through the rocket's arched entryway.

He's almost back at the edge of the rubber-floored playground when—

"Hey! Hold up!"

Quan turns around to find Justyce is headed in his direction.

"You didn't tell me your name," Justyce says, out of breath.

Quan smiles—"Vernell LaQuan Banks Jr."—and lifts his hand. "Call me Quan."

"It was real nice to meet you, Quan," Justyce says, smacking his palm against Quan's and then hooking fingers. "Even, uhh . . . despite the circumstances."

Now Quan laughs. "You're ten years old, man. Loosen up."

"Sorry."

"Don't be." Quan shoves his fists in his pockets. It's gotten cooler. "Nice to meet you too, Justyce."

Quan turns on the heel of his well-worn Jordans and heads home.

1

Doomed

Vernell LaQuan Banks Jr. remembers the night everything changed. He'd fallen asleep on the leather sectional in Daddy's living room while watching *Lemony Snicket's A Series of Unfortunate Events* (the movie), and was dreaming about Count Olaf—who'd gotten a tan, it seemed, and looked suspiciously like his mama's "boyfriend," Dwight—falling into a pit of giant yellow snakes like the one from Montgomery Montgomery's reptile room. Screaming bloody murder as he got sucked down into the scaly, slithery quicksand.

Quan's pretty sure he was smiling in his sleep.

But then there was a **BOOM** that startled him so bad, he jolted awake and fell to the floor.

Which wound up being a good thing.

Next thing Quan knew, more police officers than he could count were pouring into the house with guns drawn.

He stayed down. Hidden.

Wouldn't've been able to get up if he tried, he was so scared.

There was a commotion over his head—Daddy's room.

Lots of thumping. Bumping. A yell (Daddy's?). Muffled shouting.

Get down! Put your hands in the air—

Oww, man! Not so tight, you tryna break my arm?

Wham. *BAM!*

Walls shaking.

Was the ceiling gonna fall?

Then the tumult shifted to the left. He heard Daddy's door bang against the wall, then what sounded like eight tons of giant bricks tumbling down the stairs.

Slow down, man! Damn—

Keep your mouth shut!

Quan closed his eyes.

Chill out, man! I'm not resisti—

There was a sharp pain in Quan's shoulder as his arm was suddenly wrenched in a direction he was sure it wasn't supposed to go. A thick arm wrapped around his midsection so tight it squeezed all the air out of him . . . or maybe it all flew out because of the speed at which his body left the ground.

He couldn't even scream. Looking back, *that* was the scariest part. That his voice was gone. That he couldn't cry out. That he'd lost all control of his body and surroundings and couldn't even make a sound to let the world know he wasn't feelin' it.

It's how he feels now as he jolts awake in his cell at the Fulton Regional Youth Detention Center, unable to breathe.

Quan tries to inhale. And can't. It's like that cop's still got him wrapped up and is squeezing too tight. No space for his lungs to expand.

Can't.

Breathe.

The darkness is so thick, he feels like he's drowning in it. Maybe he is. Maybe Quan can't draw breath because the darkness has solidified. Turned viscous, dense and sticky and heavy. That would also explain why he can't lift his arms or swing his legs over the edge of this cotton-lined cardboard excuse for a "bed" that makes his neck and back hurt night after night.

What Quan wouldn't give to be back in his queen-sized, memory foam, personal cloud with crazy soft flannel sheets in his bedroom at Daddy's house. If he's going to die in a bed—because he's certainly about to die—he wishes it could be *that* bed instead of this one.

He shuts his eyes and more pieces of that night fly at him: Daddy yelling

Don't hurt my son!

before being shoved out the front door.

The sound of glass breaking as the unfinished cup of ginger ale Quan left on the counter toppled to the floor. His foot hit it as the officer with his dumb, muscly arm crushing Quan's rib cage carried Quan through the kitchen like Quan was some kind of doll baby.

The sudden freezing air as Quan was whisked outside in

his thin Iron Man pajamas with no shoes or jacket . . . and the subsequent strange warmth running down Quan's legs when he saw Just. How. Many.

Police cars.

There were.

Outside.

Barking dogs, straining against leashes. A helicopter circling overhead, its spotlight held steady on the team of men dragging Daddy toward the group of cop vehicles parked haphazardly and blocking the street.

Quan had counted six when his eyes landed on the van no less than *five* officers were wrestling his dad into.

Wrestling because Daddy kept trying to look back over his shoulder to see what was happening with Quan. He was shouting.

It's gonna be okay, Junior!

Get in the goddam van!

It'll all be fi—

One of the officers brought an elbow down on the back of Daddy's head. Quan watched as Daddy's whole body went limp.

That's when Quan started

Screaming.

Two of the officers climbed into the back of the van and dragged Daddy's body inside the way Quan had seen Daddy drag the giant bags of sand he'd bought for the sandbox he built in the backyard when Quan was younger.

Kicking.

Cut it out, kid!

Wait . . . are you *wet*?

They rolled Daddy to his back, and one of the officers knelt beside him and put two fingers up under his jaw. He nodded at the other officer, who then hopped down from the back of the van and shut the doors.

Flailing.

Screaming.

Kicking.

The taillights of the van glowed red and Quan wished everything would *STOP*. He was sobbing and twisting, and the officer holding him squeezed tighter and locked Quan's arms down.

As the van pulled off, Quan screamed so loud, he was sure his mama would hear him back home some twenty miles away. She would hear him and she would come and she would stop the van and she would get Daddy out and she would get Quan. All the blue-suited Dad-stealing monsters and blue-lit cars would *POOF!* disappear and everything would go back to normal.

Better yet, Mama would bring Dwight-the-black-Olaf, and she'd toss *him* in the back of the van in Daddy's place. And they'd lock *him* up in a snake-filled cell and throw away the key.

Quan screamed until all the scream was outta him. Then he inhaled. And he screamed some more.

His own voice was all he could hear until—

"Hey! You put that young man *down*! Have you lost your ever-lovin' mind?!"

Then the officer holding him was saying

Ow! Hey!

And

Hey! Stop that!

And

Ma'am, you are assaulting a police officer–

"I said put him *DOWN*. Right now!"

Ma'am, I can't–

All right! All right!

The grip on Quan's body loosened. His feet touched down on the porch floor just as a wrinkled hand wrapped around his biceps and a thin arm wrapped around his lower back, a sheet of paper in hand. "You come on here with me, Junior," a familiar voice said.

Ma'am, he can't go with you. Until further

notice, he's a ward of the state–

"Like hell he is! You can call his mama to come get him, but until she arrives, he'll be staying at *my* house." The woman shoved the paper into the officer's face. "You see this? This is a *legally binding* document. Read it aloud."

Ma'am–

"I said read it aloud!"

Okay, okay!

(The officer cut his eyes at Quan before beginning. Then sighed.)

"In the event of the arrest of Vernell LaQuan Banks Sr., Mrs. Edna Pavlostathis is named temporary guardian of Vernell LaQuan Banks Jr. until . . ."

But that was all Quan needed to hear. (Did Daddy *know* he would be snatched away from his son in the dead of night?)

"Come on, honey," she said, and as she ushered Quan away from the tornado of blue—lights, cars, uniforms, eyes—that'd ripped through everything he knew as normal, everything clicked into place.

Mrs. Pavlostathis. The fireball old lady who lived next door to Daddy.

"Let's head inside and I'll go over to your dad's to grab you some fresh clothes so you can get cleaned up. How dare those so-called *officers* treat you that way. The *nerve* of those whites—"

She trailed off. Or at least Quan thinks she did. He can't remember her saying anything else. He *does* remember thinking that under different circumstances, that last statement would've made him smile. He'd known Mrs. Pavlostathis since he was seven years old—she was close to eighty and used to babysit him when Daddy had to make "emergency runs" on weekends Quan was there. Despite her skin tone, Mrs. P let everyone know she was *Greek*, not white.

She was also one of Daddy's clients (*"A little ganja's good for my glaucoma, Junior"*) and, Quan had noticed over the years, the only neighbor who didn't look at him funny—or avoid looking at all—when Quan would play outside or when he and Daddy would drive through the neighborhood in Daddy's BMW.

It was something Mama always grumbled about when she'd drive the forty minutes out into the burbs to drop Quan off. *I don't know why your daddy wants to live way out here with all these white folks. They're gonna call the cops on his ass one day, and it'll be over . . .*

As he and Mrs. P made their way over to her house, Quan wondered if Mama's prediction was coming true.

And in that moment: he hated his mama.

For saying that. Wishing the worst on Daddy.

For staying with duck-ass Dwight.

Putting up with his antics.

For working so much.

For not being there.

Especially right then.

"I'll run ya a salt bath," Mrs. P said as they stepped into her house, and fragrant warmth wrapped around him like a hug from a fluffy incense stick with arms. "I know you're not a little kid anymore, but it'll do ya some good. I just made some dolmas, and there's some of those olives you like, the ones with the creamy feta inside, in the fridge. Put something in your belly. I'm sure you're starving."

In truth, food was the furthest thing from Quan's mind . . . but one didn't say *no* to Mrs. P. So he did as he was told. He stuffed himself with Mrs. P's world-famous (if you let her tell it) dolmas—a blend of creamy lemon-ish rice and ground lamb rolled up into a grape leaf. He ate his weight in giant feta-filled olives.

And when the salt bath was ready, he stripped down and climbed into the fancy claw-foot tub in Mrs. P's guest bathroom.

Quan closed his eyes.

Swirling police lights and Daddy's collapsing body flashed behind them.

Van doors shutting.

Taillights disappearing.

Would Daddy go to prison?

For how long?

What would happen now?

Quan wasn't sure he wanted to find out.

So he sank.

It was easy at first, holding his breath and letting the water envelop him completely. Even felt nice.

But then his lungs started to burn. Images of Dasia and Gabe popped into his head. He remembered telling Gabe he'd teach him how to play Uno when he got back from Daddy's house this time. Little dude was four now and ready to learn.

Quan's head swam.

Dasia would be waiting for Quan to polish her toenails purple. That was the prize he'd promised her if she aced her spelling test. And she did.

His chest felt on the verge of bursting, and everything in his head was turning white.

And Mama . . .

Dwight—

Air came out of Quan's nose with so much force, he'd swear it shot him up out of the water. As his senses returned to normal, he heard water hit tile and the bathroom at Mrs. P's house swam back into focus.

He took a breath.

Well, more like a breath took him. He gasped as air flooded his lungs, shoving him back from the brink of No Return.

It's the same type of breath that's overtaking him now.

Here.

In his cell.

And as oxygen—a little stale from the cinder block walls and laced with the tang of iron—surges down his throat and kicks the invisible weight off him, Quan knows:

He won't die now just like he didn't die then.

He can breathe.

January 12

Dear Justyce,

Look, I'm not even gonna lie: this shit is weird. I don't write letters to my mama, but I'm writing one to you?

Smh.

(Wait, can I even write that? This ain't a text message . . .)

(See? Weird.)

(You better not tell nobody I wrote this.)

Anyway, I had this dream last night and when I woke up, ~~the first thing~~ I saw was that notebook you gave me with all the Martin Luther King letters in it.

Sidenote: I really do appreciate you popping by to see ya boy before you headed back to that fancy college you go to. Ol' smarty pants ass. But for real, it was good to see you. It, uhh . . . did a lot for me. Gets more than a little lonely in here, and I don't get many visitors, so you coming through was— well, that was real nice of you, dawg.

Now back to this notebook you left. At first I thought it was wack ("THOSE" black guys, huh?), but the more I read, the more interested I got. Like it was a lot of shit in there about Manny—my own cousin!—that I didn't know because I ain't really KNOW him, know him. That was kinda wild.

And YOU! Man, we got way more in common than I woulda thought.

It was one letter in the notebook that made me wanna write this one to you. Not sure what happened (you mentioned doing the "wrong thing"), but there's a line you wrote: "Those assholes can't seem to care about being offensive, so why should I give a damn about being agreeable?"

I don't know what it is, but that shit really got me.

I've never told anybody about the night my dad got arrested. It was a couple years after you and me met in the rocket ship. I was eleven. Cops busted up in the house in the dead of night like they owned the place and just . . . took him.

And I haven't seen him since. They gave him 25 <u>years</u> in prison.

It's only one other time in my life I ever been that scared, J. It all happened too fast for me to figure out what I could do. I think deep down, I knew he was prolly going away for a long-ass time—I was fully aware of his "occupation," and while I was sure the cops wouldn't find any contraband in his actual house (he was real careful about that), he dealt in more than just green, and the net was wide, so it was only a matter of time.

I really miss him, though.

I dream about the whole scenario a lot. Did last night, in fact. And when I woke up and looked at the date? Today is the sixth anniversary.

Shit hit me harder than it usually does. Probably because it also means I've been up in here for almost sixteen months. It's the longest stretch I've ever done, and I don't even have a trial date yet. I do my best to just cruise—not really think about where I am and what it's actually like to be here. But today I couldn't help but notice how bad the food is. How heavy the giant iron doors are, and how . . . defeated, I guess, everyone up in here seems, even though a few of the others talk a good game about getting out.

I keep thinking, like: What would my dad say if he could see me now? How disappointed would he be?

Yeah, what he did for a living wasn't exactly "statutory," as he used to say. But if there's one thing he was hell-bent on, it was me NOT ending up like him. We talking about a dude who used to drop my ass at the library when he had to make some of his runs. (Head librarian had real bad anxiety and was one of Dad's clients so she took good care of me.) Don't nobody know this, but I used to eat up the Lemony Snicket "Unfortunate Events" joints like they were Skittles. You ever read those? Them shits go hard. Kinda wish I had my collection here.

Anyway, that was all him. Vernell LaQuan Banks Sr. He's the reason they tested me for Accelerated Learners and I wound up in that Challenge Math class with you.

He wanted me to do good. To go far and be better.

But then he was just . . . gone.

(Sorry for getting sentimental, but like I said before: you better not tell nobody I wrote all this. Or that I used to read books about little rich white kids.)

That night he got arrested turned everything upside down. I knew things were about to get bad because my dad had been like the duct tape holding our raggedy shit together. He paid for a lot and gave my mom money, and he really was the reason I stayed out of trouble. The minute that van drove away with him in it, I felt . . . doomed.

It's why I stopped talking to you. Everybody else too, but especially you. I woulda never admitted this (honestly don't know why I'm admitting it now . . .), but I kinda looked up to you. Yeah, you were only a year older and you were dorky as hell, but you had your shit together in a way I wanted mine to be.

I knew if I could just be like you, my dad would be proud of me.

Seeing what you wrote in that post-whatever-the-hell-set-you-off letter . . . I dunno, man. If YOU felt that way, maybe everything my dad tried to push me toward really was pointless.

Don't really matter now anyway. I'm prolly gettin' WAY more time than my dad did.

Guess it's whatever.

I don't even know if Imma send this. Maybe I should. You better write back, though. Cuz otherwise I ain't never writing you another letter again.

Got me over here pouring my heart out and shit.

Smh.

(There I go again!)

Later,

~~Vernell LaQuan Banks Jr.~~ QUAN

P.S.: I know you already knew my government name, but don't ever call me by it.

P.S.S. (or is it P.P.S.? Yo, you ever heard that song "O.P.P."? I love that song.): REMINDER—don't tell NOBODY I wrote this!

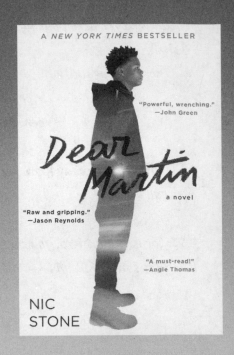
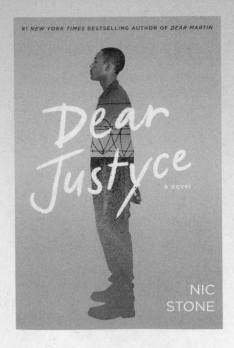
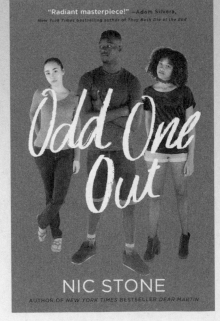